PARIS MATCH

PARIS MATCH

Kathleen Reid

KENSINGTON BOOKS
http://www.kensingtonbooks.com

KENSINGTON BOOKS are published by

Kensington Publishing Corp.
850 Third Avenue
New York, NY 10022

All Kensington titles, imprints and distributed lines are available at special quantity discounts for bulk purchases for sales promotion, premiums, fund-raising, educational or institutional use.

Special book excerpts or customized printings can also be created to fit specific needs. For details, write or phone the office of the Kensington Special Sales Manager: Kensington Publishing Corp., 850 Third Avenue, New York, NY 10022. Attn. Special Sales Department. Phone: 1-800-221-2647.

Kensington and the K logo Reg. U.S. Pat. & TM Off.

ISBN 0-7582-0577-5

First Kensington Trade Paperback Printing: January 2004
10 9 8 7 6 5 4 3 2 1

Printed in the United States of America

Acknowledgments

I am grateful to my family and friends for supporting me during this journey. I would like to acknowledge my fantastic husband, Bagley, who has helped me every step of the way. I couldn't have pursued my dream without him. Our daughters, Ellie and Susanna, inspire me each day.

I would like to thank my mother and father, who instilled in me a love of fine literature.

My dear friend Julie Lavin has always encouraged my writing. Eva Clarke, Anne McElroy and Heather McGuire listened and read pages and continually sustained me. Kit Bredrup was the first person to read the book and offer feedback. Finally, I'd like to especially thank my friend and mentor, Amy Fine Collins, who gave me valuable advice throughout the process.

Many thanks go to my agent, Kim Goldstein. I am so impressed with her talent and creativity. I'm thrilled to be working with Kate Duffy at Kensington Books, whose knowledge and experience amaze me. I'm delighted that Lisa Filippatos is guiding me through this project. A heartfelt thank you goes to Alice Rosengard. She is a terrific editor, who taught me so much about the craft of writing fiction. I'd also like to acknowledge my writing teacher, Marilyn Leahy, who always offered me her good ideas and enthusiasm.

Chapter 1

"Mother, where are my new jeans? You said they were in the dryer, but I don't see them anywhere!" demands Laura, her voice reaching a high pitch.

"Just a minute. I'm on the phone," I cry, cupping a hand over the mouthpiece. I point to the wicker basket at the top of the stairs, waving my hand sharply. "I'll see you tomorrow at noon," I say as I hang up. Leafing through the mail, I separate out some bills that need to be paid.

The phone rings again. "Lauren," Matt says curtly, "who have you been talking to?"

"The dishwasher repair man," I reply firmly.

"It's about time we had that taken care of. I won't be in for dinner tonight. Client meeting. Everything okay there?"

I look around the kitchen. Kathryn's sneakers are on the floor, Laura's sweatshirt is draped across a chair, and there's a crumb-filled plate of cookies on the counter. "Just great," I say, trying to keep the sarcasm from my voice.

Hanging up the phone, I look at the clock. The day is almost over and I haven't even had time to eat lunch. Grabbing one of Kathryn's tropical punch juice boxes from the refrigerator, I sit down, relieved that I don't have to cook Matt dinner.

"Mom," says Laura. "What's wrong with Nélie's door? I

just tried to go in there and it won't open." Laura raises an eyebrow at me when she sees me drinking from her sister's juice box.

"That's strange," I say. "I've never known Nélie to lock her door."

Pulling myself up from the seat, I notice that the blue toile cushion I made has become faded and stained with overuse. I make a mental note to clean and repair it next week.

Looking at the time again, I realize I haven't heard from Nélie this afternoon. She usually calls to leave me a message if she has other plans. My maternal instincts kick in and I quicken my pace up the stairs. Turning left down the hallway, I try to turn Nélie's doorknob and realize that it's jammed. After several attempts, I finally manage to shove the door open. Glancing around, I see the familiar objects in her room: a wall-sized poster of a Toulouse-Lautrec painting, a bookcase filled with textbooks, a photo of her natural mother, my best friend, India.

I notice that India's photo has been moved to Nélie's desk. An envelope is wedged underneath. With trembling hands, I open it. Nélie's familiar script leaps off the page. The note seems to burn my hand as I read. *I have some things I need to find out about my real mother. I'll let you know where I am when I'm ready.*

For an instant, I can't catch my breath. Fear overwhelms me. A hot, tingling sensation burns the back of my neck as I struggle to accept the grim truth. I must find Nélie before she learns the story herself.

I stare back at the note. The words "my real mother" seem to reach up from the page to slap me across the face. My fears crystallize as I contemplate my own inadequacies as a parent. The old questions about my competency ring in my ears. Each thought is troubling, tripping like the erratic beat of my heart. I tried to give her everything she needed. But my task was daunting at times. After all, I'm not her real mother.

I scratch my head, trying to quell my desire to go and get a chocolate bar to help me cope; instead, I assault my index finger, chewing the nail down to the skin. I should have opened up to Nélie, told her the truth about everything—about myself, about my dreams, about my own frustrations, about India, about the past. Instead, I strived to be perfect. Even worse, I rarely spoke of India. I portrayed her as some sort of heroine in a novel. India was my best friend, but, oftentimes, she could be difficult—more than difficult. She always wanted things her way and she nearly always got what she wanted. Trying to hide behind my vision of the perfect wife and mother, I never showed Nélie my true self. If I had, maybe she would have confided in me rather than run away.

On the surface, my friendship with India made no sense, yet our differences drew us together. I can't help but recall the Chinese myth of creation, with its references to yin and yang, the two opposing forces that make up the universe. Yin and yang, I learned, consisted of light and dark, good and evil, wet and dry. Everything has to balance to achieve order. Maybe India represented my darker yang side—the parts of my personality that were repressed. She was guided at times by sheer selfishness. No one touched her free spirit. Unlike me, India did what she wanted, when she wanted, without fear of the repercussions. In a way, I acted as a sort of anchor for her because, oftentimes, she didn't see the recklessness of her actions.

From the start of our unlikely friendship in college, I was drawn to India because she challenged every one of my beliefs. She always did what I dreamed of doing, but couldn't. We came from two different financial worlds—mine was limited, hers seemed limitless. I had never seen anyone spend money as easily as India. She once paid nearly a thousand dollars for a pair of designer jeans she found in New York. At the same time, she admired the long, black vintage coat I found at a junk shop for six dollars.

I studied hard to graduate with honors in an effort to justify my parents' years of scrimping and saving. My summers consisted of full-time work at a local fish and chips place to help pay my college tuition. I attended my classes in between various part-time jobs around campus, from shelving books in the library to working in the admissions office my senior year. Brought up to believe in giving back to the community, I helped raise money for the elderly and my church, visited my grandmother, followed a rigorous daily exercise program and tried valiantly to live up to impossible standards set by my family.

India never suffered from such a sense of duty. In fact, she never quite earned her degree. She did, however, accomplish a lot while in college. She obtained her pilot's license, rallied against apartheid, hiked the Appalachian trail, flew to South America several times, became a black belt in karate, learned the art of bungee jumping in Australia, and spent winters skiing in Jackson Hole. An unfailing sense of confidence permeated her existence.

When not pursuing adventure, India did attempt to get an education; in fact, she took her study of philosophy and ancient Greece quite seriously. Classical mythology must have appealed to her mercurial nature. Actually, we met while I was in the Metropolitan Museum of Art sketching a statue of a Greek goddess for an advanced drawing class in the spring of our first year in college. I remember how excited I was to visit New York. Despite a broken-down bus, an uncomfortable stay at a noisy Best Western and an early morning at the museum, I was in good spirits. Seated on the cold marble floor in our group's designated room, I began to work.

That afternoon remains vivid in my mind's eye. For the assignment, I had chosen a beautiful Greek sculpture of Aphrodite and Eros holding a jewelry box. Losing all sense of time, I concentrated on the folds of Aphrodite's gown, trying to be meticulous in capturing its texture. I was so absorbed in my drawing that I failed to notice a tall, attractive redheaded woman walk up behind me.

"It's beautiful," she said, looking over my shoulder. "You've done it!"

I looked up, somewhat startled. "What?" I asked.

"You're such a gifted artist. Look how well your sketch turned out." She bent down, extending her long, slender hand. "Hello, I'm India."

A loud "Shhh" emanated from one of our classmates.

As I leaned forward to shake her hand, her boots caught my eye. They were expensive-looking, made of soft black leather, with heels that looked impossibly high to walk in. Tamed by a barrette, her riotous red curly hair framed her face then fanned out down her back. As I looked at the chipped remains of red on Aphrodite's terra cotta head, I noticed that India's hair bore a striking resemblance to the sculpture's. Her cheekbones were high, set in a perfectly oval face, but her nose was slightly large compared to the rest of her refined features. Her expressive blue eyes narrowed slightly as she studied my sketchpad, judging the quality of my drawing. The scent of perfume filled the air. I couldn't identify it at the time, but now I know it was Chanel No. 5.

"Lauren," I whispered with a smile. "Are you with our group? I didn't see you on the bus."

"Oh," she muttered, effortlessly kneeling beside me. "I flew. My family keeps an apartment on the Upper East Side. New York is kind of like my home away from home. I told Professor Coleman I'd be in New York this weekend and he offered to let me join his group. Somehow I convinced him I could keep up. But after seeing your work, I'm not so sure."

"Thanks for the compliment. I love to draw. My mother's convinced I was born with a marker in my hand. But I took this class so that I could visit here. I've never been to New York City before."

"Really?" she replied. "You're going to love it. All the ex-

citement can be addictive. Where are you from?" inquired
India, drawing her well-groomed eyebrows together.

"North Carolina," I replied, stretching my legs. "I was
born and raised in a small community in Greensboro."

India shook her head, then promised to look up Greensboro on a map. Peering at my drawing again, she pursed her
lips. She took out her sketchpad to show me. "Look at my
drawing. It's simply awful compared to yours. To think that
I've spent years studying and I'll never capture anything as
well as you just did. How did you possibly accomplish this in
the last few hours?" She laughed, pointing to her work. "You
can see I tried to draw those Roman winged angels over
there. Look at his stomach. The poor boy looks like he's been
lunching on beer and french fries rather than grapes!" She
looked around, noting that there were only a few people left
in the museum. "Speaking of which, I'm starved. Let's go get
something to eat."

Sheepishly, I pointed to my backpack. "No thanks. I
brought my lunch. I'm going to finish up and then eat here."

"Absolutely not!" she insisted, grabbing my arm. "I'd love
to treat you to my favorite lunch spot. Come on! You'll be
doing me a favor by keeping me company. Otherwise, I'd
have to eat by myself and make small talk with my waiter.
This will be much more fun." She watched as I wiped the
charcoal from my pencil off my pants. "Don't worry," she
added. "The wealthiest people go to the most upscale restaurants here in patched or embroidered jeans. You'll fit right in.
Besides, you could easily pass for one of the models who are
always out and about. Just flip that long blond hair of yours
a few times and we'll get a great table."

From the moment we sat down to lunch, we realized we
shared a love of drawing and painting. Her enthusiasm was
infectious, and I found myself laughing and talking as if we
had always known each other.

Our passion for art started our friendship, but as time

went on, it seemed that India needed my stability as much I needed her spontaneity. Once I talked her out of "adopting" a painting from Alumni Hall. She had made a bet with a fraternity that she would bring the portrait of Lord Devon (one of our English founders) to a party. Persuading her that a felony might not look good on her record, I provided her, as she put it, with a "voice of reason." Besides, our solution was much more fun. We ended up spending all night in the studio drawing our own version of the infamous Lord "D," which made us campus celebrities. Our painting remained over that fraternity's fireplace for years.

For me, our time together was tantamount to a vacation from reality. As in the myths that inspired the ancient Greeks, India lived her life in a way that turned a fearful world into one filled with beauty and joy. When she died, her greatest gift to me was her daughter, Nélie.

It's difficult to pinpoint the highs and lows of the last fifteen years as Nélie's surrogate mother. I know India's death changed me forever. It's not something I'll ever get over. Even looking at Nélie can be painful sometimes. She reminds me of her mother—her laugh, the mole on her left cheek, her quirky big toe, the sparkle in her eye, the way she laughs at Snoopy comics, the way she moves her graceful, long-limbed body. Like India, Nélie has an aptitude for languages; she can speak three of them, and recently, she had begun studying Chinese. She's remarkably independent in her thinking and, like her mother, has a penchant for helping the underdog. India would have been so proud of Nélie's years of volunteer work helping abused dogs and cats at our local animal shelter.

My self-induced trance is broken by the sound of Laura's voice. As her slim figure glides into the room, my nail-bitten hands go immediately into my lap. She has her long, strawberry-blond hair tucked neatly behind her ears. Her straight nose and the tiny telltale cleft in her chin make her look like a miniature version of Matt. Sometimes her presence surprises me, because it seems that only yesterday she was three feet tall, sitting on my lap, demanding that I read her another story. These days, she wears a second gold hoop earring that she knows antagonizes me.

She doesn't look me in the eye at first when she enters the room. I notice she's wearing a midriff top with hip-hugging blue jeans, an outfit that she cajoled her father into purchasing for her last weekend. Too upset to comment, I watch her hesitate and then survey the room.

"Mom?" she says with a puzzled expression. "What are you doing in here? Where's Nélie?" Her eyes narrow when she sees the note in my hand. "You're not going through her things or anything, are you?" She looks indignant.

Ignoring her recent penchant for challenging my authority, I absently wipe a tear from my eye. "I just found this note. Your sister has run away."

Laura grabs the paper from my hands, studying each word. "Why did she just leave? It doesn't make sense." She frowns, crinkling her freckled nose.

"It's my fault."

"Yours?" she says with a smirk. "Mom, how can you think that? You always did everything to please her."

I stand up, folding my arms across my chest to stare out the window at the large magnolia tree. A white picket fence edges the manicured flower beds where I spent last weekend mulching and weeding. The fence's irony is not lost on me. For an instant, an image of three little girls playing out on the front lawn comes to mind. However, the note in my hand quickly removes all doubt that my daughter is not playing safely within my reach.

"I should have told Nélie more about her real parents." I exhale. "I guess I was waiting for the right time, but it never came."

My mind races over my many conversations with Matt about telling Nélie the truth about her parents. He always warned me that it would be a mistake. Every time I spoke of India, he shook his head and said, "Lauren, it's a bad idea to rehash the past. The truth will only mess her head up. Don't do it." Against my better judgment, I withheld so much information from her that it pains me now to think of it.

"What are you going to do?" Laura asks plaintively, her voice losing some of its teenage defiance.

"I need to find her," I reply, my voice cracking. *Think like her*, I tell myself. Several destinations in Virginia and New York come to mind. Going over the likelihood of these possibilities, I quickly discard both, thinking that she could still visit them within the confines of her suburban life. Suddenly, it occurs to me that Nélie may have confided in her closest friend, Margaret. Propelled into action, I run out to the front hallway, reaching for the phone.

"Laura, run and find me the school directory downstairs. It's on the top shelf in the kitchen. I need to talk to Margaret. Hurry!" I demand, willing myself to stay calm and think rationally. Within seconds, I find out that Margaret's not at home but studying in the language lab at school for her finals.

"Laura," I say, hanging up the phone, "I'm going to run over to school and talk to Margaret. She's got to know something. Anything." I pull Laura close, squeezing her tightly for support. "I love you," I whisper in her ear. "Stay here and wait for your sister to get home. I'll be back as soon as I can."

Laura seems about to protest, then nods her head in acceptance.

I race to grab my purse, find my car keys and head outside. Pausing at the bottom of the steps, I call out, "If your father phones, don't let him know what's happened yet. I'm hoping Nélie hasn't gone far."

Just thinking of Matt's reaction makes my head spin. "She's trouble, Lauren," he always says. "Just you wait and see."

The high school is nearby. Trying to remain calm, I reverse the car too hard down the driveway, practically running over a long row of bushes. In frustration, I pitch the car forward again, causing the wheels to screech, then back it down carefully. Driving up the tree-lined street, I am greeted by the oasis of familiar landmarks: the Browns' house with several bikes scattered on the driveway; a white flag with a watermelon (which the girls think looks more like a pizza) hanging from the Murrays' porch; the small triangular park with the old metal swing set where I used to take the girls when they were little. I think over the events of the past week, carefully searching for clues in Nélie's behavior. Was there anything unusual that happened? Or was this a decision she had been planning for months?

Last Friday afternoon, Nélie had asked to borrow my car to head to the local mall with Margaret to do some shopping.

"Hi Mom," she'd said, taking off her sweater. "I'm beat. We had a review for our Chinese final and I swear I'll never get all the sounds right. It's such a complicated language and culture to understand, especially since I've never been out of the United States." She glared at me, having issued this reminder that I had refused to let her go abroad last summer on a school trip.

A pang of guilt coursed through me, thinking that India had traveled all over the world by the time she was eighteen. Swallowing my trepidation, I simply said, "You'll get it, honey. You have a natural aptitude for languages."

Margaret chuckled. "I don't know why you're studying Chinese anyway. How often are you going to use it? You're going to be hard-pressed to find anybody in Greensboro to converse with."

"Who says I'm going to spend the rest of my life in Greensboro, North Carolina?" Nélie shot back, looking at me out of the corner of her eye.

"No one," I replied calmly. "When you're in college, I would encourage you to spend your junior year abroad. I think you'd love it."

Nélie smiled at the thought. "I sure would. By the way, Mom, can you lend me some money? I want to buy something for tomorrow night."

"What's happening tomorrow night?" I inquired, eyeing Margaret, who couldn't hold back a smile.

"Teddy Jansen's having a group of us over. That's all," added Margaret, who seemed to have developed curves overnight. "I'm making Nélie come this time. She's no fun anymore. Every time I ask her to do something, she's either baby-sitting or studying in the language lab."

Realizing that Nélie did more than her fair share of babysitting for her nine-year-old sister, I didn't question her at all. "You know what, Nélie," I said, retrieving my wallet, "I should be paying you something to baby-sit. I'll give you some money to put toward an outfit. I just got a check from Mrs. Mawbry for refinishing her bathroom."

"Mrs. Mawbry," howled Margaret. "Isn't she the lady who wears those tight spandex outfits and all that pancake makeup?"

Nélie laughed, mimicking her walk. "She's married to that ninety-year-old rich guy. Why are you working for her?"

"She's perfectly pleasant," I said, trying to be professional.

"Oh Mom!" cried Nélie. "She's got awful taste and you know it. Did you paint the bathroom in some jungle print?"

"Close," I replied, shaking my head. "She wanted a sea of pink flamingoes to remind her of her Florida roots."

We all burst out laughing. I added, "I tried to tell her that maybe she should choose something else, but she was adamant."

Without warning, Kathryn came in. Her blond hair was pulled up in a ponytail, emphasizing her heart-shaped face. Her enormous blue eyes sparkled beneath a thatch of white eyelashes. When Kathryn was a baby, she had a head of blond curls. Strangers stopped me regularly, saying something like, "She looks just like Shirley Temple. You should put her on T.V."

"Nélie," she cried, rushing over to give her big sister a hug. "You're back! Wanna help me do my fingernails?" She giggled, then held up her hands caked with glitter glue in an array of colors.

Nélie examined her fingers. "Lovely, daaaahling," she said with a drawl, mimicking a Hollywood starlet. "What are you making?"

"A cover for my report on my kindergarten buddy. It's supposed to be like a biography but mine's more creative— Alexandra loves winter and ice-skating, so I made a glittering snow scene. Making everything white was boring, so I jazzed it up a little bit."

"Does that stuff come off?" asked Margaret with a look of amazement. She peered at her watch, pointing out the time to Nélie. "We've got to go if we're going to make it back by dinner."

Nélie giggled. "Sweetie, I think you're gonna need a box of soap to get that stuff off your hands."

"Come with me, Kathryn. I think I've got something that'll work," I chimed in, pulling her alongside me.

"Hey Nélie, wait!" cried Kathryn, running for her sister. "Will you take me to McDonald's for lunch tomorrow? Pleeease!" Kathryn grabbed Nélie's black T-shirt with her glitter-crusted fingers.

Unfazed, Nélie merely smiled, then bent down to be at eye level with her. She kissed Kathryn on her cheek and said, "Sure. I get off work around noon. I'll come get you when I'm done, if I can take Mom's car."

I nodded.

"You're the best!" cried Kathryn, looking up at Nélie with adoration.

That night, Nélie returned home from shopping while we were seated at the breakfast room table eating dinner. She placed her packages by the door, then walked to the sink to wash her hands before joining us.

Matt looked up, eyeing her warily. "You're late," he said, pointing to his watch. "You know your mother puts dinner on the table at six forty-five P.M."

"Matt," I implored, "nobody's punching a clock around here. I told Nélie she could go." I turned around, pointing to the plate I had waiting for her.

"I've suddenly lost my appetite," announced Nélie, turning to leave the room.

Matt stood up. "Oh, no you don't, Nélie. Please sit down and eat dinner with your family." His eyes narrowed, giving his handsome face a sinister appearance.

"Sit next to me," Kathryn motioned, sweetly oblivious to the tension.

Throughout dinner, Matt directed several questions at Nélie that she answered politely before trying to excuse herself from the table. He asked Nélie to wait, but sent Laura and Kathryn upstairs, promising to call them for dessert shortly afterwards.

"What did you buy at the mall?" he questioned, wiping his mouth with his napkin. He leaned forward, peering at Nélie.

She replied calmly, looking him squarely in the eye, "I bought a new outfit for a party I'm going to tomorrow night."

"With what money?" He tapped his foot on the floor.

"My savings from working at The Grille," she answered sharply. She went on. "Mom also gave me some extra to pay me for baby-sitting Kathryn on Saturday nights."

"You did what?" Matt exclaimed, giving me an accusing

stare. "Why would you do something like that? She shouldn't be paid for helping out around here. All of the girls are expected to do their fair share."

"I gave her some of my money, Matt," I said. "If I had a baby-sitter, I'd pay her an hourly rate. What's the difference?"

"You never used to pay your mother, did you? She should be grateful for what she has, not constantly trying to get more. It's always the same with you. It's never enough. You just don't get it do you?" he carried on angrily, his lips narrowing in disapproval. "You're spoiled rotten just like your . . ."

"Don't say it!" screamed Nélie as her eyes filled with tears. She fled the room.

"How could you?" I cried, standing up to face him. "This time you've gone too far. Her mother is dead, Matt. All she has left is our memories of her. Don't you dare criticize India around Nélie." Disgust filled me. "You never knew India well enough to understand her."

"I have to look at a brown-haired version of India everyday," he snapped. "Poor little rich girl India must think this is pretty funny, that I'm supporting her daughter!"

"She's our daughter!" I asserted desperately. "What's the matter with you? Why are you acting like this? Nélie did nothing wrong. She's a good kid, Matt, yet you act like she's some troubled youth! She's a straight-A student, editor of the yearbook, holds down a job to help pay for college, and she's been accepted to Princeton. Why can't you look at the big picture instead of constantly picking at her over little things! So what if she's a few minutes late for dinner, for God's sake. Lighten up!"

The next morning, on his own accord, Matt made breakfast for Nélie.

"Honey, I'm sorry I lost my temper last night," he said, giving her a hug. "It's been a long week at the office and I didn't mean to take it out on you."

Nélie nodded, then said, "What are you making?"

"Ze best French toast in North Carolina," he said. "Mademoiselle Nélie, s'il vous plait. I'll serve you somezing zo delicious you'll sink you're at ze finest bistro in Paree!"

Nélie laughed, then handed him her plate.

Hearing Matt's pseudo-French routine reminded me of the many times we spoke the language together when we were first married. Watching him flip Nélie's toast in the air, I was able to catch a glimpse of the man I married—handsome and charming.

Later that morning, Laura helped Matt wash his car, then accompanied him on his errands. Kathryn and I headed out to my makeshift studio in the garage.

"What are we gonna do today, Mom?" she asked, reaching for a brush and watercolor paints on the counter.

"I've got some wineglasses to finish for a client," I replied, sorting through a set of order forms. "I want you to paint this rose outside. Use that sketchpad over there. Really look at the shape, Kathryn. That's the key to creating a life-like image." I handed her a vase of flowers that I had picked that morning in my garden.

"Mom," she said, staring at me. "Why don't you paint anymore?"

"I do," I replied, grabbing a wineglass. "See these? Mrs. Jackson's going to love them."

"Not those. I mean real pictures, like oil paintings. I've never seen you paint anything as pretty as what's in the living room. Why? I've heard people asking you to." She cocked her head to one side, then stared at me. "Grandma told me you're a gifted artist."

I shook my head. "Honey, she's my mother. Of course she thinks I'm gifted. But I'm not sure how good a painter I really am." I smiled at her. "Now, go on and get started. I'll come over and show you how to study the sunlight on the petals."

I tried to retreat to the safety of a mindless project. Some of Kathryn's questions had already been running through my mind. Why hadn't I painted anything serious for fifteen years? After college, I had wanted to make painting my life's work. I loved the challenge of creating something beautiful. Hours would go by unnoticed as I worked in Henri Gustave's studio in the evenings. On weekends, I would head out to places like the gardens at Versailles to sketch and paint the geometric patterns of the hedges.

When I lived in Paris with India, it was a happy time for me. Each day took on a similar pattern. Mostly, I walked to Gustave's studio in the early morning just as the pâtisseries were opening up. I ordered my favorite hot chocolate to go and munched on a warm pain au chocolate as I made my way to work. Usually, India and I would meet at a round table to discuss ideas with Gustave before we worked on a canvas or cutout.

Gustave had such amazing talent that I was energized just being in his presence. He would demand that I mix just the right color for a section of canvas, teaching me how to achieve a wider range of hues. Or, when we worked on panels for a church project, he would draw the sketch, then I would copy it to learn his technique. I experimented with bright color, often defining a sky with fuchsia or bright orange. Gustave always told me that I had an excellent sense of detail and that my use of color was, in fact, my strength. He encouraged me to find my own style and express it on canvas. When I worked with him, I began to believe I could have a future as a professional artist. I used to picture myself living in a small apartment in Paris, traveling to the countryside on weekends to paint like the Impressionists had before me. There was a fancy gallery on Rue St. Honoré where Gustave used to exhibit his work. Some days, I dared to dream that my work would be displayed in that same gallery.

Every day around two o'clock, Gustave took a nap, so

India and I would break for a leisurely lunch in the park. Oftentimes, our favorite place was the gardens of the Musée Rodin, where we would eat cheese slathered on a baguette and sip a glass of red wine out of a plastic cup. It was so inspiring to stare at *The Gates of Hell* or *Balzac*. But it was the beauty of those pink roses that made me repeatedly take out my sketchpad, trying to recreate them on paper.

Sitting on the stone bench on a sunny afternoon, I can remember feeling sublime surrounded by Rodin's art combined with those beautiful roses. India and I used to watch the tourists walk by us with their cameras in hand, circling the statues. In the late afternoon, the park became quiet; I remember those times best when I could concentrate on my drawing disturbed only by the crunch of the gravel as an occasional visitor passed by us. Reluctantly, we would head back to Gustave's studio to paint for several more hours before ending our workday. Several times a week, we gathered at a café around the corner with five other artists to exchange ideas. Other artists would question India and me on why we chose to follow Gustave's commitment to create beauty rather than doing work that showed man's foibles or expressed deeper emotion.

When I wasn't painting on weekends, I enjoyed getting to know Matt. I had been living in Paris for nearly three years when he moved there. It was so much fun meeting him on Saturday mornings to go look at Napoleon's tomb, see the Musée Picasso or take a walk through the beautiful Park Monceau. We would wander the streets until we selected the perfect café where we would enjoy a leisurely lunch. Back then, Matt had a spontaneous, playful side. Like the hot, summer night when we walked home from dinner. Spying a fountain, he whisked me around back and we just jumped into the water in our evening clothes, kicking and splashing each other until we spied a policeman running toward us. We ran all the way back to his apartment. He was so incredibly charming. Sometimes he would meet me at the studio with a picnic basket and we would eat dinner in a nearby park. After the crash, my life changed dramatically. Within two weeks, I had assumed legal guardianship of Nélie, married Matt, said goodbye to Gustave and returned home to live with my mother in Greensboro until we could find a place to live. Those early years were filled with the more practical aspects of a new marriage and motherhood. I spent hours holding Nélie, taking her to the park, reading her stories, playing games with her and singing her to sleep while she cried for her mother. It was a difficult time living with my mother, who wanted her share of attention, too.

When Matt worked late, Mother used to fix me a drink and ask me to sit in Dad's old chair. We would talk about her bridge club, her work for the church bazaar, her life with Dad. I would listen patiently, trying to provide her with the love she had been missing during my absence. She repeatedly told me how much she loved having us home again. To her credit, she prepared meals, baby-sat, ran errands—anything she could do to be useful. But living with her had its disadvantages. Matt and I had no privacy and our relationship became strained until we found our own home.

I wanted to paint, longed to pick up where I left off with Gustave. But somehow, my work seemed flat. My colors lacked any richness. The ideas seemed to become stale in my new basement studio. Sometimes, while Nélie napped, I would just sit downstairs for hours painting one small leaf or hedge. When I tried to blend my colors the way Gustave taught me, I became frustrated and angry, often smearing a white canvas with blue paint. Over the years, I painted small scenes on canvas, but there was a spark missing in the final product. It just wasn't good enough anymore. When I reviewed those canvases with a critical eye, it was as if I had gone backwards and those years under Gustave's vibrant tutelage had never taken place. The harder I tried, the worse my work became so I let go of it for a while.

Before long, I became pregnant with Laura, then Kathryn. We moved again to a larger home. When I would try to sneak time in the garage to paint on canvas, something always seemed to go wrong with my children. I remember looking carefully at my work and deciding that it still wasn't good enough to justify spending time away from them. At that time, I truly believed I had no talent, that I could never live up to the standards set by Gustave. The group of paintings in my garage seemed an embarrassment. I refused to paint anything for several years.

After my mother had let it slip that I had been trained as an artist, one of my friends asked me to help raise money for Laura's school. She begged me to put together some ceramic pieces for them to sell at my own booth. Nélie and Laura were so enthusiastic about my new ideas that I felt encouraged. Ceramics were a different medium from painting so I took a deep breath and headed back into the studio. First, I fashioned the bases for several lamps, then painted them with polka dots and unusual combinations. As I worked, I actually started to have fun. Simple wineglasses took on a whole new meaning for me. I drew floral vines and zebra stripes, whimsical figures and patterns. To my amazement, every one of my pieces sold and I received so many compliments that it made me feel good again about myself as an artist.

As for painting on canvas, I've been too afraid to try again. My visions for landscapes still turn dark and cloudy in my mind. It's as if a part of my life carries a scar that I've refused to even examine. I never consciously made the decision to give up my passion; it just happened. Where did my dreams go?

Several hours later, Matt and Laura returned home, both enjoying an easy camaraderie that seemed to come naturally to them. It made me wish he could treat Nélie with the same care and understanding. Laura was laden with packages from the mall. I motioned Matt to meet me in the backyard, out of earshot of the girls.

"What were all those packages Laura was holding?" I asked.

He grinned. "You know, you look cute with that streak of blue across your cheek." He leaned over, trying to kiss me, but I ducked away.

"I'm serious. It looks like you bought her half the store. Why? You just came down so hard on Nélie for buying an outfit. It's not fair. You have two completely different standards for our girls."

"Not necessarily," he said, shrugging. "Laura's a good kid. She spent the morning helping me around the house. I gave her a little reward."

My chest heaved as I tried to steady myself. "Then do the same for Nélie. Take her out and spend some time with her. She'd love that."

Matt reached over, trying to pull me close. "You know, you're very persuasive when you want to be," he said, trying to nuzzle my neck.

I pushed him away. "Will you please try harder with her?" I begged. "We're all she's got."

He stared hard at me. "Lauren, for the record, I've been a damn good father to Nélie. I've done more for her than her own father would have! But it's never enough for you!" He turned away.

"You're right," I said gently, reaching for his arm. "I'm sorry, Matt. It's just that I worry about her sometimes. She's old enough to start questioning things now."

He smiled, then took me in his arms and kissed me gently on the lips. "I'll try harder," he promised, running his hands through my hair. "I love our life together, Lauren. I'll see if Nélie wants to do something together next weekend if you think it'll help."

"Thank you," I said, looking into his eyes.

*   *   *

A loud horn blares behind me, focusing my attention back on the accelerator. I immediately turn left, then right into the back parking lot of the school. A student clad in soccer clothes gives me directions to the language lab. I race down two flights of steps, walking through an endless corridor. Opening the industrial-looking door, I find nearly all of the cubbyholes filled. Margaret's blond head grabs my attention. She happens to look up; the instantaneous look of fear on her face tells me she knows something.

Telling myself to calm down, I hope that reason will persuade her to tell me what I want to know. I make my way to where she's sitting, motioning her to come with me to a place where we can talk in private. We find a small, windowless room littered with textbooks which offers us a modicum of privacy.

I remove the crumpled note from my pocket, handing it to Margaret. "I just found this note in Nélie's room. She's run away."

Margaret pauses, then says, "Oh, my God, why? Oh, Mrs. Wright, I had no idea." She reads it over, shaking her head. Her cheeks are flushed with anxiety.

"Where did she go?" I ask, losing patience with Margaret's Academy Award-winning performance. "I need to know."

Margaret shakes her head. "I don't know, Mrs. Wright."

Lunging forward, I put my face just inches from hers. "Answer me, dammit! She could be in real trouble. There are things she could find out about her real parents that will hurt her deeply, Margaret. I've got to get to her first!"

Margaret's eyes turn into black moons with only a hint of blue remaining. "What are you saying? I don't understand!"

"You don't need to. If you care about her at all, please, I'm begging you, tell me how to find her."

With a deep sigh of resignation, Margaret rolls her eyes and then says, "She's gone to Paris. I'm not sure exactly where. She wanted to know more about her real mom, Mrs. Wright."

Tears well up in my eyes. *I knew it.* I feel overwhelmed by Nélie's defection.

Seeing my reaction, Margaret quickly adds, "It's not that she doesn't love you, Mrs. Wright, she says that she just has this giant hole inside her. She says she'll never know who she really is until she can find out more about her mom." Sensing my anguish, Margaret softens, giving me a sympathetic look.

I look up, then say, "Thank you for telling me the truth."

Certain I need to be on the next plane to Paris to find my daughter, I race home. The trip back to the house is a blur. A vision of our old apartment in Paris flashes through my mind, awakening long-forgotten memories.

Laura is waiting at the door for me. "Mom, what happened? Did Margaret know anything?"

"Yes," I reply, throwing down my purse. "She says she's gone to Paris. Where's the phone? I need to call the airline."

Her voice rises several notches. "Mom, are you crazy? How do you know for sure that she's gone to Paris? I can't believe you'd be that stupid! You're just going to drop everything and head off to some city where you think she might be! Call the police or something."

"You sound just like your father," I snap back, watching her place her hands on her hips.

"My dance recital's on Saturday. We've been rehearsing all year. I'm supposed to get an award. You promised you'd be there!"

"Laura," I sigh, walking over to grasp her shoulders. "Sweetie, you know how much I love you. I've never missed one of your recitals. But Nélie's in trouble. She needs me more right now. Can you please try to understand that?"

"What about the rest of us? Don't we count?"

I want to shout—*please don't make me feel any worse than I already do.*

Instead, I say calmly, "You know how proud I am of you. Your dad will be there and so will Kathryn. You've also got your grandmother coming. I think your cheering section will be plenty big." I kiss her forehead and smooth back her hair. "Laura, please try to understand. If Nélie has gone to Paris, she may find out things that'll really hurt her. Perhaps even shatter her world. I can't let that happen. There are things I should have told her about her family but didn't. She'll feel completely betrayed by me."

"What things?" she asks, her eyes wide with speculation.

"I can't tell you, silly," I reply, trying to lighten the mood. "We'll all talk about it soon, I promise."

Chapter 2

I pick up the phone and dial Matt's cell phone. "Nélie's gone!" I say. "She's run away."

"What?" he cries instantly. "Are you sure?"

"She left us a note saying she'd be in touch when she's ready." My voice cracks.

"All right. Let's stay calm and figure out how to find her. I'll call the police," he offers.

"No," I exclaim. "Not yet!"

The conversation seems disjointed as I spew forth the relevant details on the whereabouts of our other girls, about my need to go after Nélie myself, my hunch she's gone to Paris, and my plan to hop the next plane to New York.

I hang up quickly, careful not to let Matt shatter my resolve. I head to my bedroom to pack, trying to assuage my own guilt at leaving my husband and two daughters. The wall of shame creeps back up to surround me. A part of me wants to go—needs to go. It's a feeling I can't explain. It's as if sirens are clanging inside my mind, calling forth unresolved conflicts from my past.

The pale yellow walls of my bedroom seem to embrace my troubled senses for a moment. A notebook on my bedside table reminds me of the lists I write each day; it's a ritual that I must complete every evening before bed. Gazing around the room, I look at the floral curtains, the beige woven carpet and the large old trunk of my grandmother's. The gold-framed oil painting of a ballet dancer, a copy of a Dégas, never fails to delight me. India gave it to me as a birthday present after I moved to Paris. She also gave me a Matisse, which I placed in storage when I left Paris. I've thought about getting it over the years but it would raise questions with Matt that I've refused to think about. In the righthand corner, the overstuffed blue and white striped armchair, where I frequently curl up with a good book, offers me a safe haven.

Silver-framed pictures of the girls line my dresser. There's Nélie's senior portrait, an old photograph of Laura and Kathryn dressed as a peanut butter and jelly sandwich for Halloween, my wedding photo, a picture of my parents smiling in front of the home where I grew up. I'm drawn to an old photo of a nine-year-old Laura grinning after completing her year-end ballet performance. Her expression is silly and uninhibited.

Looking at Laura's picture, I'm reminded of a time when life was a lot less complicated. These days, I'm desperate to maintain some sort of balance in our relationship. At fourteen, she's caught in the throes of raging hormones and peer pressure. Sometimes, she fiercely demands her independence by challenging my authority; at other times, she needs me terribly.

If not for a school conference, I would take offense at Laura's frequent churlish remarks. Her teacher and I met last month to discuss Laura's progress. She shared Laura's recent homework assignment that required her to write about the person she admired most. Much to my surprise, she had actually chosen to write the report on me.

Lauren Wright is more than just my mother—she's someone I admire most because of her devotion to her family, her friends, her church and her community. She always thinks of others before herself. When Mrs. Chambers, a family friend, became ill and was confined to her bed, my mother brought her a home made dinner regularly, visited several times a week and helped raise money to pay her medical bills. She also volunteers her time at the local hospital, church and senior center.

My mother is always there for our family and I know I can always count on her. In my opinion, helping others is more important than making a lot of money at your job or being famous.

Her words brought tears to my eyes. Being a full-time mother doesn't afford me much praise by either society or my kids. Mostly, I hear about what I've done wrong or what I haven't done. Laura's report made me feel good about myself. But if she thinks so highly of me, why does she challenge me all the time?

Taking a deep breath, I move away from the picture, focusing my attention on the task at hand. Instinctively, I go searching for India's gold pin, which I keep in its green suede case buried in my bottom drawer. Six months ago, I began allowing Nélie to wear it on special occasions. Laura became jealous, so I loaned it to her for a dance last weekend.

Still trembling from the shock of Nélie's disappearance, I weed through piles of sweaters to find the familiar object. I greedily unzip the case to find it completely empty. Knowing Laura was the last person to borrow it, I call her.

"Laura," I say. "Can you come here?"

"Yeah, Mom. What's up?" she asks, her hands clenching when she sees my suitcase.

"Where's India's pin?" I ask, while sorting through a pile of shirts.

Her cheeks flush. "*Mother*, it's still at Claudia's house. I forgot to bring it home."

"You what?" I reply, irritated. "Come on, Laura! You know how much that pin means to me!"

"Oh please," she replies sarcastically. "It's just a pin."

"It's not just a pin," I assert. "It was India's pin. I told you when you borrowed it to return it to its case right away. Why didn't you do it?" I question anxiously, waiting for her response.

"What's the big deal?" she says, placing her hands on her hips.

Willing myself to be patient, I say, "I want to take it with me. Call Claudia and see if you can go over to get it."

Laura frowns at me, then turns around, slamming the door. Taking a deep breath, I catch my reflection in the mirror, wondering at the woman I see there. Who am I? The face that stares back at me looks anxious, angry and disillusioned. Was I always this way? Turning to the side, I suck in my stomach, thinking that it was once flat as a board. Black rings make my eyes look sunken rather than exotic. My blond hair is plastered to my head in a makeshift style. I lean toward the mirror to take a closer look. The eyes that stare back at me appear as empty as black holes in the night sky.

Before long, Laura throws open my door, carrying the pin. She scowls at me, dumps it on the bed and walks away without a word. I reach for the pin—a two-inch solid gold cricket with tiny emerald eyes. The wing is bent. I stifle a cry to Laura to explain how she broke it. Now is not the time for more arguing, I tell myself rationally, as I run my fingers over the gold object. India used to wear it everywhere when we lived in Paris together. I had nearly forgotten about it until Nélie started asking to borrow it. Placing it on my black sweater, I quickly finish the job of packing, placing my notebooks carefully in the stacks of neatly folded clothes.

I call Matt's travel agent to make arrangements for the next available flight to Paris. My best option, I discovered, is to fly out of Kennedy Airport tomorrow morning. Needing a place to stay in New York for the night, I call my old college friend Paige Riverton. Paige seems overjoyed at our impending reunion, apparently forgetting the crisis that prompted her invitation. Then again, that's Paige, who can always find a reason to have a party. Her enthusiasm lightens my mood—but not for long.

Knocking on Laura's door, I crack it open, calling her name softly. Her room is unusually neat for a teenager's. Her books are organized in their shelves by subject; hairbrushes, barrettes and hairbands line the top of her hand-painted dresser; the blue-flowered comforter is pulled up. A row of stuffed animals in various shapes and sizes decorate her pillows, reminding me that she's still just a kid.

"Hi!" I say, sitting on the edge of the bed. "Can we talk before I go?"

"No," she says sulkily.

I push on. "India's pin is important to me. I don't mind if you borrow something of mine as long as you return it in the same condition that you found it. I know that's not asking too much. You're really responsible when you want to be." My last statement hangs in the air.

She reluctantly turns from her desk to face me. "Why are you going? Why does *she* always come first?" Laura's petulant expression hurts me.

"Laura, that's not fair and you know it. I've never played favorites with any of you. I've always tried to give each of you what you need. Right now, Nélie needs more than you and Kathryn. I made a mistake by not telling her enough about her real family. She needs to hear the truth from me, not some stranger. Does that make sense?"

"Why are you wearing that pin?"

"You mean, how can I wear it, since you broke its wing?" I ask, eyeing her warily.

"Whatever," she says grudgingly, staring down at her sneakers.

"The pin reminds me of India. It's time I face my memories so I can share them with Nélie."

"I just don't get it. It's like India was this goddess or something. I know she was Nélie's mother and she died young, but you act so weird about her. Why?"

Her words strike a chord in me so deep it hurts. I pause, grasping for the right words. "When India and I lived in Paris together, I remember feeling so passionate about life. I lost that feeling when she died. Does that make sense?"

"Not really," she blurts out. "Aren't you happy with Daddy?"

"Of course!" I respond, too quickly. "I'm just worried about Nélie, that's all. How could you ever think such a thing?"

She shakes her head. "Just things. Like the way you two yell at each other all the time." She looks down, fiddling with a button on her cardigan.

I want to tell her that she's right. That I'm not happy and I don't really know the man I married. I wonder if I ever really knew him. But I can't explain these feelings, even to myself.

I shrug. "I've got to go now, sweetheart. I'll be back before you know it. You guys have fun with your daddy."

She nods while I kiss her on the cheek. Turning toward the door, Laura says, "Mom."

"Yes?"

"Don't go."

"Laura, I have to find her. You know how much I'll miss you. Have your dad take lots of pictures Saturday night."

She turns her back to me. I close the door, wondering if I'm making a terrible mistake by leaving. I head downstairs, checking my watch repeatedly, wondering why Kathryn isn't back yet. I can't leave without saying goodbye. I walk through the kitchen to stare out the window again as my anxiety mounts. When I envision telling her about Nélie, I anticipate her sadness, which upsets me further.

As I walk around downstairs, I instinctively touch the

framed pictures of the girls lining a silk-skirted round table in the living room; my hand moves along the top of an uphol-stered chair covered in a bright leaf pattern. A large, colorful oil painting of a pond decorates the top of the fireplace. I painted that picture when I lived in Paris. It brings a smile to my face whenever I see it. I don't think I've painted anything this good on canvas in fifteen years. Where did the time go?

Moving into the family room, I take in its "lived-in" look that I love, from the scattered color photographs of our fam-ily to the kids' artwork everywhere. My eye catches an or-ange ceramic dog that Kathryn made for me last Mother's Day. My border of painted blue swirls below our crown molding gives the room a whimsical look. Instinctively, I walk over to the brightly patterned sofa and start fluffing the cushions. Looking at my watch, I note the time as I impa-tiently wait to talk with Kathryn.

Afraid I'm going to miss my plane, I phone my mother, but there's no answer. Hanging up in frustration, I decide I can have the cab take the girls and me to her house on my way to the airport. I search for the number for the local cab service. Matt marches into the kitchen while I'm on the phone.

"What are you doing?" he says, his eyebrows drawn to-gether in confusion. He paces back and forth in front of me. I cup the phone and signal for him to be quiet.

"Hang up, now, please!"

"Don't start, Matt. It's not going to change my mind!" I reply forcefully, slamming the receiver down.

"Lauren!" he says. "This is crazy! I'm not going to let you fly off to Paris alone. You've no idea where she's gone. We need to call the police and have a detective help us." He loosens his blue patterned tie.

"No!" I cry sharply, noticing the beads of sweat on his upper lip. "Just give me a week. I know I can find her. She's upset and she needs me now more than ever!"

"If she needs us so badly, why did she just take off?" He

sighs. "Our real daughters wouldn't do this. Nélie's just like her mother—spoiled and selfish."

Tears prick my eyes. "How can you be so insensitive? She's a seventeen-year-old kid who's trying to find some answers!" I reach for the phone, my gaze daring him to stop me. "Either you can take me to the airport or I can call a cab. Why can't you be more supportive?"

When I stare at him directly in the eye, he's the one who looks away, running a hand through his brown hair. I watch him, noticing his conservative suit, necktie and brown loafers. Many people have told me how lucky I am to have such a handsome husband. I peruse his straight nose and athletic build. He shakes his head.

"All right!" he says. "You win. We'll do this your way. But if you don't find her in a week, then we're getting the police involved."

"It's not a competition, Matt. I wish you'd be more understanding."

"Lauren, I love you and I'm concerned that you're making a mistake by doing this alone," he explains, leaning against the counter. "All right?"

Relief floods through me. I reach over to touch his hand, knowing that he's trying to understand my motives.

I say softly, "I need to get going. Laura's upstairs. Kathryn's at a friend's house. She should be home any minute."

Matt nods. "What time's your flight?"

"Six-thirty."

"Then we need to leave here in fifteen minutes," he says, moving away.

Moments later, I hear a car door slam, and I rush outside. Kathryn arrives, her pigtails bouncing on her bright yellow sundress. She carries her tie-dyed book bag over one shoulder.

"Mom!" she cries, rushing forward to give me a big hug. That greeting is what makes all my hard work worthwhile.

"Hi sweetie," I say, kissing her cheek. I wave to her ride, then walk inside with Kathryn. "Did you have a good time at Haley's house?"

"Yes!" she says. "We played soccer in her backyard. I scored two goals against her brother."

"That's terrific!" I say, putting my arm around her. "Come on inside for a minute. I need to talk with you."

"What's wrong? You look worried about something."

"Come here," I say, taking her hand and sitting her at the kitchen table. While I talk, I open the refrigerator to get her a cold drink while she helps herself to an apple. "Nélie left us a note. She's gone away, and I need to find her."

Kathryn's eyes fill with tears. "I don't understand. Nélie would never leave me without saying goodbye or telling me where she's going."

My heart aches as I watch her face fall. I fight my own tears that threaten again. "Your big sister loves you, Kathryn. I know that—she's just confused right now. I'm the only one who can help her sort things out."

"Mom, are you leaving, too?" she asks quietly, her eyes full of confusion and fear.

"Oh, sweetheart," I cry, rushing over to her side, giving her a hug. "It's just for a few days. I promise I'll be back in no time."

She places her head on my shoulder. "I don't understand. Why did Nélie leave? We were supposed to go to the mall on Saturday."

"Kathryn, I'll have Grandma take you. She would love that—just the two of you. Can I call her and ask?"

"I don't want to go with Grandma! You take me. You never leave—that's not fair." She stamps her foot.

Matt stands in the doorway, watching our exchange. He folds his arms in front of him, sending me a look of complete disapproval. I hesitate, questioning my decision, then listen to my inner voice, which tells me that I need to go after Nélie, that my other girls will be fine with my mother and Matt caring for them.

I kiss her cheek. "Your dad's going to be here. You guys are gonna have loads of fun without me. I'll bet he'll let you order in pizza and eat McDonald's."

Kathryn runs out of the room.

"Kathryn!" I cry anxiously. "Please!" I hear the door to her room slam. Checking my watch, I hesitate, thinking again that I can't leave. It's crazy to go after Nélie myself. Taking a deep breath, I phone my mother to explain what's happened.

"I knew from day one that kid was going to be trouble," she says.

It's a wonder Nélie didn't run away sooner. I shout, "Mother, I need your help right now! Will you please come over and stay with the girls so Matt can take me to the airport! Please!"

"Well, if you put it that way. I'll be there in less than ten minutes."

"Fine. Bye."

Slamming the receiver down in frustration, I look up to see Matt with a self-righteous look on his face. My mother always had a soft spot for him. "Who was that?" he asks, as if he didn't know.

"Mother. She'll be here in a few minutes to help out."

"What did she say?"

"None of your business," I snap. "You don't have to take me. I can call a cab."

"Lauren, stop this nonsense. I said I'd take you. Now, let's get going!" He walks over to pick up my bags. "I'll be in the car. Come out as soon as she gets here."

"Thanks for your help," I reply sarcastically.

Chapter 3

Sitting on the 737 bound for New York, I feel a strange sense of déjà vu. What does Nélie know about her mother? Where should I start with the story? Contemplating my crimes, I wish I had let Nélie go to Spain last summer on a school trip. Nélie was furious at my refusal and didn't speak to me for a week. Why didn't I say yes?

I was afraid she would die in a plane crash just like her mother. At the time, my excuses seemed original. I argued that it was our last summer vacationing in Maine together, that graduation would change things, giving her more freedom to do what she wanted. In truth, my refusal was based solely on my fears.

Taking out a compact, I powder my nose, unmindful of anyone who would care to watch. My forty-two-year-old face has a broad forehead and straight nose that seem rather ordinary. If not for nearly almond-shaped eyes balanced by thick blond hair, I would blend into a crowd. India once called my eyes "exotic" and used to question me incessantly about them. I remember wanting to claim something musty and foreign, exotic and interesting, such as that my father came from Bangkok, my mother was British and we lived on a houseboat and spent our weekends jetting off to Belize. The reality was that my father was a retired insurance executive and my mother a former school teacher.

My memories of India have lingered on the edge of my consciousness, especially in the past year. She lived life freely without hesitations or fears and, while I knew her, I tasted freedom, adventure and the promise of infinite possibilities. I reveled in our Paris days, in our naiveté in the joy we derived from walking along the Seine, painting for Gustave and indulging in late nights filled with endless conversation about improving our brush strokes. For that brief time in Paris, I wasn't even required to fulfill life's basic needs: food, an apartment or a car. As it happened, Julian DuBusé paid for everything for India, and I, as her roommate, received many of the benefits.

It was India who had arranged for our internship with Jules Gustave, whom many in the art world considered a genius. We were only supposed to work with him for a year, but the time was gradually extended as he allowed India and me an opportunity to be his hands as his arthritis worsened. Each day, I learned something new under his often gruff tutelage. He never failed to intimidate me with his bursts of temper. Some days, after one of his creative tantrums, I'd have to talk myself into going back into his presence. His mood swings were sudden, like the onslaught of a thunderstorm, and then afterwards, he would calm down and proceed to work with an intensity I'd never seen before.

As time went on, Gustave allowed India and me to try some of our own ideas, while he made suggestions. Thanks to him, I learned how to make certain complex compositional decisions, create vivid color and find the beauty in everyday objects. I remember being so inspired by the three-dimensional images that he added to a canvas. He was always refining his own concepts, reaching for a higher level of design. Gustave had a kind of energy that ignited everyone around him. I felt like a human sponge, soaking up every bit of knowledge that I could.

Before I knew it, four years had passed.

I remember one of the days from my last week in Gustave's studio. After a late lunch with Matt in the park, I headed back to my work. It was a beautiful afternoon and the air was only slightly damp. I remember thinking how much I loved the city of Paris. When I walked into Gustave's work space with the vaulted ceiling, I contemplated spending the rest of the day cleaning everything up. The place seemed a mass of chaos. Paintings were stacked against the walls and paints had been placed hastily on a long wooden bench. India's work area matched the rest of the place. My corner, however, was organized with all of my brushes clean and my paints stacked by color, according to how I planned to use each of them. India used to tease me relentlessly about this, oftentimes coming over to playfully switch two colors just to irritate me.

No one noticed my late entrance since Nélie proved to be the center of attention. Pauline Gustave, a short, robust woman with long gray hair knotted in a bun, was scooping Nélie up in her arms, promising her some delicious lemon cake.

"Hi, everyone," I said, removing my jacket and placing it on the hook behind me. I grabbed my smock and went straight to the canvas I had been working on, hoping India wouldn't question me too much about Matt. I knew she wasn't crazy about him, so it was easier not to talk about it. That day, I had planned to achieve brighter hues of blue on one of Gustave's paintings. Working furiously on my palate, I looked over when I heard Gustave raise his voice.

"The color was supposed to be mauve, India. Not black," he said, glaring at her. His arthritic fingers were hidden in his jacket pocket.

"It suits her better, don't you think," India replied thoughtfully, standing back a bit to look at the nude she was finishing for him.

Gustave moved away and paused for a moment. He shook his head in disapproval. "You can't edit my work based upon your moods," he said sharply.

"I'm not!" she shouted.

"Watch your temper with me, India." Gustave turned his back to her.

India put down her paintbrush. "I'm sorry," she said softly. "You're right. I'll change it back to mauve." She immediately began making the color change.

Gustave nodded, then wandered over to inspect a canvas I had produced on my own. Over the last year, he had finally allowed us both to try some of our own ideas, while he finetuned the details. I hunched up my shoulders nervously as he inspected my abstract portrait of Pauline, a harmonious blend of blues and greens.

He smiled and nodded his approval as he studied the painting. I knew he liked it. "Lauren, you paint extremely well," he said. "You have a gift for color that you use in a way I've never encountered."

He glanced over at one of India's paintings of a nude jazz musician. "Indeed, you both paint extraordinarily well. India, your work may provoke the viewer. Lauren takes ordinary subject matter and makes it extraordinarily beautiful."

India came over and stared at the canvas I was working on. She said softly, "Your colors are spectacular. I've never seen anything like it. I knew you had a gift when I first met you." She paused and looked over at me, raising one eyebrow. "If you weren't my best friend, I think I'd hate you. You're even too *nice*. I'm not nice and I don't want to ever be nice!" She punched my arm playfully.

Gustave threw back his head and laughed. "India, I can always count on you to liven things up around here. Ever since you were a child, I knew you had spirit. Tell me, how's Julian?"

India sighed, then leaned against a chair. "Married," she snipped.

"So, what's the problem?" Gustave took a gnarled hand out of his pocket and placed it on her shoulder. "He loves you, you know. You can see it in his eyes."

"Does he?" she replied, a hint of a smile curving the corner of her mouth. "She's worse than a pit bull. Why can't he just leave her?"

"You know why." He paused, then looked over at several canvases. "Now, how about finishing some of your own work so it'll be ready for the opening in a month."

"What? But I'm leaving tomorrow. I can't possibly finish." India shook her head.

My heart pounded in anticipation. "Are you serious?" I gasped.

Gustave looked at both of us. "It's time," he said quietly.

I looked over at India and said in a rush, "We can do it! There's only one more of Gustave's nudes to finish. I have a new idea I'd like to try. Why don't you go to New York after the show? That way we'll have enough time to get everything done."

India said nothing.

I knew something was wrong. Indeed, it was strange for India to be acting so subdued. I planned to talk with her about it that night. Instead, she left to run errands and I volunteered to take Nélie home and put her to bed after I finished painting. That night, India arrived with a bottle of wine, a baguette, a round of brie and a chocolate bar for dinner for us. We ended up by talking about how I could balance working for Gustave with caring for Nélie that week. India knew how much I loved Nélie so she detailed few instructions, except one: she was very particular about her daughter trying different types of foods. I did have to gently remind her that Nélie was only two years old. Finally, we headed to bed without a word about her abrupt departure.

The following night, around ten o'clock in the evening, I awoke to the sound of my phone. It was Julian.

"I'm sorry Lauren," he said.

"About what? What? What's the matter?"

"India's plane. It . . . it blew up over the Atlantic."

Rescue workers were searching the waters for some sign of life, but they had only found bits of debris. It was unlikely, they said, that anyone had survived the explosion.

That horrible night, I knew instantly that I needed to take care of Nélie. At that moment, she became mine as if I'd just given birth to her myself. Fortunately, two months earlier, India had drawn up papers naming me the legal guardian should anything happen to her. Now that she was gone, her foresight seemed surreal.

That was fifteen years ago, and I'm just now beginning to realize that my adventurous spirit died with India. After the crash, I wanted calm, safety, control over my environment. I wanted a family and, most importantly, security. A week after India died, I married Matt and made arrangements to return home. The months ahead were challenging, as Matt and I struggled to find each other while trying to help this child cope with the loss of her mother.

Maybe my first mistake was moving back home to Greensboro, a conservative community where four generations of my family had lived. It was 1982 and Ronald Reagan was president. Greensboro was a place where "family values," at that time a catchphrase of the Republican Party, had meaning. My life in this small southern community consisted of such hallowed traditions as Aunt Jean's homemade pecan pie on Sunday nights, the monthly church bake sale, regular visits to the senior center, Mother's bridge club meetings, the annual fall arts and crafts fair and the Garden Club's daffodil show.

Sudden parenthood awakened that same sense of over-responsibility in me that I had begun to relinquish through my relationship with India. Pragmatism became my playfellow and reality, while less exciting, felt calm. I needed to be in control to cope with India's death, a new marriage and motherhood.

At twenty months, Nélie had been old enough to know that I was not her real mother. I remember how many times she woke up in the middle of the night crying for her mother. Her little face was soaked with tears as I struggled to explain that her mother rested peacefully in a better place. The words, "I want my Mommy," challenged every religious belief I had ever harbored. Why did India die so young? I sat up many nights with Nélie, holding her, soothing her brown hair back from her forehead. Sometimes, I sang to her in French; only then would she fall asleep.

A year after India's death, Matt and I began to grow apart. He accused me of saving every bit of love I had for Nélie, depriving him of my time, attention and caring. I needed to save my marriage. So I asked my mother to baby-sit two nights a week while Matt and I enjoyed time alone together. At first, it was a disaster because Nélie still cried hysterically every time I left her. It used to break my heart, but I knew that Nélie needed a stable home life now more than ever. Matt and I continued to go out, trying to rekindle our love.

The task of mothering Nélie was daunting. I felt unprepared for my role, often taking it too seriously. I remember the time Matt expected me at an important client dinner. Nélie had a fever, and her cough sounded deep in her lungs. Worried about leaving her, I made a last-minute visit to the pediatrician. He prescribed an antibiotic, while assuring me that she would be fine without me for a few hours. But Matt believed I had committed the ultimate sin by being late for a client social meeting. He was furious, and I heard about it for weeks afterwards. When he eventually lost that client, somehow, he believed that I was ultimately responsible.

Suddenly, the taxi stops short, jolting me forward. I quickly smooth my hair and wipe imagined lint off my black pants, fearing that my outfit's too casual for this elegant apartment building on Manhattan's Fifth Avenue. I head inside, where I am greeted by a fortysomething manager who eyes me warily, then demands to know who I'm here to see.

"Paige Riverton," I reply nervously, noticing a black and white marble floor, a potted tree and a colossal vase filled with fresh lilies, curly willows and snapdragons on the front desk. He punches a number into a phone to confirm that Mrs. Riverton is expecting me.

"Gary'll take you," says the manager, gesturing to another gray-suited man for him to take my bag.

An elevator opens up and I step inside, feeling claustrophobic in its tiny interior. The man's stiff posture doesn't lend itself to any kind of pleasantries. On the thirtieth floor, we get off in front of a pair of mahogany doors. Paige opens them immediately, dressed in men's silk pajamas, her frosted hair professionally flipped at the ends.

"Lauren darling, I'm so glad you're here," she says, wrapping me in a warm embrace. She smells like rose-scented nicotine.

"Oh, Paige, it's great to see you, but I wish it were under better circumstances. Thanks for letting me stay on such short notice. I hope I didn't ruin your evening," I say, self-consciously pulling several strands of hair back behind my ears.

"I'd forgotten how sickeningly sweet you are! Will you come in and sit down. I've made coffee." Paige nods to the doorman. A housekeeper steps forward to take my coat and bag from me.

As I walk into the marble entranceway, I'm greeted by an oil painting of a mother and child. It looks like a Mary Cassatt but I don't want to ask. The living room is formal, with its mixture of floral chintz and elegant upholstered furniture. A glass coffee table is covered with colorful books neatly stacked in rows, a small bronze head of a man and a glass trophy of some sort. Everything appears perfectly arranged, making it a setting fit for a magazine cover. The apartment boasts a dramatic view that I take in briefly until Paige ushers me into a sitting room with floor-to-ceiling silk curtains.

Before I take a seat, I ask Paige whether she minds if I call Matt to check on the girls. Our conversation is brief; he tells me everyone is asleep, and that they're managing just fine without me. His words chip away at my already battered self-esteem and he knows it. Controlling my anger, I hang up and turn my attention back to Paige, who has brought in a tray of coffee and a pack of Marlboro cigarettes for hors d'oeuvres.

"I always smoke in times of crisis," she announces with a glint in her eye. "Let me see your hands."

"Not a pretty sight, huh?" I shrug, surveying my freshly bitten nails. "I've been better for a while. I did it on the plane."

"Look at the bright side—your vice won't kill you."

I nod, observing my old friend, thinking that right now she could grab a purse and head to a cocktail party. With a New York flair for the dramatic, she lights a cigarette, waving the match in the air several times before flicking it into the ashtray. She blows a waft of smoke up in the air as if that will eliminate the smell from the room. The years have added a few extra pounds. Her hands appear swollen beneath four gold, emerald and diamond cocktail rings. It almost looks as if she couldn't decide which ring she liked best, so she bought them all. Her hands speak for the rest of her, as if to say "I'm rich. What else can I say? I married well."

Paige tries to lighten the mood. "Can we talk? Let's talk, Lauren." She glances at my shoulder. "I haven't seen India's pin in years! It looks . . ."

"Broken?"

"Just a little bent in the wrong places, that's all. I always thought it looked more like a grasshopper than a cricket anyway. So tell me, what's happening?"

Through tears, I can't keep myself from laughing. "As I told you on the phone, Nélie left me a note. I think she's on her way to Paris."

"It could be worse. She could have picked Cleveland." I give Paige an ironic smile, realizing she truly believes there's no other city on earth comparable to New York.

"I want her to come home."

"Let me get this straight," Paige says, adjusting her pajama top. "A seventeen-year-old girl heads to Paris, in the spring no less, and you think she's alone looking for her dead mother? What planet have you been living on? She's probably going to meet up with some boyfriend. I hope he's good-looking. You can't go to Paris at seventeen unless you're in love."

I shake my head. "I could tell by her note that she's not thinking straight."

"The hell she's not. She's young and foolish like her mother—like we were. There's a whole world out there and just because you've chosen not to embrace it doesn't mean she's going to do the same. You've got the poor kid holed up in a small town. How much fun can that be? You once jumped at the chance to go to Paris with India when you were twenty-one. Don't you remember?"

"If you put it like that." I wonder why those years seem like a lifetime ago.

"You know what your problem is," Paige says, plunging forward as if our separation over the past fifteen years had never existed. "You're too damned serious these days. You're not auditioning for the role of June Cleaver in some 1950s sitcom. Loosen up a little. Let the kid have fun. She's no dummy. She'll come home when the money runs out."

"Or find someone to pay her way. She's beautiful, just like India," I say, momentarily watching the lights. The housekeeper returns with a silver pitcher full of water, pouring us each a glass. I'm hot and tired, and the ice water relieves my parched throat.

"For God's sake, Lauren, half the women in France would have longed to have had a man like Julian DuBusé pay attention to them. India and I used to call Julian *The Conductor* behind his back. I swear if he'd given the signal, groups of women would have broken into song for him. But, despite his overwhelming charisma, I do think he loved India. It was that lunatic wife of his that caused the problem. She was a real nutcase."

Taking another sip of ice water, I say, "I want more for Nélie. She's been accepted at Princeton."

"So what," says Paige as she crushes her cigarette in the ashtray. "This calls for another one. I doubt Bert will catch me. But if he does, he'll make me get another patch. See," she says, lifting the arm of her pajama top. "I could buy stock in the company."

I start laughing. It's as if the years fade away and we're back in Paris again, only this time without India. None of my friends at home show me their faults; they're all too proper, just as I try to be. Maybe I should have given them a closer look at my hands. Right now, it's such a relief being with someone who's not afraid to admit she's got problems.

Paige's monologue runs on. "I hope you taught the kid about birth control. India failed that course and look what happened—a single mother at twenty-five. I couldn't imagine having a kid at all, let alone when I was that young. It makes me want another cigarette just thinking about it."

I think back over the years trying to pinpoint my conversations with Nélie on the subject. "We talked about sex. I remember the time I tried to sit her down and she said she already knew everything. I figured that was it."

"You mean to tell me you didn't take her yourself to have her fitted for a diaphragm? Or put her on the pill? Half of her genes are India's. Oh my God, why didn't I think of it before? What if she's already pregnant and that's why she ran away?"

I stand up suddenly. "Damn it, Paige. It never even crossed my mind—what if you're right? And she's too afraid to tell me. India never told her own parents about Nélie, if you can believe it. Her mother died never knowing she had a grandchild."

"And her father?" asked Paige, squinting through all the smoke.

"She made me swear never to let Nélie within a hundred feet of him."

"Where does he live? What did he do?" Paige leans forward, searching my face for answers.

"I think he was a politician or something."

"You'd better hope he's not the President or you can kiss your daughter goodbye if he finds out."

"Not funny," I say, suddenly feeling cold.

Chapter 4

Sleep proves elusive as my mind wanders aimlessly through corridors long closed. Until tonight, I haven't really thought about anything more than the endless tasks of everyday life. My *To-Do* lists stare at me, reminding me of my daily goals. Raising three daughters has kept me boxed in the present, unable to reflect on the decisions I made along the way. It's so easy to get caught up in going through the motions of daily life without really living it. Sometimes it feels as if there aren't enough hours in the day once I drive carpool, attend soccer games, swim meets, and dance recitals and the list goes on. I keep a black leather calendar that tracks the time of each day's activities but even then, appointments have been cancelled, promises broken, and dreams forgotten in the myriad details.

I think of the stacks of papers lining my desk. There are files with labels like *Egypt, Scuba Diving, The Caribbean, Art*. Within their confines lie numerous magazine articles cut and readied for my review. But, again, my mind wanders to the present to avoid looking at the past, remembering India and why she made the decision, obtaining my promise early on, not to tell Nélie about her father until she was old enough to understand. Was I wrong to withhold this vital information? Nélie's father lives; he didn't die in the crash, as I had quietly led our daughter to believe. But Julian DuBusé will never acknowledge Nélie's existence. His character is too weak, his need for material gratification too strong, his allegiance to his and his wife's money too powerful for him to even recognize that a part of India still exists and lives on. Had he ever truly loved India? I remember the events leading up to that night when India made me promise never to tell Nélie about Julian. The faces from fifteen years ago awaken in my mind, and I can see the twilight as we walked home from a day spent at a museum that delighted me with its wealth of Dégas paintings. On our days off, India and I would spend time sketching there and studying the great Impressionist artists' work to see how they fashioned a figure or portrayed a scene.

That afternoon, I had spent an hour staring at Manet's *Déjeuner Sur L'Herbe*, a controversial painting in its day because it showed a man lunching with two naked women. I looked at the painting from different angles all over the crowded room, noticing that the women's eyes met mine at each location.

When India viewed the painting, she laughed, wondering why critics had made an issue out of two naked women. She said, "It looks like they're having a perfectly enjoyable afternoon. What was the problem?"

"It was a big deal back then," I replied, pointing to the naked figures. "Manet broke the rules. Before this, artists only painted nudes as angelic-looking figures. Here, Manet shows them as real women, enjoying themselves. It probably offended society matrons who found nudity shocking."

Her face reddening with anger, India shot back, "Why do people listen to society's conventions? It's ridiculous! We're all supposed to follow these rules of conduct and if we don't . . ."—her voice rose several notches—"then we're called sluts or whores. Even worse, our children are called bastards and they're never quite looked at the same way. It's wrong."

People turned to stare at us as India ranted on about morality and stereotypes. I calmly suggested that we leave. After a few more curious stares, we left the picture behind. Once outside, India's lighthearted mood returned with the warm smell of late spring in the air. We walked home at dusk. India's mane of red, curly hair blew in the light breeze. Her lilting voice sounded so sophisticated, a combination of British and South African because she never pronounced her 'th' right. My mother, a schoolteacher, would have corrected each one of her sentences.

Horns blared on the street as we walked along, crossing over a small bridge. After traveling several blocks, we spied several steamships of different sizes and varying degrees of luxury. One line called the *Bateaux Mouches* seemed the most lively, lit up with yellow tabletops set for dinner and a band playing a French version of a Michael Jackson song. India snapped her fingers to the song, twirling around on the sidewalk.

"Let's go!" she said, dancing to the music. "I think they'll take passengers."

"But, I can't," I replied nervously. "I promised Matt I'd meet him for dinner."

India shrugged, "Make him wait. Don't be such an easy catch for him—men like a challenge." Sensing my hesitation, she added, "Come on. It'll be fun!"

I nodded. Then we headed toward the ship. The interior ticket area looked like a bordello with its red walls, red leather seats and ugly statues of Greek gods. Despite the dubious entranceway, tickets were expensive and we didn't have enough money. Not one to be daunted by this minor inconvenience, India flirted with the ticket-taker until he let us in for free.

We didn't realize that the band was part of a wedding reception that filled the other half of the boat. Moments after we pushed off for a ride up and down the Seine, the teenage ticket-taker and his equally young-looking friend joined us.

Red wine flowed easily, helping to ease the headache of indulging in polite conversation with our new benefactors. We dined on lamb and potatoes. As we floated along, I caught sight of a glint of gold trim on elegant buildings lining the river. After dinner, India leaned forward, her expression suddenly serious.

She lit a cigarette, then blurted out, "Julian asked *her* for a divorce and plans to tell his children about us. They're all old enough to handle such things. Oh, and I've found the most wonderful wedding gown. You should see it. It barely reaches my ankles. Perfect for a garden wedding, don't you think?" She took a long drag, holding up her drink for the evening's young patron to fill her glass again.

I hesitated, choosing my words carefully. "I find it hard to believe that *she*'s going to let him off the hook that easily. What are the divorce laws here? Doesn't there have to be a legal separation?"

"He promised me he'd take care of everything by the first of June. It's now the third week in May. I consider it almost done."

Frosted white cake appeared in front of me. I was stuffed, but dipped my finger on top to take a taste of the icing. Greedily licking my finger clean of a blue flower, I focused my attention back on the conversation. "India, I know everything's going to work out, but maybe not this fast, or this easily. She's an heiress to one of Europe's biggest retail fortunes, with a reputation for being tough. Their divorce could get messy. Besides, Julian has three children to think about."

"I've written her a letter," India announced passionately, a wicked gleam in her eye.

"You did what?" I exclaimed, nearly spilling red wine all over myself.

"I won't let her stand in the way of our happiness. She

doesn't love him—he doesn't love her. It's been a marriage of convenience for years and I've waited long enough. I may even go to my father."

"I thought you hated your father."

"I do, but I love Julian more. Besides, despite our differences, Father has an unfailing sense of family loyalty. He sees me as the one who cast him aside. Anyway, the point is, I have connections of my own."

Her face had an intensity I'd never seen before. Fascinated, I watched her long, slender fingers toy with the stem of her wineglass. I stared into her slanted blue eyes, trying to understand how her mind worked. India was impulsive, often recklessly so, and I worried about the repercussions of what she'd just done. I seemed to be the only one worried as India grabbed the bottle, filling her glass with red wine.

"Just what do you expect your father to do?" I asked, holding up my glass for a refill.

"Father knows how to make deals with anyone. You see, he has a gift for maneuvering people right where he wants them."

"He can't be that good. You two haven't spoken in years."

India smiled. "Not since I led that candlelight vigil against apartheid on campus. We got into a terrible fight and he demanded that I make a public apology for my actions. I refused and that was that. He likes to support those in power; I like to help the oppressed. I suppose we'll always be at odds. I like to think of myself as his conscience."

"You must be desperate now, to call on him," I said, seeing the irony of the situation.

"Desperately in love." India sighed, unmindful of the young ticket-taker vying for her attention. She rewarded him with a smile, a squeeze on his arm and a promise that she'd come back sometime soon.

That night, Matt and I had a fight. I returned to his apartment tipsy and giggling. He greeted me at the door as I waltzed in.

"Where have you been? I expected you back two hours ago," he said, his necktie missing and white shirt unbuttoned. Having been surrounded by long-haired bohemian artists for several years, I found Matt's conservative appearance appealing. His look was familiar, southern and preppy, with short brown hair, a straight nose and clear blue eyes. He wore horn-rimmed glasses when he worked and his square jaw boasted a tiny cleft.

"Oh," I giggled, "India and I got sidetracked on the way home. We took a trip down the Seine on one of those tourist boats." I used the word tourist to deliberately distinguish myself as a *real* Parisian. I didn't dare tell him that India had flirted her way onto the vessel for free and then we had danced and drank at someone's wedding—we never did get the name of the bride and groom.

"You what?" he asked, running his hand through his hair. Shaking his head in disapproval, he said, "Lauren, why would you do something idiotic like that? Obviously, you forgot we had dinner plans."

"I'm sorry I'm late," I said, wrapping my arms around him. "Forgive me," I added, kissing his neck. With his shirt unbuttoned, I caught sight of a chain and asked him about it.

His anger momentarily diffused, Matt replied, "It's a St. Christopher's medal that once belonged to my grandmother. I forgot I had brought it to Paris with me."

I reached for him again and he brushed me away. "Lauren, you reek of cigarettes, which I don't find particularly appealing right now."

"Oh," I replied in a small voice. "I'll take a shower."

"Do that," he replied. "I'm starved—let's go get some dinner."

Obediently, I took a shower, not daring to tell him that I'd already eaten.

For the next week, I stayed at Matt's apartment. Half my clothes were there; the other half were at India's place. My mother would have been horrified, so it was easier never to tell her of my exact living arrangements.

That Friday, India and I were working on a painting of a nude reclining on a bed in an Odalisque manner. Gustave, who had studied and worked with Matisse, wanted to recreate Matisse's paintings of nudes in the 1930s giving them his own design. Our mentor was growing increasingly ill, his hands gnarled from arthritis. India and I talked about how much longer we would stay on, deciding we'd give it six more months before making plans; we felt we owed it to Gustave to work with him as long as he wanted us to stay.

While painting the nude's fluorescent pink background, India told me about a gallery opening. The artist's work had received high praise from the critics, which made us both curious—and, perhaps a bit envious. As it turned out, Matt was heading to London on business, so I was on my own.

After work, I decided to head to India's apartment to shower and change before the opening. In a pensive mood, India put on the stereo, cranking it up so the music practically bounced off the four walls. The sound of the drumbeats, with their fast-paced tempo, created an air of excitement. Early summer's warm breeze blew through the balcony doors. India then lit two jars of incense, giving the room a heavy, musty smell.

"What's that?" I asked as I brushed my hair.

"Heat and Passion," she replied. "I'm getting in the right mood." Dressed in a golden sari, her hair wild and flowing, she looked like a red-haired lioness eager to meet her prey.

India stared at me. "*She* thinks I'm the fool. That I'm no match for her. She's wrong," India said, lighting another long, thin cigarillo, a habit she'd picked up from Julian.

Melodrama filled the air as the drums beat on, unmindful of the fact that we were in an elegant section of Paris surrounded by art and antiques, some of which looked as if they had belonged to Napoleon himself. I actually lit up a cigarillo myself. I looked at the clock on the Louis XIV table and realized we only had a few more minutes if we were going to make it to the opening on time. It was India, for once, who noticed the time before I said anything.

"Let's get going," she said, putting her cigarillo in the ashtray.

Suddenly, it occurred to me that her child couldn't be sleeping through all this incense burning and drum beating. "Where's Nélie?" I asked.

"Upstairs asleep with Madame Richard. I'm fortunate to be living in the same building with a sixty-year-old grandmother who's just aching to baby-sit. Julian couldn't have found me a better apartment."

India's flippant description of Madame Richard amused me, considering that dear Julian was fifty-three. Granted, he was gifted with such aristocratic features and charm that age worked in his favor. India was young enough to be his daughter, but she'd have failed to find the humor in such a comparison, so I stayed quiet.

The gallery was located on the Left Bank. As an artist, I was eager to see this work, since it had drawn such high praise from the critics. Crowds of people gathered in the gallery, from the Bohemian to the well-dressed society matrons. I walked inside. The lingering smell of cigarettes made the air heavy. A waiter offered us a glass of wine and I took mine, grateful for something to hold while I attempted to make conversation with strangers. Without Matt's comforting presence, I always felt a little awkward and shy in such situations, while I knew India would flit through the crowd like a cricket, kissing everyone, making loud exclamations of joy when she saw an old friend and dragging me along behind her. She said things like, "You look fantastic tonight," and "I've been meaning to call you, I promise. . . . How was the sea? I always find it so revitalizing to go there . . ." She was a master of the art of small talk and it was truly a gift.

As usual, I lost India to a man wearing a black sweater and boots. Looking around, there appeared to be no immediate prospects for conversation so my attention was drawn to the wall-size canvases of an artist named Isu (pronounced E-soo), which sounded to me like the name of a car.

Above the quiet hum of conversation, I heard comments like, "extraordinary," "fresh," and "luminescent." I studied the canvas and wondered at the gullibility of mankind. Did these people really know what they were talking about? Perhaps it was me, but all I saw was a black canvas with a lightning bolt cut through it. Each canvas looked the same as I squeezed my way around the room, wondering how the crowd could sustain such long conversations about work that seemed so uninspired.

"I see the mark of human suffering in this work," said a Frenchman with a raised eyebrow.

"Really?" I reply. "Where?"

"It's in the lines, separating dark from light. Reality from dreams. Hope from despair. Isu is a genius."

A familiar voice whispered in my ear, "Who in their right mind would buy any of this stuff?"

"Paige!" I said with relief. "What are you doing here? I thought you had a date."

"Oh him, he's over there in the leather jacket. I knew you and India were coming, so I told him that I had to see this opening. This Ishew guy has a lot of nerve charging money for this junk. I wouldn't even want these in my garage!"

I laughed, giving her a hug. "I'm so glad you're here. I thought I was on my own tonight."

"Where's India? Wait a minute, don't tell me. Our India is probably talking with the artist himself, promising to buy something. I personally think that all-black canvas over there would look great in her living room. I think I'll go and offer

Ishew double what it's worth so India will spend more of Julian's money."

"It's Isu," I corrected her quickly, looking around the room for the artist.

"Whatever. His real name is probably John Smith. Oh wait, we're in Paris. I'll bet it's Jacques something."

I wandered down the hallway and turned left, seeking a break from the innumerable pseudo-art critics. A portrait caught my eye, and I was drawn to the clean lines on the canvas. The subject stared back at me, his face furrowed in concentration. Who was this man? What was he thinking about? I wanted to know more about him. Looking pensive, his hand tucked under his chin in concentration, he had a story in the lines of his face. The use of color drew me to him, but once I was there I wanted to stay.

"Do you like it?" said a male voice.

"Love it. Who's the artist?" I replied, focusing on the detail of the subject's eyes.

"An American painter named Jean Whitfield."

I looked over at the man standing beside me, dressed in dark pants and a white shirt. He looked serious, almost reminding me of the portrait in front of me. His hair was dark, his nose large, but attractively so, and his brown eyes had impossibly long lashes. I said, "To me, this is how art should be. I can see the person—I want to know more."

"So I can assume you're not going to be taking any of Isu's work home with you this evening." He took a long swallow of his red wine.

"I can't afford it."

"And if you could?" he questioned, watching me intently.

"I don't think it's really my style."

"Is that your polite way of saying you hate it?"

I looked into his eyes, and felt as if he were someone I could have trusted. I didn't have any reason to feel this way. I just did.

"The truth is I think it's awful. It's too trendy. This kind of work will make Isu famous for a time, but it won't last. Now, something like this portrait will. It's not as fashionable right now but it has a timeless quality to it."

"I agree. That's why I'm back here. What's your name?"

"Lauren."

"I enjoyed meeting you, Lauren. I hope we'll meet again."

I headed back to the party to look for India, hoping to catch a glimpse of her. The wine was making me feel light-headed, so I went in search of some cheese and crackers. Engaged in conversation with the man I had just met, Paige signaled me to join them.

"Lauren," said Paige with a glint in her eye. "I'd like to introduce you to someone very special."

I smiled warmly. "We've met."

"You have?" Paige looked confused as the man and I exchanged glances.

"I just realized I didn't catch your name."

"This is the soon-to-be-world-famous Isu," Paige announced proudly, waiting for my reaction.

My embarrassment was so intense that it felt as if someone had just ripped my clothes off. A blush started at my toes, moving swiftly up my body, taking root in my neck and face. Speechless, I stared at him, wondering what I should say. I had just told him that his work was awful.

"Are you all right?" questioned Paige, grabbing my arm.

"Fine," I replied quickly, wanting to make a quick exit.

Isu smiled and handed me a glass of wine from the tray. "Are you enjoying the opening?"

Chapter 5

The evening wore on and the crowd thinned considerably, so I wound my way to the back of the gallery. Where was India? I wondered, immediately noticing that she wasn't standing in the center of a group of followers all clamoring for her attention. I ruminated on my conversation with Isu, quickening my pace so I could find India and ask for her advice. An apology seemed completely inadequate in the wake of such candor. Why did I have to use the word awful? Couldn't I have said something more constructive, such as that perhaps he should use a brighter color palette? While this work was not my style, I could sort of see what everyone was talking about.

The slight ache in my feet turned into an uncomfortable throbbing sensation and, considering the black sandals I wore, it was no wonder. My search for India became more deliberate as I circled the gallery again, hoping not to run into Isu. When I saw she was nowhere in sight, I headed down the back hallway to find the bathroom. The sound of India's voice caught my attention, and I wondered what she was doing.

Taking my sandals off, I followed the sound into a small sitting area where I heard another woman speak. My instincts told me to leave, but my conscience was no match for my curiosity. The room was littered with half-filled wineglasses along with several ashtrays swollen with cigarette butts. Napkins holding half-eaten crackers decorated a side table. Aside from the lingering odor of cigarettes, I smelled turpentine. A loud remark captured my attention again. The woman's conversation sounded like a hiss as I tried to decipher the torrents of French. Peeking through the door, I saw India talking to an impeccably groomed middle-aged woman with bright red lips. Given the woman's sneer and the harsh exchange, it had to be Julian's wife, Madame DuBusé.

"You're a stupid American!" Madame DuBusé muttered, her lips pursed in disgust. She paced back and forth, her red suit and designer scarf held perfectly in place by a gold tiger-shaped pin.

India started speaking Chinese, which I couldn't understand. As she shifted back to French, I listened to her say, "*Madame*, I'm no more American than you, so your comment is irrelevant." I heard the sound of the match as India lit a cigarillo.

"Just what did you hope to accomplish with that letter of yours? My family will stay together no matter what. I'll not have you tarnish my reputation. I've tolerated you for years. Do you think I haven't known? I've even seen the bills on your apartment. You spend money like it's water."

"I want to get married," India announced.

"Men don't marry women like you," she snapped, inches from India's face.

India backed off. "You're wrong," she replied, her voice rising several notches.

"Am I? I don't think so. Your relationship's been going on for years. What's different now? Julian's no fool. He wouldn't trade our children's legacy for you."

"That's not the point. Julian doesn't need you anymore," India said. She flopped down on a chair, her battle seemingly won.

Madame DuBusé corrected her. "That's your mistake, my dear. My father started the company and taught Julian the business. When he died, he left me the seventeen buildings that hold our stores. If Julian tries to relocate, he wouldn't have ready access to the factories that supply our stores. Poof!" she said, waving her arm in the air. "You see, Julian and I are bound together financially whether you like or not. Without me, he'd be some poor old man who couldn't afford things like those rubies you're wearing in your ears. I wonder if you'd find him so attractive then."

India raised one eyebrow. "Why do you want him when you know he doesn't care about you anymore?"

"He's mine. And you have no family of your own, except a love child with no proper heritage." She cocked her head, her voice lowering several notches. "Don't look so surprised. I know everything about you, India. You see, I have a key to your apartment. I've been inside. I know what clothes you wear, what foods you eat. I've even met Nélie."

"You've no right to invade my privacy like that," said India, her voice sounding more shrill.

"I have every right! I wanted to see for myself if you were any real threat to me. Your daughter is quite lovely, by the way."

Silence.

"Stay away from my child. This has nothing to do with her."

"It has everything to do with her. I don't want her growing up and one day making financial demands on us. You were wise to leave Julian's name off the birth record. I'll make you a deal. You stop this ridiculous notion of a divorce and you won't have to worry about your little girl's safety."

"Is that a threat?" asked India.

"Yes, I think it is," replied Madame DuBusé.

"And if I think you're bluffing?"

"You may choose to see it that way."

"Get out of here," India ordered.

"I will expect to see an answer before the week is out."
I watched her turn and walk away. My anger surfaced; I
felt guilty listening to something that was none of my business, infuriated that this woman dared threaten my friend,
regret that India had chosen such a difficult path for herself.
We couldn't help whom we loved, could we? I felt depressed
that India remained trapped in a hopeless situation.

It was Paige who brought me back to reality as she waltzed
up the hall and I noticed that her dress was a bit tight in all
the wrong places. Her flushed round cheeks, however, glowed
with excitement as she motioned me forward.

"Where's India? I just saw, I think, Julian's wife leaving.
What are you doing standing there all alone looking like you
have a mouthful of delicious information to spill? Hey
India," shouted Paige. "Are you all right?"

"What do you think?" India called from the sitting room.

"Give me a minute." Paige departed, then returned moments later with two bottles of wine. "This calls for some
emergency reserves. I feel like I missed the real show, so you
two have to fill me in." She walked into the room and looked
at India; Paige's brow was furrowed in concentration.
"You're not going to make Madame DuBusé's Christmas
card list this year. I don't want you to be upset about this—
it's okay."

"Oh, Paige," India said, laughing. "I really do love you.
Both of you. Where would I be without my two best friends?
Madame DuBusé is probably going to have me thrown into
the Atlantic before long."

Paige adjusted her frame on an oversized velvet armchair.
"Well, you might not be the only one in the Atlantic. Miss
Manners over here may be swimming in a sea of despair with
you. We can't take you anywhere, can we, Lauren? She's in-
sulted a near-genius."

"What did you do?"

I stammered for a moment, unable to look India in the eye. Feeling immediately defensive now that the truth was out in the open, I said, "I was looking for you to ask your advice on how I go about making an apology to Isu. I told him, indirectly of course, that I think his work is awful."

"Awful?" India questioned, lighting another cigarillo. "How so? I just spent twenty-five thousand dollars on a canvas."

"You did what?" Paige said, standing up. "Have you lost your mind and Julian's money?"

India was quiet for a moment. "It's not just Julian's money. It's *their* money, or so she told me tonight. She says she knows everything about me." Silence ensued as India's face took on a look of desolation. Her eyelids drooped for a fleeting moment. She looked at her long, slim, white fingers. Was she thinking that they would never be adorned with a wedding ring? Was she struggling to admit even to herself that she needed society's approval?

"I've got it!" Paige said, breaking the silence. "Send Isu's canvas to Madame DuBusé. You bought the black wall-sized canvas, didn't you? Oh wait, I almost forgot, they're all black. So, let me see, what do we think of when we think of black?"

"Death," India said immediately.

"Despair," I answered.

"India, I think you should send Isu's portrait to Madame DuBusé with a note that says, *Thinking of you*. I mean, after all, she's paid for half of it."

The three of us broke into peals of laughter. A leather-clad Frenchman appeared in the doorway looking for Paige. She departed with him, leaving India and me alone. We stayed in that little room a bit longer, sensing the oppression of melancholy.

"You heard the whole thing?" she said calmly.

"I didn't mean to," I replied.

"Yes, you did. But I'm glad you heard. At least I'm not alone in my misery. What a fool I am to love Julian. He's a weak man; he always will be. I suppose this was his way of taking care of things."

"I'm sorry," I said quietly.

"Don't be. This mess is my own fault. I'm sure some psychiatrist would have a field day with this, saying it was connected to something like my penchant for unavailable men." She shook her red hair, making it fan out behind her on the sofa. "I'll never love anyone else. Why am I such a fool?"

I had no answer for her. A silence descended upon us that required no comments. I saw India draped over the sofa, leaning on her elbow, her sari still elegantly in place. As an artist, I wanted to capture her brooding figure on canvas; the subject's pain-filled expression would tell India's story: a young woman desperately in love with the wrong man.

Chapter 6

When the following dawn breaks, I have trouble separating reality from memory. In the murky light of morning, the trip to Paris seems overwhelming. I look over at my notebook: the clean white pages offer me some solace. My list continues for a half page, with notations on breakfast and goals for the day. I hope Margaret's confession was truthful.

A knock sounds and Paige bursts into the room. The smell of cigarettes and steaming coffee assails my senses.

"Good morning. I've made reservations to join you," she announces, coming to sit on the edge of the bed. She grabs the notebook. "What are you doing?"

"My list for the day."

She glances over my notations. "The only thing you haven't planned is when you go to the bathroom."

I roll my eyes. "At least I get everything done this way." I change the subject. "Now, what were you saying?"

"I'm coming with you."

"Really?" I say, sitting up, inordinately pleased. "That's great news!" I feel like a young child who's just been told her parent is accompanying her on a class field trip.

"Absolutely. I wouldn't miss this for the world. Besides, did I mention that we keep an apartment in Paris? Nothing fancy, just a comfortable place that doesn't need much up-keep."

I wonder at Paige's definition of nothing fancy.

The next few hours are filled with a profusion of details, from baggage check to passport approval to our seat assignments. Unaccustomed to international travel, I sink into my seat ready to make a list, focusing on my plans for finding Nélie. My hope for quiet time does not last long, however, because Paige's feelings about traveling coach are painfully obvious; I feel as if I'm on the set of a television commercial. She informs me that her seat isn't leather as in first class. Then she checks to see how much leg room exists and finds someone's bag blocking her from stretching her legs. There is, of course, no service, because the flight attendants are preparing for takeoff, not worried about whether she has a bottle of water. When for the third time, she fails to get the attention of a passing flight attendant, Paige moans loudly and starts critiquing her fellow passengers.

"Paige," I remind her calmly, "I told you to take that last seat in first class."

"No, no. I'll be fine, really. I promise I can do this," she whines in a petulant voice.

"Do what?"

"Sit sandwiched in this seat for the next eight hours with only the thought of a cardboard chicken dinner and a cheap glass of wine to comfort me."

I remain silent during her ramblings, knowing I'm unable to pacify her tender sensibilities. This is my first trip overseas since India's death. As I look out the darkened window, thinking of India, a feeling of unease comes over me. What had India been thinking the night she boarded the plane to the States? Did she smell the same things I smell—a slightly acrid odor inside the pressurized cabin, stale air, the faint aroma of someone's perfume? Did she hear the click of the overhead compartments as the flight attendants prepared the cabin? Were people talking all around her, discussing plans for a future that they would never see? Disliking the direction of my thoughts, I find that even Paige's complaints sound comforting.

Watching her chew some white mints, I ask, "Can I have one, please?"

Paige laughs. "I'm not sure you'd want one. These are my nic-o-mints. Since I'm not allowed to smoke, my doctor prescribed them for long trips. They take the edge off the hassles of flying."

"See." I laugh, holding up my gnawed fingernails. "There aren't any left."

"That's quite an accomplishment. Maybe I should try it." Paige examines her long, hot-pink manicured fingernails. "Then again, maybe not. Just try not to shake hands when you meet people."

Raising one eyebrow, I retort, "At least I don't smell."

"Tsk, tsk," Paige says. "And I thought you'd lost your bite. It's good to know you won't win the award for southern belle of the year."

"Well, I certainly wouldn't win one for being mother of the year either," I add dryly.

Turning my attention to the window, my calculations tell me that Nélie is probably in Paris now. She's smart enough to have some sort of plan. More than likely, she's looking up a friend from school or has a list of youth hostels in her pocket. Could she be with a boyfriend? Someone I've never met, certainly, because none of the young men she's brought home seem like the type to suddenly whisk Nélie off to Paris. I wonder again how long Nélie had been planning this trip.

Paige practically launches herself out of her seat. "Will you look at that girl! She looks like a human pincushion. Her mother should be charged with neglect. She's even got an earring in her bellybutton."

I look up from the pages of an in-flight magazine and stare at the girl.

Paige adds, "Now that's a fashion emergency. Where's Joan Rivers when I need her?"

"She thinks she looks pretty hot."

"I can remember thinking India was ahead of her time double-piercing her ears. She used to wear those ruby earrings Julian gave her and two little gold hoops. I was so jealous. Back then, I could barely afford to put paperclips in my ears let alone real jewels."

"I think you've made up for it since then, Paige," I respond rationally.

"Have I?" Paige says, holding up her ringed fingers. "Money is a strange little bitch-goddess. There's always someone who's got more."

"I thought it was success that was the bitch-goddess. Since when have you been reading D.H. Lawrence?"

"I've read parts of his work." She looks down and wipes something off her black designer pants.

Sensing her discomfort, I plunge ahead. "Which parts? What's that supposed to mean?"

"I read the sections of his work that were relevant. That's all," Paige replies, her voice rising in pitch several levels.

I notice her black, polka-dotted high heels as she taps her foot. It's a wonder she hasn't started complaining about her sore feet, I muse, thinking that's probably next. Paige looks like an advertisement for a fashion magazine while I'm comfortable in a black turtleneck, khaki pants and loafers.

"Do you have a problem with that?"

"So you read the Cliff notes? Why didn't you just read the book?" I frown, wondering what Paige is trying to prove.

"You can't be serious. What an absolute bore that would be. I had this dinner party that was being covered by *W* magazine. One of my guests moonlighted as a gossip columnist. I wanted her to write something about me that said how well-read I am."

"Did it work?" I inquire, gratefully taking a sip of the

oversized bottled water Paige had insisted I buy at the news-
stand.

"Sort of," Paige replies dryly. "She used three whole para-
graphs to describe the puff pastry dessert with the warm
chocolate center. At the end, she remarked that I was a gra-
cious hostess who regaled my guests with my own brand of
humor. Whatever that means." Paige leans back in her chair,
yawns and stretches. "And to think I studied for a week for
that party."

I laugh. "I still think you got the review you wanted."

Paige shrugs, then orders up a glass of wine from the
flight attendant. "Not really. She never once mentioned my
fifty references to D.H. Lawrence. Entertaining is a tough
business. Everyone knows that." Paige ticks off the details
about *the* florist, the tents, the chairs, the caterers, the guest
lists, the designer of her dresses and all of the rest of the
preparations. Next, she lists each of her most recent parties,
from a 1970s disco party to one with an Arabian Nights
theme.

"So how many parties have you had this year?"

Paige hesitates and starts counting. "Almost two hundred.
And you?"

I count them in my mind. "One cocktail party for my
neighbors and three dinner parties with friends over the past
year."

"You're kidding? I hope."

"No, I'm not kidding," I reply defensively. "I have three
kids, Paige. Matt and I love the quiet. We have a lake house
where we spend time with the kids and catch up on some
much-needed rest."

Even to myself, I sound boring, the paragon of an uninter-
esting suburban housewife. I wonder why I feel tired all the
time. Is it the responsibility of motherhood? Or a life that
holds few challenges? My life is filled with the mundane,
making me feel sad. Granted, I'm not interested in winning

the cocktail party Olympics like Paige, but I wonder at our choice of entertainment. Boating at our lake house did provide some help for my restlessness. Being on the water calmed my soul, yet was it enough? Certainly not for Nélie, who wanted more, needed more from her young life.

"Lauren," asks Paige, "are you happy with Matt?"

Those words reverberate in my brain. Of course I am, I want to say. I have everything good life has to offer: a loving husband, three beautiful daughters, a lovely home. My friends are just like me—conservative, traditional, locked into our idealized world of a suburban utopia where I can go to Harris Teeter and buy fresh-cut fruit and ready-made fried chicken for dinner. Where I take my dry cleaning to a place called Scott's Cleaners that's only a few blocks away. Where my life takes place in a two-mile radius because I've chosen to stay safe and embrace the familiar, the comfortable, the secure.

"I don't know," I say quietly, uttering words that assault everything I've spent the past fifteen years building. Seeing the look on Paige's face, I quickly set up a diversion. "Maybe if I'd been invited to one of those two hundred parties, I would be." I say this in a half-joking manner. "Perhaps I wasn't exciting enough to make the guest list." My voice takes on an unfamiliar edge. "After all, who in *W* magazine would know Lauren and Matt Wright?"

Paige shakes her head. "How many times did I invite you over the years? You never once came to anything! You always phoned at the last minute with some excuse—a kid's sick, Nélie has a dance recital. You have no right to blame me for your decision to move down south. If you remember, I'm the one who told both of you not to move back at first. I suggested you rent a place in New York, have some fun in the beginning. India was about fun and life, like a cricket hopping from one adventure to another, bringing her merry band of followers along. She wouldn't have wanted you to stop living just because she did."

Silence. A magazine claims my attention.

Paige breaks my quiet. "Will you look at this dinner! I think it's lasagna. I couldn't make out the other choice. What do you think? Let's just hope this isn't our last meal. Boy, that would be a rip-off. I'd love a nice piece of sautéed salmon and a little Caesar salad to go with it." She describes various labels of her favorite chardonnay and why she likes each one.

I nod patiently and let her talk.

After a thirty-minute monologue, Paige adjusts her black jacket and yawns. "You know, Lauren. I'd forgotten how truly nice you are. I haven't heard one complaint yet. And none of that fake social stuff like you buttering me up just because you want something. That's why I'm here to help."

"Help?" I laugh. "Let me see. You've cut down the plane, the service, our fellow passengers, my life, my husband, and we still have three hours to go. What's next?"

"Your outfit. I need to take you shopping, mademoiselle. If I had a figure like yours, I sure as hell wouldn't be wearing those conservative pants and a turtleneck. I'd wear that midriff over there. I would even consider piercing my bellybutton. Shopping cures all evils. I know this marvelous little boutique I'm taking you to once I recover from the jet lag."

"I'm here to find Nélie," I remind her firmly.

"Like I said, Lauren—if this is the kid's first trip to Paris, she's not going to be bubbling over with joy when she sees you. She'll be out, I hope, with some hot-looking man."

"You never thought the French men were that good, looking. Too skinny."

"No, there were a few of them I liked. Julian, for one, and that artist with the name that sounds like a car."

"Isu," I exclaim. "I remembered him last night. I wonder if he's still painting in Paris."

Paige yawns again. "I'd think he'd be out of a job by now. How many all-black canvases could he possibly sell?"

Her yawn makes me tired. My shoulders ache. I stretch my legs out in front of me. "Did India ever send her picture to Madame DuBusé?"

"I don't know. I'm sure if it's worth anything, Julian will have it hanging in the apartment of his newest love." She adds, "I've seen him over the years from a distance with various women on his arm. All of them beautiful, all of them young." Paige removes the wrapper from her blanket, placing it around her legs.

I muse, "Was he in love with her?"

"India was a clever one. She'd have kept him interested," she replies, putting on hand cream.

"How can you be so sure?"

"He still wears the ring she gave him. I saw it once on his right pinky finger."

"So we think he really loved India. Could that mean he might want to see Nélie?"

Even as I express my hope, I know I gave my name and address to India's attorneys before I left. So, Julian could have found us if he had wanted to see his daughter. My mother has lived in the same house for the last thirty years. I would have gotten word that some Frenchman had been making inquiries.

"What do you think? Madame DuBusé doesn't want Julian's love child anywhere near her real family. I'm not placing any bets on Julian. He's not shown any interest until now."

"What if Nélie finds Julian and he rejects her?"

"Lauren, Julian has done nothing for Nélie. Hasn't it been fourteen years of rejection? He let *you* raise her. He never wanted to be her father. That's not going to change now. Nélie wanted the truth. You can't protect her any more than you already have."

"But," I say, "Nélie will soon know that Julian did nothing to find her . . ."

I curse Julian for his total indifference to his own daughter. If he'd wanted to do something, he could have found a way to contact me. Madame DuBusé wouldn't have had to know. Funny, how my perspective has changed now that Nélie is seventeen. For the first years after India's death, I feared Julian would take Nélie from me, staking his rightful claim. Now, I'm angry that my daughter will soon know she has a blood relative who refuses to acknowledge her existence. In a way, it casts a tawdry light on their love affair.

If only I'd shared India's side of the story with her, perhaps Nélie would see things from a different perspective. She would have seen first the love that brought her parents together despite the odds. It was all so innocent when it began. India wrote to me that she had met someone interesting, an older man who was unfortunately married. She hadn't wanted to have anything to do with him. He had pursued her, sending her a yellow rose each morning with a silly note in English. I remember how India liked him thinking that she couldn't understand French too well.

Any woman would have had a hard time resisting such a man, especially Julian, who was titled, wealthy, powerful and handsome. He was the embodiment of any schoolgirl's dreams, even in his fifties, even married, even the father of three. Julian, like India, had a coterie of people around him all the time, but he always dropped everything for her. If only I had described to Nélie the look that came over Julian's face when India entered the room. His eyes would light up and he'd grin almost stupidly at her. Perhaps it would soften the hurt of his flawed character.

What if I were to ask Julian to talk with Nélie, explain his need to protect her from his proud wife? Would Nélie accept his reasoning without examining the plethora of loopholes?

The fact is that Julian never wanted her and never cared enough about her to check on her well-being over the years. Nélie is bound to be hurt by his abandonment. It's one thing to think that your loving father died, but that he would have been there for you if he could have. This idea seems far more palatable than the reality.

Chapter 7

Armed with a map, a list of youth hostels and a photo-graph of Nélie, I sit down on a sidewalk bench to think about the most effective strategy for reaching as many places as possible in the next few hours.

Once there was a little bunny who wanted to run away.
So he said to his mother, "I am running away."
"If you run away," said his mother, "I will run after you.
For you are my little bunny."

The words from *The Runaway Bunny*, a book I read to Nélie a thousand times as a child, echo through my mind.

"If you run after me," said the little bunny,
"I will become a fish in a trout stream
and I will swim away from you."
"If you become a fish in a trout stream," said his mother,
"I will become a fisherman and I will fish for you."

I must think like Nélie, I tell myself. If I were seventeen years old and on my first visit to Paris, I would get my few belongings situated, then go in search of the place where my mother used to live, maybe ask questions, find out if anyone in the building remembered India. If Nélie had gone through my things stored in the attic, she might have found the address. India's old apartment building seems the most effective place to start the search.

Picking up speed, I observe a small café on a street corner, its front decorated with rows of tiny round tables and chairs filled with chatting patrons. My mouth waters as I pass by, taking in the scent of freshly baked bread. Tempted to stop and get something to eat, I realize I don't have much money so I start searching for an exchange booth.

My pace is brisk, but I allow myself a few glances in some shop windows. The shops on Rue St. Honoré are expensive, with designer names; the gold C catches my eye and I recall that India always frequented this type of shop. I peer in the window, noticing a glass case filled with purple snakeskin handbags. Several security guards stand watch over the entrance. I still wonder where these Celine shoppers can actually wear stiletto-heeled boots, a crochet halter top and low-slung pants.

Several blocks later, I pass by a patisserie, and my mouth waters again. The window has rows of freshly baked croissants and baguettes placed upright, looking more like a basket of gladiolas. Starving, I go inside to find my favorite, *pain au chocolat*, which I greedily purchase. It takes a few minutes of fumbling to count out the correct amount, but I manage. As I bite into my croissant, the chocolate flavor sends tingles of delight to the roof of my mouth. Guilty at this pleasure, I nearly throw the croissant away but remind myself that I must eat to keep going.

My feet hurt by the time I spy India's old apartment building, and I feel a funny catch in my throat. The whitewashed building on Rue Lauriston appears nondescript in this fashionable part of the city. It occurs to me that India's building had a lower courtyard filled with flowers and stone benches. I remember that I need a key to gain entry. I wonder whether anyone is going in this time of day. An hour later, I notice an immaculately groomed middle-aged woman in a smart pink suit inserting her key into the outside door. I rush across the street and call to her.

"Pardon, madame, *s'il vous plaît!*" I say, watching her furrow her brown-penciled eyebrows in disapproval.

"May I help you?" she asks.

"Oui," I reply. "I'm searching for my seventeen-year-old daughter. I think she may have come here. Do you have a moment?"

She looks at me carefully, her eyes narrow and she nods. This is one of those times when I'm grateful for my conservative appearance.

"Merci," I respond, feeling strange speaking even these few words of French. Even to my own ears, my accent sounds very American.

"I used to live here about fifteen years ago with my best friend, India. She was about six feet tall with long red hair. Would you know anyone in the building who might have lived here then or known her?"

"I've lived here since nineteen sixty-nine. Yes, I remember your friend. Who could forget her? Such a beautiful young girl to have died so young."

Relief flows through me. I say in a rush, "My name's Lauren Wright. I live in the States."

She nods and says, "Yes, I can tell by your accent. You may call me Sophie." She unfolds her arms and extends her hand in greeting.

Squeezing her bony fingers, I say, "You see, India had a daughter named Nélie." I pull out a photograph of my family and point to her. I then pull out Nélie's senior portrait. "I raised her as my own. She's run away." Suddenly, the fatigue, the stress, the reality of being in Paris in India's old apartment building overtakes me. Tears flood my cheeks.

Taking pity on me, Sophie takes my arm, her bony fingers

gripping me as she walks me over to a stone bench. She reaches into her pocket book, pulling out a handkerchief. "This is one of the benefits of being from my generation. In my day, everyone carried one of these."

"Merci," I say, embarrassed.

"To my knowledge, you're the first person to come here inquiring about India. The younger people who can afford to live here all work. Many of the older couples travel. I'm here all the time. I've not seen anyone who looks like your daughter. Perhaps things happen for a reason. Will you come upstairs where we can talk?" She stands up and smoothes her skirt, her movements brisk.

I nod, sensing she may have something to tell me. I can't fathom my good fortune in finding her. She leads the way up the stone steps to the second floor. A vine clings to the metal balustrade and I see pockets of yellow and pink flowers as I look behind me.

The complex is quiet. I remember how India used to play her bass-toned drums, unmindful of anyone else. We were young, thoughtless, interested only in our own escapades. People like Sophie must have been appalled when we came and went from the apartment in the middle of the night. Perhaps her memory of these incidents has faded over the years.

She walks quickly with the quiet dignity of a woman who knows how to take care of herself. When she shows me her profile, I note the lines around her eyes and the white strands of hair peeking out of her black bun. Her apartment looks just like her—immaculate and elegant. There are hints of red throughout the living and dining rooms in the curtains, pillows, patterned rug and paintings. A growling, stubby dog bares his teeth, but she soothes him with a treat and a pat on his head.

"When my husband died ten years ago, George became my roommate. But they don't like him at the salon. The owner claims he bothers the other customers, which is rubbish. Now Lauren, please let me put on a pot of coffee." A realization that Sophie is a lonely lady in need of attention dawns on me and I wonder how I can politely decline her offer. She may be so starved for company that anyone, even a stranger, will do.

The next twenty minutes are filled with pleasantries, but my nervousness increases when I watch her arrange a plate with some cookies and take out china cups.

"Sophie," I say politely, "was there something you wished to tell me? Is that why you brought me here?"

"Oui. I know you're anxious about your daughter," she says patiently. "But what I have to say is important. Please have a seat."

Understanding that Sophie won't be rushed, I follow her instructions and head into the living room. She arrives what feels like an eternity later, and I curse my own politeness. Sneaking a glance at my watch, I decide to give her ten more minutes of my time before I abandon etiquette and head on.

"How do you take your coffee?" She busily prepares each cup, her trembling hands not spilling a drop of liquid.

"With cream, please," I reply automatically.

Her lined hands pour a healthy dose from a flowered pitcher into a cup and she hands it to me. "Cookie?" she offers, smiling at me.

"No, thank you," I say as I watch her bring the cup to her lips. "You were saying you had something important to share with me?"

"How old was India when she died?" Sophie asks, her penciled-in brows furrowed in concentration.

"Twenty-seven."

"And her daughter was how old when you took her into your care?"

"Twenty months," I say, recalling a vision of Nélie as a baby snuggled in my arms.

"Oh, the poor little thing. She would have known. Was it

very hard for you?" She adds another teaspoon of sugar to her cup.

"Yes, Sophie, it was," I reply curtly, trying to quell my annoyance.

"How did you manage such a thing so young?" I wonder if Sophie is going to ask about Nélie's father.

"When India died, I got married immediately and brought Nélie back to the States to my mother."

"No wedding? My dear, how sad. To cope with your best friend's death, a new marriage and then motherhood and then, a new place to live with family, no less. It seems overwhelming."

"It was. Now, Sophie," I say gently, "you've been very kind in bringing me here, but I've so little time to find my daughter."

Sophie beckons George over. "Come here, my love," she says as she hands him a dog biscuit. "Such a nice dog." She pats him on the head, then puts her coffee cup down to stare intently at me. "The apartment that you and your friend shared fifteen years ago has been unoccupied since then."

"What?" I say. "I don't understand."

"A housekeeper comes in once a month and cleans the place. Over the years, I have seen a gentleman come and go from time to time but that's it. I have often wondered about him. He's a handsome man and I wonder why he keeps the place. Could it have anything to do with your friend?"

"I wonder if India's things are still in there. I only took a few things when we left, but I assumed her personal items would have been removed." I don't want to mention Julian's name at this point. It seems premature.

"I talked with the cleaning lady once, and she said it was a shame no one enjoyed all those pretty things." Sophie pauses for a moment. "The housekeeper seems like an honest woman, like someone who wouldn't help herself to anything if you know what I mean. But, even so, I wouldn't be surprised if some things are missing. Fifteen years is a long time."

Of all the things I expected her to say, this isn't one of them. Could India's apartment still be intact? Julian may not have sold it or brought anyone else there. It seems impossible, yet it would support my hope that he was truly in love with India and devastated by her death. Think of what this could mean for Nélie. To come here to see for herself where her mother lived, to feel just for a period of time that she was in India's world.

"Is there any way I could visit? When does the cleaning lady come? Or is there some sort of manager here?" I perch forward at the edge of my seat.

Sophie folds her hands in her lap, composing her face into a neutral mask. "This building has been here for years. I can show you how to pick the lock, like I do when I forget my key."

"Can we go now?" I demand impatiently, unwilling to indulge in any more conversation.

With a knowing look, she says, "Well, I wonder if you're prepared to see your friend's things again."

Her words sober me for a moment. It's been fifteen years since I've dealt with India's death. Perhaps there's a reason things work out the way they do. Am I ready to see the apartment? To connect with my friend, my past, my youth seems like a gift.

"I'm all right, I promise," I reply, reassuring her that I won't fall apart.

"I'll not keep you waiting any longer. Shall we give it a try?"

"Yes," I reply eagerly. "You're very kind."

"Oh my dear, you place too much trust in my ability to pick the lock. However, I'll do my best."

My heart pounds as I tremble in anticipation outside the

door. We start picking at the lock and, at first, it seems hopeless. Sophie runs back to her apartment to retrieve several sharp objects to assist us. She complains that this lock is different from hers. Just as I decide to call Paige to ask her advice, Sophie wrangles her key in the lock and shoves the door open. The apartment smells stale, but I'm undeterred. In a rush, I walk right into the living room, then abruptly stop. The curtains are drawn but the evidence of our life together in Paris still exists. I glance around, stunned to see several objects once cherished by India in the same places where she'd left them. The small glass dolphin remains on the coffee table; a color photograph of Henri Gustave decorates the antique dresser. My hands begin to tremble and tears well up in my eyes. I thought I could handle this, but I reach for Sophie's arm to steady myself. She tells me it's all right to cry.

"I was so happy here," I babble, trying to control myself from the onslaught of memories that have overtaken me. "I can't believe this."

"Maybe we should come back tomorrow, dear," Sophie offers, gently taking my arm to lead me back out the door.

"No," I respond quickly. "I'll be okay, I promise. I need to be here right now."

She nods her understanding. "Just think of how those archeologists in Egypt felt when they discovered the hidden tombs in the desert."

Her remark, which bordered on the ridiculous, helped me regain my composure.

"They're still here," I exclaim, pointing to the wall of India's African tribal masks.

Sophie eyes me warily. "My word," she mutters, her hand reaching instinctively for her throat. "How interesting."

As I walk over to examine the female mask carved out of wood with its features decorated in tiny white shells, I gingerly wipe away my tears. I remembered how India used to love showing them to guests, having each person guess what kind of ceremony each mask may have been used for. India always had a keen understanding of African art, and she loved the primitive beauty of the wooden sculptures. On a table to the left was a sculpture of a woman nursing a child, which India always proclaimed "remarkable" and "fantastic."

Sometimes, depending on her mood, India would have everyone take their shoes off when they entered her sanctuary. She used to tell Julian she liked to observe different cultural traditions at different times. Julian referred to this shoe-removal custom as one of her "international oddities" and it drove him crazy. India's followers, on the other hand, used to try to impress her by bowing and removing their shoes for dinner parties. They thought they were adhering to her unique brand of respect for another way of life, when in actuality she was playing some silly game. Once she told me that she just didn't like the wear and tear on her white carpeting.

India and I enjoyed such luxury. The art and antiques Julian showered on his love would have been well beyond my budget even today. I remember Julian never hesitated in giving India any trinket she wanted, even if he disapproved of the purchase. Except the time India brought home a parakeet. That bird could repeat just about anything. When India taught him to say "Julian is a bastard" as a joke, Julian found the bird less than amusing and ordered him banished from his sight.

I need to see more of the past unfold before me. It's surreal suddenly unlocking these memories and recapturing this part of my life. This is the first time I've actually allowed myself to really remember who I was—who we were.

"Let me check the closet," I say, propelling myself forward.

I head back to the master bedroom, thinking it will be empty. India's closet surprises me. Many of her favorite dresses are still hanging up—the golden sari she wore the night of the opening, her black silk tank dress, the turquoise patterned silk she'd bought in Thailand. Her collection of high heels is neatly shelved on racks. I walk over to her dresser, fingering all of the crystal bottles of perfume.

As I walk to the window in the master bedroom, the courtyard opens before me. The view is still lovely. I can recall India sitting on one of the benches, smoking her cigarillo at dusk, sipping on a glass of wine. We would sometimes talk for hours, not caring if anyone heard, just enjoying ourselves until late evening, when we would go out for dinner. Our conversations ring in my ears, and I am ready to again spew forth my thoughts on Victor Hugo or Oscar Wilde. I remember too India's flair for the dramatic; at times, we would even act out scenes from the books we were reading.

Shifting my gaze, I see that her bed, covered in a white matelassé, seems pristine. My need to find Nélie intensifies because I want her to see this apartment and know Julian's love for her mother and yes, maybe for her, too. Maybe he couldn't face removing India's things from these rooms. Julian's foible might turn out to be his one gift to his daughter.

I must find Nélie, I think.

"Sophie," I call. "Come look at India's closet."

When there's no answer, I walk back into the living room and see that she's left, closing the door behind her. Checking my watch, I decide to give myself another half-hour in the apartment before I start my search of the local youth hostels. I must cover a few more bases before I quit looking for the day.

On the coffee table in the living room, there is a black and white photograph of India and Julian. It looks as if it could have been taken last week. They seem inseparable, posing cheek to cheek, as if one begins where the other ends, their smiling faces unaware of the tragedy that lay ahead. I touch art books, photographs, a china monkey, handling the familiar objects reverently because each contains a pathway to a memory long forgotten. I can almost smell India's cigarillo in the air and hear the drumbeats of those long-ago nights. I close my eyes, trying to conjure up India and bring her back to Nélie, who still needs her so desperately. Before I sink into despair, my inherent pragmatism returns in full force, demanding that my attention return to my daughter. With a last look around, I depart from the apartment, turning the lock on the doorknob. Now I feel like I've only dreamt its existence.

I head outdoors, checking my list of youth hostels. For the next several hours, I cover ten different locations around the city, each time showing a manager or desk clerk a picture of Nélie and leaving Paige's phone number. This method yields no immediate rewards, and, feeling fatigued and frustrated, I head back to Paige's apartment.

The housekeeper informs me that Paige has gone off on an errand and will return shortly. Recalling Paige's description of her apartment as "nothing fancy," I survey the surroundings. The sparse accommodations include a Corot hanging over the mantel, a butter-colored leather sofa and chairs, fifteen-foot ceilings with elaborate moldings and a view of a neighboring park.

I head to my bedroom, marveling at everything from the canopied queen-size bed and blue silk draperies to the whimsical painting of a jester paying court to a young woman seated in the woods. I dial my number in Greensboro, relieved when Laura answers the phone.

"Mom!" she cries. "Where's Nélie? Have you found her?"

The urgency in her voice reminds me why I'm here and how torn apart my family has become.

"Not yet, honey. But I'm making a lot of progress," I reply.

"I wish you'd come home! You missed my recital and I'm going to fail my English final if you don't help me. It's not fair!"

"Laura," I plead, "I miss you too! I'm so sad I can't be there for you right now. You know, your grandmother used to help me with my English papers. She was an English teacher remember? Make sure you talk to her about it tomorrow."

"Yeah," she responds with a loud sigh. "Sure."

Kathryn then gets on the line. She starts to cry. "Mommy, I miss you! Why can't you put me to bed tonight? Grandmother got mad at me today. She said I made a mess of my bedroom doing an art project. I don't understand why you're not here!"

Tears fill my eyes. "Oh sweetie, I miss you so much. I hate that I'm not there either. I'll be home really soon, I promise!"

When I hear Matt's voice, I feel uneasy and say, "No luck. I've visited twenty-five youth hostels and left word at several restaurants. I met one of India's old neighbors who was very helpful."

Matt clears his throat. "I talked with a local detective this morning. He said he could start an investigation tomorrow morning, perhaps speak with Nélie's friends and see if any of them knows anything."

His decision surprises me. "Why?" I say. "You know how small our community is. The last thing I want for people to think is that Nelié's a runaway or some troubled teenager. Please just give me twenty-four more hours."

"What if you're wrong and she's in trouble?" Matt argues. "I'll wait one more day but that's it."

"I know I can find her," I say breathlessly. "I miss you and the girls."

"Sure. You know I don't approve of this scheme of yours. It's too chaotic. Flying off to Paris at a moment's notice. Then to stay with Paige, of all people."

The last comment annoys me. Am I speaking to my husband or my parent? He can't stand it when I think for myself, make my own decisions, trust my own instincts. He always wants me home to wait on him, playing the roles of wife, mother, hostess, maid, cook and bedmate.

"If it weren't for Paige, I'd have no place to stay or any connections in this city. She's been extremely helpful," I say, feeling the need to defend myself and my friend.

"How helpful can she be? You don't have a single concrete lead."

"Something will turn up. I'm certain of it." My confidence rings hollow even to my own ears.

"You'd better watch out for those Frenchmen," he warns.

"I'm here to find my daughter."

I click off the line, feeling depressed. Maybe I'm just tired, I tell myself. Fortunately, Paige walks in, looking refreshed and disgustingly cheerful.

"Hi!" she says pleasantly. "I feel like we've been missing each other. Fill me in." She sits on the bed, absently smoothing the comforter in place around her.

I notice her immaculate appearance and ask, "Did you get your hair done?"

"Yes. Do you like it? I have this wonderful hairdresser here named Claude. Have you heard of him? It's nearly impossible to get an appointment, but he just adores one of my friends. He works on every name actress and model in the city."

My eyes feel dry. "I'm going to need a whole body makeover once I find Nélie and put this behind me," I say, glancing in the mirror and looking at the fine lines of fatigue around my eyes.

Even the thought of explaining my day to Paige seems exhausting, but I manage to share the relevant details, omitting the fact that India's apartment is still intact.

Paige says simply, "You're a good mother, Lauren. Remember that through all of this. India was lucky to have you for a friend and Nélie was lucky to get someone like you to raise her."

"Do you really think so?" I ask, my emotions raw. "I've spent so much time focusing on what I did wrong. It's a wonder Nélie didn't shrivel up and die of boredom." Maybe the fatigue is catching up. These words bring a misting of tears to my eyes.

"That kid better appreciate all you've done for her over the years. Just think, she could have gotten me for her mother. She'd be a platinum blond chain-smoker living in New York with hobbies like shopping and bar-hopping. At least you've made sure she's got a good set of values behind her before she does those things!"

"Thanks, Paige," I say. "I think."

Chapter 8

Having searched ten more youth hostels, I become filled with doubt and frustration. What if Margaret wasn't telling the truth and Nélie has run away to a different part of the world? Could she still be in the United States? What about my other children, Laura and Kathryn? I miss my girls terribly, but calm myself knowing they are safe at home with their father and grandmother.

"If you become a mountain climber,"
said the little bunny,
"I will be a crocus in a hidden garden."
"If you become a crocus in a hidden garden,"
said his mother, "I will be a gardener.
And I will find you."

The gallery. I head to the Left Bank. My pace quickens as I wonder if I can gather any information there. Nélie might be trying to recreate certain aspects of India's lifestyle, perhaps visiting galleries and museums, and discovering for herself the many wonders of the city. Perhaps Paige is right and Nélie may not be literally searching for India, just following some preconceived notions of her own about what her mother might have done. Simply being in the city may be all the information she needs.

The building looks sleeker than I remember, set back from the street and decorated with a black wrought iron bench and a ficus tree. In the front window, I can see a framed portrait and several landscape paintings encased in gilded frames. A marble table with carved gold legs holds a sculpture of a nude which looks like a statue of Aphrodite. This can't be the same gallery, I think, admiring a landscape reminiscent of Monet's waterlilies at Giverny. Certain I am in the wrong place, I walk inside to inspect the artwork further.

When I close the door behind me, a bell rings, signaling my entry. Out of sheer curiosity, I walk over to the wall where the landscape hangs, looking for the artist's name and a price. A woman dressed in beige asks if I need assistance. I inquire about the cost of the painting. She nods, returning moments later with a list of prices in francs. Once I make the conversion, the number shocks me, making me wonder how this can be the same gallery where Isu had his opening.

"May I speak with the manager for a moment? It's important."

Probably thinking I'm a potential client, the woman nods as she motions me forward to the back office area. Instantly, I am reminded of the gallery opening when I listened to India's confrontation with Madame DuBusé. Along the way, a wall of black-framed photographs catches my attention. I am impressed again by the quality of the work. A picture of a row of trees casting their reflection on a body of water intrigues me. The woman heads to an office, holds a quick conversation, then gestures for me to enter.

The man who stands to greet me seems familiar, but eerily so, yet he bears no resemblance to anyone I met fifteen years ago. Dressed in black pants and a blue shirt with cuff links, he shakes my hand, then asks me to have a seat. He looks professional with an underlying air of nonchalance that belies his elegant surroundings.

"How can I help you?" he says politely, staring at me with eyes laced with compassion rather than the impatience I had anticipated. I tell my story quickly, unclear why this man makes me nervous. Yet the timbre of his voice eases my discomfort. I end up telling him more details than absolutely necessary.

"I've not seen her," he replies. "I will phone you if she turns up here."

Giving him the phone number of Paige's apartment, I reply easily, "Thank you for your interest."

"Your French is too good for you to be a tourist. Have you ever lived here?" He searches my face.

"Yes. Fifteen years ago." Uneasy with the intensity of his gaze, I shift my attention to a pencil drawing of a ballerina. It looks like a Picasso, but I can't be sure.

"What made you leave?" He pauses and corrects himself. "Forgive me, Lauren. May I call you that? That question is none of my business."

"Certainly. I'm sorry, I don't believe you told me your name."

"It seems my manners are not what they should be today. I'm Jean Whitfield." He smiles, revealing a dimple in his right cheek.

The name sounds familiar, but I can't place it.

"I came to an opening here featuring an artist who called himself Isu. You wouldn't happen to have heard of him?"

"Why do you ask?"

"The evening left a strong impression."

"How so?" He looks at me with a curious expression.

"Many reasons. Specifically, my friend bought a piece of his work, and she rather admired him."

"What if I told you Isu died that same night?"

"That can't be! How tragic. What happened?" I say in a

rush. I feel as if another piece has been taken from my past. My heart thuds in my chest. I watch Jean as he goes on to say, "I believe he was killed by a lovely American woman." He watches my face and our eyes meet. The tension rises as I hold his gaze unable to move or look away.

The memory registers as I replay our meeting in my mind. *"This kind of work will make Isu famous for a time, but it won't last . . ."*

I feel a blush creeping up my neck to my cheeks, even now. "You must think I'm awful, don't you?"

"Quite the contrary. I admired your honesty. It's a rare thing. You see, I was a struggling artist like you. Only I was untrained, with no job. After I showed up here for three months straight, the owner of the gallery finally agreed to hire me. Just by luck, an eccentric old woman came to the gallery and saw me painting a black background. She told me she wanted to have a room in her house with all-black canvases to celebrate what she called her 'dark moods.'

"I thought she was crazy, but she offered me too much money to refuse. I tried to liven up these paintings with the arrows and white streamers. She thought they were marvelous, so who was I to argue? She showed them to all of her wealthy friends, some of whom were critics, which helped get me the opening you attended. Isu was born because I didn't even want to use my real name on the work. None of the fashionable set questioned the integrity of the work. As a matter of fact, no one did until you . . ."

The years fall away, and I smile warmly at him.

"Where did you go? I went to talk to Henri Gustave the week after that opening because I remembered your friend telling me you studied under him. But as soon as I mentioned your name, Gustave became furious—I remember exactly what he said. He thought you were one of the most talented student artists he'd ever worked with. That you had a gift and it was going to be wasted."

His words shock me. I breathe in deeply to maintain my composure. Suddenly, I want to deny my association with Matt, the small town I live in, the suburban life I lead. Had Henri Gustave really thought I was talented? How could that be? He rarely gave me any compliments. A lump rises in my throat, but I swallow it quickly, remembering why I'm back.

"I must be going. I have to continue the search for my daughter," I announce, then, drawn in by his patient demeanor, I continue on. "When my friend India died, I raised Nélie as my own. Everything seemed fine until she ran away two days ago. I'm not sure about anything anymore. It's hard being back in Paris after all this time."

"I understand."

"Do you?" I regret the words once I say them. Why do I want this man to understand what I'm going through? My problems are none of his business. I notice a few flecks of paint on his hand, as if he didn't quite wash them off after leaving the studio. A strange sadness overtakes me when I think that I haven't painted seriously in years.

Jean again promises to call me if he sees anyone resembling Nélie. "I'll make inquiries," he declares.

For some reason, I believe he will help me.

"Thank you so much," I say politely, heading for the door. "You've been wonderful to listen for so long."

"No problem," he replies. "I'll see what I can do."

That afternoon, I give Paige a brief synopsis of the day. "I met with Isu. Only he doesn't go by the name Isu anymore."

Paige interjects, "Oh, I get it. Like the artist formerly known as Prince." We laugh and I continue my report. "Actually, his name is Jean Whitfield and he now owns the gallery."

"Please tell me that he's not fat and bald like the rest of the men our age. I remember him as being so handsome. I'm sure that's why India bought that ugly painting in the first place. She always had good taste in men."

"Did you contact any of your friends here for advice on how I might handle this situation?" I say anxiously.

"Yes, I was on the phone all morning. I have the names of four trendy restaurants that might hire an American girl with no working papers. Each could pay her under the table without government interference. If I were Nélie, I would try to hostess or waitress at this type of establishment."

"You're terrific!" I cry, rushing over to give her a hug.

"This may be the first concrete lead I have. Let's go."

"Wait a minute, Lauren," says Paige. "I think you need to rest a bit. We can go in the morning. You haven't stopped moving since we arrived."

"I'm fine, Paige. I promise. One of the first principles of motherhood is sleep deprivation. I'm used to it. I just need a few minutes to freshen up." I survey my appearance and decide to change shoes because my feet hurt.

While I'm changing, Paige says, "Have you called home? I'm surprised Matt has let you do something on your own for two days."

I remain silent, pretending I didn't hear her remark as I splash my face with cool water. Her comment makes me wonder about the animosity between them. I realize how much I had wanted to visit Paige over the years, but Matt always had some business trip or made plans for us. Our visit never took place, and after a while the invitations stopped coming. Once I had three children, it didn't seem right to leave them with a baby-sitter or my mother for the weekend just so we could attend a party.

Over and over, my mind replays my conversation with Jean. Did Henri Gustave really think I could have made it as a professional artist? A tear runs down my cheek before I can stop it. I wonder what might have happened to my life if I'd stayed in Paris fifteen years ago.

Chapter 9

Seated at a corner table, I observe a mixed crowd of people, all of whom appear rich, chic and without a care in the world. A group of women stand in a circle by the bar area, chatting, laughing and smoking cigarettes. One woman tells a story, her hands gesturing in the air for emphasis while the others pipe in a sentence or two. Like her friends, she's dressed casually, wearing tight black pants, a cream-colored halter top, and spike heels. Her sleek, long ponytail and over-sized hoop earrings gives her a sophisticated look. Smoke emerges from her mouth between sentences.

I have an absurd urge to join their group. What would it feel like to be free for a few hours? I could dress the way I want and perhaps enjoy a spontaneous evening that didn't end with a polite kiss on the cheek and the words, "So nice to see you again." I'd like to do something stupid for once, not worry about my reputation, my mother's reputation, my children's future or whether every single neighbor would find out about my actions by morning.

The glass of red wine goes down smoothly as I lean back in my seat. Paige emerges from talking with the manager. As they walk over to our table, I automatically pull out pictures to give him my explanation. He smiles when he sees Nélie's picture.

"You've seen her," I exclaim.

"Oui," he replies. "She was here this afternoon to speak with the manager. Is there a problem?"

"No," I say easily. "I'm her mother and she doesn't always tell me what's she's doing anymore. We had a fight over a boyfriend, you understand?"

"I have a teenager myself," he says with a sympathetic look. "Don't worry, I'll tell her you were here looking for her."

"Please don't," I cry, unconsciously touching his arm. "I'm not sure what my plans are. I'm just glad to know she's well. Maybe I'll write her a note. Do you have her address?"

"No, I don't have that kind of information. You'll have to come back tomorrow and speak with the owner."

Relief floods through me. I think I'm close to finding my daughter. But I still don't know if the young woman he's seen is really Nélie or someone else. If she is Nélie, what shall I say to her? How will she react to seeing me? When I share the fact that India's apartment still exists, Nélie might be so excited that she'll forgive my shortcomings as a parent. And if I do find her tomorrow, I need to decide whether to let her stay here. I suppose I'll make that decision after we talk. But, it also means I'll be going home to Greensboro, to my life, to a structured existence, to the suburbs. Suddenly, a ball of fear forms in my stomach.

"Shall I order a bottle of champagne so we can make a toast to finding Nélie?" Paige whispers.

"No, thanks. We haven't found her yet, Paige, so I'm not quite ready to start celebrating. But I'll have another glass of red wine."

Just as I look up from the menu, I spy Isu (Jean, I correct myself) coming through the doorway with a beautiful, dark-haired Frenchwoman on his arm. Jean looks well-dressed in black. I admire how easily he moves through the crowd.

Paige leans forward, blowing smoke out of the left side of her mouth. "Who are you looking at?"

Returning my gaze to meet hers, I say casually, "No one in particular."

She follows the direction of my eyes. Always a bit too perceptive, Paige recognizes the former Isu immediately.

Raising an eyebrow, she says, "India was right. Her unknown artist Isu must now be selling quite a bit of his work to be dining in such a fancy restaurant. Just hold on."

"Where are you going?" I ask nervously.

"To invite him to join us for a drink." Paige stands up and waves.

"Will you sit down. He's probably here for a romantic evening. He doesn't want to see us."

"Sure he does," she answers confidently. With a wink, she adds, "There aren't any more tables left in the lounge." She strides forward to greet Jean and introduce herself.

In a matter of minutes, Jean joins us along with his date, Monique. He takes a seat beside me, asking politely if I've heard anything about Nélie. I share our latest findings, surprised that he seems genuinely pleased by the news.

"What do you plan to do once you find her?" He reaches over and grabs a handful of nuts from the dish on the table. I notice the arm of his tailored black jacket, thinking he looks more like a successful businessman than an artist.

"I don't know. I haven't thought everything through," I reply, watching his hands and unconsciously looking for some paint flecks.

"I meant to tell you the other day that Julian's a client of mine," he offers quietly, looking me in the eye. "Perhaps we could get together to talk about this." The waiter comes over to take our drink order. Jean orders a whiskey and a glass of wine for Monique.

"Would it be too much trouble?"

A frown creases his brow and he looks at me quizzically. "Not at all."

"Lauren tells me you've done quite well for yourself," says Paige with a wicked smile.

"I get by," he counters easily. "My work pays the bills now. I'm fortunate to be able to do what I love and make money at it."

Paige laughs. "Everything I love to do costs money. But that's another story. So, what have you been painting these days, Jean?"

At the mention of his artwork, Jean's face lights up. "Mostly, I do portraits. But lately, I've been developing my skills as a photographer."

Monique, who appears meticulously groomed with her sleek, jet-black ponytail and bright red lips, sits forward in her seat. She places her red-clawed hand on Jean's. She says, "Jean's being very modest. He has a five-year waiting list for his portraits. He's a genius."

I take a sip of my wine. "That doesn't surprise me. I admired those landscape photographs I saw in the gallery the other day." I turn to Monique. "We had a mutual friend, India, whose hobby was discovering young talent. We used to go to estate sales, auctions and gallery openings on weekends when we lived together in Paris years ago. In fact, we met Jean at his first opening."

"So that's how you know each other," says Monique, eyeing both of us.

Jean sits up. "Lauren wasn't quite sold on my work back then." He winks at me.

I blush, changing the subject. "Do you represent other artists at the gallery? I noticed several sculptures that weren't yours."

The waiter returns with drink orders and Paige takes charge, ordering a round of appetizers for the group including duck, veal and salmon toast points.

Jean nods his approval at her selections. "I try to give struggling artists a chance if I can. But I really set limits on how much I'll sell at any given time; I'll only represent two or three contemporary artists and no more than a handful of paintings by Gustave, Picasso or Matisse; if I do more, then I don't have enough time for my own work. Sometimes it's easier for me to buy work directly at an estate sale. But, you know, about ten years ago, I went to this estate sale outside of Paris. It was hot, so nobody came. Besides, the old man who died had a reputation for being cheap."

Warming to his topic, Jean takes a sip of his drink then continues his tale. "But, oddly enough, I had heard the man loved to buy shoes. He used to buy dozens of pairs of the same style shoe. Rumor had it that he would bring an extra pair of shoes to restaurants so he could change them while he ate. Anyway, I went to the sale and found—"

"Don't tell me," Paige interjects. "New shoes?"

Jean laughs. "Actually, I found a painting of a jester at a carnival. Something about its colors must have appealed to me. Either that, or I didn't want to go home empty-handed. Anyway, I bought it. I shoved it in a corner of my studio and then forgot about it. One afternoon, I was cleaning my studio and found it again. When I held it up to the light to see what it was, the colors looked odd. Once I scratched away a few chips of paint, I realized that there was another painting underneath. You can imagine my excitement when I thought of the possibilities, especially given the man's rumored wealth and his idiosyncrasies."

The waiter interrupts Jean's story as he places several trays of food in front of us. As the others lazily chat while serving themselves, Jean whispers, "You know, your eyes light up when you talk about art."

"Art was always my passion," I blurt out. "But it's been such a long time since I've expressed myself creatively. I keep these files at home on places I'd like to go, things I'd like to do. It's really hard with young children. To leave them, I mean."

"Where would you go?" he inquires politely.

"I've always wanted to go to Egypt, see the pyramids and tombs for myself. Maybe ride on a camel. I've also wanted to study Middle Eastern and Islamic art." I shrug, embarrassed by how unsophisticated I must sound to him.

But Jean nods, listening carefully without judgment. He smiles, then says, "Lauren, I applaud your devotion to your children. They're only young once. Egypt will always be there for you to explore. But have you found time to indulge your passion for art at home?"

"My friends have asked me to do decorative work but . . ." I pause. "I haven't painted on canvas for years. I suppose I'm my own worst critic."

"Lauren, you're an artist whether you've indulged your passion or not. You were Gustave's prize student. You must reach inward to find your creativity again and express it. It's so important. Without self-expression, how can you be happy?" Jean stops himself, then laughs. "Forgive my unsolicited advice."

"No, really. It's okay. You're right."

His message is clear. Why don't I make time? I know the answer to the question, but I refuse to blame Matt for my own problems. As I question my decision to give up painting on canvas, Jean stares into my eyes, making me uncomfortable under his keen observations.

"Please finish your story," I say for all to hear, immediately bringing all eyes on us.

"Ah, yes," he smiles, a light sparkling in his eyes. "The process was tedious, removing layers of paint, but you might say it was worth it."

"My heart can't take it, Jean. What did you find?" says Paige, greedily nibbling on a piece of duck.

"It was a Picasso." Jean shrugs. "I guess the old man covered it over so no one would know he had it. Rather odd." Monique takes the last bite of a salmon toast point. "My father happened to come into Jean's studio soon after this discovery. He's an avid collector of Picasso's work so once he saw the painting—he bought it on the spot for more than a million dollars. Jean, I still think you should have charged him more. To this day, he claims he stole the painting from you."

"Your father's a good client, Monique, and a generous man."

"Speaking of which, he wants me to talk with you about buying that painting by Henri Gustave that you recently acquired."

"Which one is that?" I ask impatiently, sitting forward in my seat.

"I think it's one of his nudes." Jean raises an eyebrow. "You know, Lauren, I meant to tell you that there's a retrospective of Gustave's work showing at the Pompidou."

My eyes light up. "You're kidding! I'd love to see it."

Turning to me, he says, "I'll take you, then we can talk more about Nélie." He shifts his attention to Monique. "Lauren was one of Gustave's best students. She worked with him in his last years when his health was failing. He told me he considered her one of his most talented assistants."

"Oh, my God," says Paige loudly. "Lauren, you never told me that!"

I blush profusely. "No, really, I haven't painted seriously in years. Jean, I think you're being too kind."

"No, I'm not," he replies curtly.

A pang of sadness overtakes me when I think about my abrupt parting with Gustave. I've never given myself a chance to examine the impact he had on my life and my artwork.

Clearing her throat, Monique chimes in. "Jean, I think our

table's ready by now." As they take their leave, Jean squeezes my hand, promising to call about our museum visit.

Paige stares hard at me. "I forget that you came here to study under Gustave. His work is selling for a fortune these days. So he thought you were gifted, huh? Why doesn't that surprise me?"

"I don't know—he never told me that. He wasn't a particularly easy man to get along with. He yelled and screamed a lot. As he got older and his health detiorated, he became even more difficult. I can only remember a few times in that last year when he actually gave me a compliment." I sigh, remembering how many times I went home in tears after one of Gustave's tirades.

"But you must have learned his techniques. Four years is a long time."

"Probably. He was a genius. It was the way he thought when he envisioned a canvas. I don't know. It's been so long since I painted seriously."

"What happened?" says Paige, picking up several fallen capers from the table then placing them back on her cracker.

"India died and I had other responsibilities," I respond quickly. "But since I've come here, it's as if time's started again. For fifteen years, I've looked for the comfortable and safe route without challenging myself. Look at you, Paige. You kept going, made great choices. Now, you're still so full of life. That's what I love about you. I guess the creative part of me was on that plane with India without my even knowing it."

Serious for once, Paige says, "Lauren, is it India's death that held you back or your relationship with Matt? There, I said it, don't shoot me!" She holds up her hands in mock dismay.

After a long silence, I finally reply, "I can't answer that right now."

"Well," says Paige, shaking her head, "you certainly wouldn't be lonely for long, that's for sure. Call me uncouth, which, I might add, many people do,"—she chuckles—"but I can't believe you didn't even notice how he looked at you all night. Monique did. That's why they left."

"I'm married," I say dismissively. "He was just being polite."

"Are you sure about that?"

"Paige," I reply dryly, "I'm a housewife with three kids. I drive a Suburban, live in a redbrick Georgian house with a manicured lawn and do volunteer work in my spare time." With a laugh, I add, "He belongs with someone like Monique."

"Have you looked in the mirror lately? You have the kind of beauty that's lit from within. And those cheekbones of yours don't hurt."

Annoyed, I snap, "I'm here because I need to find Nélie. That's it." The need for a banal conversation seems appropriate so I add, "Are you hungry? I think I'll have the chicken. What about you?"

Paige signals the waiter who comes to take our order. She's already talked the maitre d' into letting us eat dinner in the lounge, since the restaurant is so crowded.

"Forgive an old friend for interfering, but Lauren, why did you abandon painting? You have a gift; you ought to share it. Gustave was considered the premier colorist of the twentieth century, his work is legendary. He handed down his techniques to you. You could create some beautiful work if you wanted to. Why haven't you done it?" She leans forward in her seat, staring at me.

"I stopped painting when India died, to raise Nélie and have a family." I tap my foot on the ground nervously.

"Why couldn't you do both?" exclaims Paige. She purses her lips in agitation.

"I can't," I cry stupidly, rubbing the knot of tension in my temples.

"Why not? Your kids are almost grown. Pick up where you left off!"

"I'm afraid to," I answer in a low voice. "It's not that easy, having your work judged, being in the spotlight. It makes me uncomfortable!" I take a deep breath. "Besides, after India died, my life changed and so did the quality of my work. I tried for a while but I found no joy in painting. My work just wasn't good enough anymore." A tear rolls down my cheek. I quickly wipe it away, embarrassed by this public display of emotion.

Paige reaches over and grabs my arm for support. She says in a low voice, "Gustave knew you had talent. That doesn't just disappear. In one of the few unselfish acts of her life, India arranged for you to study with Gustave. It was the opportunity of a lifetime. Why throw it away? Why not honor her memory, and Nélie, and show the world your talent?"

Would it be possible to remember everything Gustave taught me and to paint again?

Sensing my inner struggle, Paige returns her attention to our food which has just arrived. "Will you look at this, roast beef, mashed potatoes and green beans. We're in Paris. I left all those California healthy rules at home." She gestures to the waiter for more wine. "Now, what are we going to do about Nélie?"

The chicken dominates the plate. I fear slicing it will send a piece onto the tablecloth so I cut a series of small pieces. "I don't know how to approach her. We need to be in a place where we can talk privately. I'm afraid that if I send her a letter asking her to meet me somewhere, she may disappear again."

"This is sublime," Paige extols, holding up her fork with a chunk of red meat. "Why don't you just come back tomorrow morning to speak to the owner? They should know her work schedule. She may not start for another few days, which gives you more time here. You can decide what to do after that."

Despite the relief I feel knowing Nélie's in Paris, I wonder how she's going to react when I find her. The words, "I'm sorry," sound inadequate even to my own ears. These past few days have opened my eyes to a different view. She needs to know so many things. Where do I begin?

That night, I decide to call Matt to tell him I think I've found her. He offers no congratulations but simply demands to know when I'm coming home.

"I don't know," I reply. "It depends on Nélie."

The Pompidou, which looks like an oversized glass elevator with interior conveyer belts, stretches out before me; an open stage designed as a fruit stand catches my eye. I'm drawn immediately to the colors and shapes, wondering at the message. Jean and I pass by rooms filled with paintings by Picasso and Matisse.

When we come to a wall-sized collage by Matisse, I'm startled to recognize the bird-like shapes similar to those used by Gustave in his work. I stop for a moment, pausing to peer at this collage.

"You know, Gustave studied under Henri Matisse in the nineteen thirties. They became great friends, often spending time together at the cafés of La Rotonde or La Coupole," I say, looking at Jean thoughtfully. "When Matisse became ill, Gustave worked with him to create many of his famous *papiers découpés*."

Jean nodded. "I've always thought these collages were Matisse's finest achievement, like mini experiments in color and light."

Moving on, we take the escalator to the third floor to see Gustave's work. As I enter the room, I see bold strokes of color and such beauty contained on canvas that it takes my breath away. Momentarily stunned, I recover from this pleasant assault on my senses, tentatively moving forward to see the wall of nudes.

Trying to maintain my equilibrium, I say, "See this? India

and I painted her two months before she died. Gustave had become ill. His fingers were nearly useless, so we created the portrait according to his specifications. It was important that his vision carry on. Gustave, like Matisse, wanted his art to show only life's beauty."

Jean peers at the picture. "You drew the original, didn't you?" His tone sounds accusing.

"Yes," I admit readily. "I wanted to complete his concept. He was a genius when it came to color."

"He trusted you not to put in your personal style or take credit," Jean counters, turning to face me.

"Of course. Gustave did the same thing for Matisse."

"No," says Jean. "I got to know Gustave in the years before his death. I sold many of his paintings at my gallery. Gustave took direction from Matisse for years. He would never have dared to do the original work."

"So what's your point?" I demand impatiently.

Sweeping me aside, Jean stares at me intently. "Do you realize that you have the ability to use what Gustave taught you and go further in your own concepts?"

"I'm here to find Nélie," I say firmly. "My art career is secondary to the health and well-being of my daughter!" I add angrily.

Jean raises his arms in mock surrender. "Okay! I hear you, but I won't give up. Let me tell you what I know. There's a café upstairs with a fabulous view where we can sit down and talk."

We walk through the rest of the exhibit, then head upstairs for something to eat. Once inside, we take our seats and order. Then Jean fills me in on his relationship with Julian DuBusé. He begins to tap his fingers on the table, creating an innocuous drumbeat to his next words. "Julian hasn't changed much over the years. He's grown richer, perhaps more powerful. He's got many friends in high places. Madame DuBusé may have political aspirations for him. Nélie would be a most unwelcome intrusion on her plans."

"Will he see her?"

"Honestly, I doubt it. If he hasn't already shown an interest, I see no reason for him to change."

"Can you arrange for me to talk with him? I don't want him to do much, maybe just share some happy memories of his time with India. I'm not sure how Nélie's going to react to his indifference. She hasn't found out about him yet. At least, I hope not."

Jean looks surprised. "You never told her?"

Once again, I'm stung by the realization that my course of mothering had been horribly wrong. As if on cue, a large platter appears before us, filled with an array of cheeses, ham and slices of bread. "This looks wonderful," I comment politely, relieved at the momentary distraction. "No, I was afraid for her safety. Madame DuBusé has a reputation for being tough."

"You're right. Madame seems to have a network of people everywhere who carry out her wishes. If she has an enemy, the papers run damaging stories about them. She knows rumors can be dangerous. But enough about her; she can't be that powerful or else Julian would stay at home more often. I'll try to arrange a meeting for you as soon as possible. I know you're eager to find your daughter and go home."

"Yes, of course," I reply. Pleasantly relaxed and feeling certain that Jean will take care of things with Julian, I agree to return to the gallery to look at his latest acquisitions.

By the time we emerge from the restaurant, it is late afternoon. We walk easily together, unhurried, enjoying the warm spring weather. Winding our way back to the gallery, we observe several customers admiring Jean's work, and we exchange a knowing glance. He greets one of them, answering a question about the painting's setting. Suddenly, it seems as if everyone there has a question for Jean. Once he dislodges himself from his customers, he grabs a set of keys from his desk and leads me to a utilitarian back door that looks as if it leads to a regular supply closet. Inside the small room, there are two walls lined with shelves containing various artifacts.

"I sell certain pieces of art on consignment," he explains. "If I have an extremely valuable piece, I have to keep it back here and only show it to select private clients." He carefully unwraps two pieces of art, holding them close as if they are babies. "Here they are," he exclaims, then walks us to a private back room located down a corridor beside his office. "I had this area built several years ago. I've found it's a nice way to show the art under proper lighting."

The room has only one window, with a series of spotlights on the ceiling. I watch as Jean flicks a switch that illuminates two pedestals. He places each piece of art on a pedestal. Once the spotlight hits the art, it has the same effect as if it were in a museum, only I have the privilege of a private viewing.

He faces me, then says, "Well, what do you think? I'm bringing Egypt to you."

I'm touched by his gesture. For some reason, my throat constricts. Trying to calm myself, I focus my attention on the first piece of art to the far left. "This looks like a man mashing grain through a sieve to make beer. The woman is grinding grain into flour. I read somewhere that beer and bread were the two main staples of the Egyptian diet."

"Very good. Now, who should I sell it to?"

"A museum, of course, Jean. You can't deprive others of such an important part of our history."

"It takes too long for many museums to make this kind of purchase. They have so many people involved in the decision-making process. Fortunately, I'm in no hurry. Take a look at this," he says, pointing to some intricate ornaments.

"They're magnificent," I cry, staring at the elaborate beading. "These bracelets are so fascinating. It makes me wonder about the woman who wore them. To think that they are more than two thousand years old, with all of the beads still intact. They must be worth a fortune."

"Indeed, they are, which is why I can't put them out front, even in glass cases."

A knock on the door interrupts our conversation. A woman appears. "Jean, there's someone here to see you. Her name is Paige Riverton. She says you know her."

"Send her back here."

Paige sweeps into the room, elegantly clad in a slate blue suit with a matching crocodile bag and pumps. Reassuring me that everything's all right, she says, "Lauren, may I speak to you alone for a moment?"

Jean immediately takes his leave. "No one will disturb you in here. I'll be at my desk."

"Thank you," I reply before turning my attention to Paige. "What is it?" I say breathlessly.

"Matt's called the apartment several times today. He wants to know where you are. I think he's ready to get on a plane and come here himself. I told him you were out making inquiries, but he says he wants to talk to you immediately."

The blast of reality intrudes upon my senses. "I'll run home to call him. He'll calm down. Sometimes his temper gets the better of him. I'm sorry to put you through it."

"You're not going anywhere until you tell me what you were doing in here." Paige walks over to survey the pieces of art on the pedestals. "Okay, we've got some guy mashing potatoes or something on this one. The woman looks like she needs an appointment for a facial and a manicure. Will you look at those bracelets? Some woman should have sewn those onto her wrists when she died. They're awfully pretty."

Tears of mirth ripple down my cheeks. "Should I even try to tell you about each one?"

"No, thanks. I like my version better. Let's go home before

I have to entertain Matt, too. Make sure you sound exhausted and upset about Nélie when you speak with him."

"Don't make me feel any more guilty than I already do!" I snap.

"Lauren, you haven't done anything wrong by having lunch with Jean. I think it's good for you to see a different perspective on things."

"What's that supposed to mean?"

"Nothing. But I hardly qualify looking at Egyptian statues as anything to be worried about. But, more importantly, when are you going to talk with Julian?"

"Jean said he would call him this afternoon. I hope as early as tomorrow. I would like to see him before I contact Nélie. Did you go to the restaurant?"

"I saw her."

"Oh, my God! Why didn't you tell me?"

"That was the other reason I interrupted your private art history class. By the way, does he give out grades?"

"Not funny. Go on."

"Does Nélie have a boyfriend at home?"

"She dates a number of young men, but I've never seen her bowled over by anyone. Don't tell me."

"He's about six feet tall. Dark hair. Blue eyes. I give the girl credit. She's got good taste just like her mother. But he doesn't sound southern, nor do I think he's from Greensboro, North Carolina. And he's certainly not in high school."

"They must have met on the plane."

Paige giggles as if she's still a teenager. "Why didn't I see anybody that good-looking on our plane? Seriously, it must have been love at first sight or something. They seemed awfully involved to me, if you know what I mean. She's certainly doesn't seem unhappy nor ready to pick up the phone to call you."

I rub my hands over my eyes. "What do I do now?"

"We'll talk about it on the way home. My driver's out front."

How would India have handled this situation? Her reaction may have been understanding, happiness, even excitement for Nélie. Yet, I don't feel any of these emotions. Until three days ago, I trusted Nélie's judgment, but now I'm not so sure that she's making the right choices. Yet, she's seventeen years old. I can't control her destiny, just as I couldn't control India's. This realization hurts, reminding me of the time ten-year-old Nélie made me a ceramic heart for my birthday that said, "I love my mommy." India's little girl, no, my little girl is a young woman with a mind of her own. She needs to move forward in her own life, not the life I envision for her. It's so hard for me to let go, to allow her the freedom to be herself.

Back at the apartment, I pick up the phone to call Matt at work. His greeting is curt, which makes me want to slam him with a similar obnoxious response. His anger is palpable. "Where have you been? I've tried to reach you today."

"I think I've found her. I've arranged to meet with Julian. I hope he'll see me."

"I don't believe it! Where is she?" I hear the relief in his voice, which relaxes me.

"She's gotten a job at a trendy nightspot that seems pretty upscale, so I'm not worried about that. Paige went by there. I think she's met someone."

"Who?"

"I don't know, but I want to talk with Julian before I confront Nélie. She's an adult, Matt. We can't force her to come home. I'm not sure what to say to her."

"Lauren," he responds gently, "one thing at a time. First, let's make sure it's her."

The conversation turns to events at home, with Matt filling me in on what's been happening. He's going to tell people that we surprised Nélie with a trip to Paris as her graduation present and we'll be back in a few days. Fortunately, Nélie had enough sense to complete all of her requirements for a diploma, but I assume she had planned to miss the ceremony with all of her friends. He wants to know when I'm coming home.

"I need at least another week to get things settled. I'll return then with or without Nélie." When we hang up, I stare at the receiver for a moment, wondering why I feel so detached from my home, from my life in Kirkwood, after only a few days.

What will people say when they find out Nélie and I have suddenly gone to Paris? Potential conversations come to my mind with phrases like, "That's not like her," or how about, "There must be something more to the story. Why would Nélie miss her graduation ceremony?" A few malicious comments may enter the rumor mill, such as, "I wonder about that girl. Her mother wasn't married, you know. It's a secret, but I heard she had an affair with a married Frenchman." The talk will start out simply enough, but speculation could inspire too many inaccurate conclusions. Too many people there have too much time on their hands.

"Did everything go all right?" Paige asks.

I stand up to go stare out the window of my room. "He's fine now. He was relieved to learn that we've found Nélie. I plan to talk with her after I meet with Julian. We're telling people that I gave Nélie a surprise trip to Paris for her graduation. Do you think anyone will buy our story?"

"Honestly, no. It's too out of character for you. But who cares what other people think. They can say whatever they want. It doesn't matter. You know the truth and you have the right to share it with whomever you choose."

I turn to face Paige. "Why do I feel like Nélie's disappearance is going to be the topic of conversation at home for the next few months? Maybe I should live in a place like New York."

Paige laughs. "Where anything goes. People can walk down the street naked and no one would care. Then again, someone could be knifed on the sidewalk while many people would just keep walking by. It's a tough city, Lauren. At least in your neighborhood, it sounds as if people care. There's something to be said for that. I don't even know half the people in my building."

"Yes, but my quiet southern oasis can be so stagnant. Even the brick houses look the same. They each have an immaculately groomed lawn and the standard Suburban parked in the driveway. The University of North Carolina sports teams provide the main excitement. Do you know that when a family moves into Kirkwood, a neighbor greets them with a bottle of wine or home-baked cookies or even a potted geranium?"

"How horrible!" Paige mocks.

"Can you be serious for just a minute?" I say sternly, giving her the same look of disapproval I used to use on my girls when they were five years old. "In New York, you can be anonymous. It's not like that in the south. People *know* us. They know my family, my aunts, my uncles, my grandparents. I'm accountable for my actions. I hate the fact that Nélie's disappearance is going to cause a wave of speculation so high that it will supercede everything else for a period of time. It's one thing saying you don't care what others think; it's another living it."

I sigh heavily. "The funny looks, the questions, the rumors. Questions like, is she pregnant? People may draw their own conclusions, convinced that Nélie is just like India. They'll say poor Lauren and Matt, after all they've done for her, just look at how that ungrateful girl has treated them. Our lives will be put under a microscope by groups like the ladies' bridge club that meets at my mother's house Wednesday evenings. Mrs. Woodlands is going to wonder where we went wrong and decide that we should have attended church every Sunday rather than missing it on select occasions. I want Nélie to have choices but I also want her to be able to come home to Greensboro."

"Lauren, have you considered the fact that as much as Nélie loves her family, she realized that Greensboro can never be a place she calls home? That's why she left the way she did."

Tears fill my eyes. "Why do you say that?"

Paige adopts a serious tone and says gently, "I don't think she ever meant to hurt you, Lauren. She may not care what the people of Kirkwood think of her. There's a whole world out there. She wants to take advantage of it. Just because she's left the community she grew up in doesn't mean she doesn't love you or she didn't love her childhood. She's young, and she's gone out to find herself, her real mother and a place where she belongs."

Folding my arms tightly around myself, I lean my forehead against the window. I can't control the flow of tears that roll off my cheeks onto the carpet. "Why do I feel like my illusions about my life have all been shattered? I don't know what to think anymore."

"You have choices, Lauren. Remember that. You seem to think that someone is standing over you preaching all these rules that you live by, whether it be someone like Mrs. Woodlands or your family or this list of aunts and uncles that you mentioned. It's time you made your own rules. It's your life, too, and you have to live it as you see fit. This isn't about Nélie. She did you a big favor and opened the door for you just as India did all those years ago. You can look at the broken glass, decide what's worth keeping and glue some of it back together."

"Do you have any rubber cement?" I quip. "I'm all out."

Paige laughs. "I'll buy you some in the morning. Now, you

need to get some sleep. You're exhausted. We've found Nélie, Lauren. That should help you rest easier." She gets up, yawns and then gives me a hug goodnight.

`After shutting the door, I change into a pair of sweatpants and a T-shirt. My mind swirls over the events of the day, but I find myself concentrating on something Paige said that keeps reverberating in my head. *This isn't about Nélie. She did you a big favor and opened the door for you just as India did all those years ago.* Is it truly a door that Nélie opened or a Pandora's box?

Chapter 10

For better or worse, Julian lives ignoring the fact that he is Nélie's biological father. He has the power to help Nélie deal with his existence in a positive manner if he explains things properly. The explanation need not be complicated, just an indication that he wants a real relationship but finds it an impossibility due to his wife. I still find it hard to believe that he could so completely abandon Nélie without a word or letter of inquiry.

My father was a quiet man, distant and aloof sometimes, but he possessed a certain kindness that always let me know he was there if and when I needed him. Not an overly demonstrative man, he did try to show me he loved me by that occasional pat on the head or the fifty-cent pieces he gave out on report card days. While I took my problems and concerns to my mother, Dad was always in the background, watching, listening and providing a presence in my life that I often took for granted.

Solitude gave him the comfort he needed, but life cannot take place solely in a book or at the end of a fishing rod. Over the years, perhaps it was I who was the harshest judge of his character. He was never quite the man I wanted him to be. Certainly, he provided for us, giving us a nice home. But he lacked the dynamic personality I wanted him to have. On

Father's Day at school, he was always there, but he seemed a bit uncomfortable in the navy blue suit he wore only on special occasions. He pulled at the collar from time to time, stayed seated in the back of the room and spoke only when probed with questions. He hated to draw attention to himself. It wasn't until he passed away during my sophomore year of college that I truly appreciated the lessons he taught.

He was there. My father was always there, watching and waiting, and that in itself provided comfort to me in my formative years. Home by five o'clock each night, he sat in his favorite armchair by the fireplace in the living room, while Mom worked with me in the adjoining kitchen on homework and school projects. She got up repeatedly to check the pots on the burners or coax some tasty sauce into shape. From time to time, Dad inquired and I had the pleasure of explaining what I was doing. While the events and activities that characterize our relationship seemed ordinary, I was happy enough, and often I take solace in those peaceful times. Especially now, as I prepare myself to face Julian.

Oddly enough, Julian has all the qualities I had wanted my father to have: he's handsome, charming, witty, sophisticated, wealthy. The surface character seems very appealing. Just showing up at a school event Julian would have caused quite a stir among Nélie's friends. He would have arrived in a chauffeur-driven car, black probably, and he would have been impeccably dressed in a hand-tailored suit and custom-made shirt with gold cuff links. The teacher would have fluttered to his side, asking him to speak first about his profession. He may have said something charming such as, "How does one begin to talk about running a multinational company: we're diverse, but we make everything from leather into goods such as shoes and handbags to furniture. You see how many of you are wearing something leather right now?" All of the classmates would vie for his attention, each one proudly summing up his or her leather wares. The students' display of shoes would have dominated the discussion.

Julian's world has a magazine-like quality to it, and he seems far beyond my reach. Seated in a waiting room, I am among several other visitors ready to take my turn talking to this titan of business. While it is luxurious, I find Julian's choice for a meeting place cold and impersonal. When Jean arranged this meeting for me, he told me Julian had insisted on meeting at his office. I can't help but think that Julian views his relationship with Nélie as impersonally as an everyday business discussion. Calm down, I tell myself, he's her father. He has to want to see her just once, if only to reconcile his own conscience.

After I've been waiting twenty minutes, a woman comes forward, smiling and telling me to come with her. The mighty Zeus awaits, I muse. I do not return her smile, indicating in my own small way that I am not enamored with her boss. As for Julian, he probably perceives my visit as a privilege.

The moment I see him, I think how little he has changed. In fact, he's probably more handsome than I remembered him. He must be approaching seventy. His hair has more gray in it, but he has such an aristocratic bearing that age has only added to his appeal. His smile appears welcoming, albeit polite. I walk into an off-white office the size of a gymnasium, furnished with art, antiques and white sectional sofas. He sees me gazing at them and says, "Do you like them? This is how we do business nowadays. My son hates the coldness of a conference room, so we had these sofas put in for everyone to gather together for meetings. He claims it generates creativity. I'm not quite convinced."

"They're lovely. Has anyone spilled coffee on one yet?"

After a polite laugh that does break the tension, he motions me forward. "I remember you well, Lauren. Please come over here and sit down. Speaking of which, may I offer you something to drink?" Julian's always been a gentleman, I think.

"No, thank you." On the way over to the sofa, I spy several silver-framed pictures of Julian's wife and children. They are displayed with pride. His supposed sense of family emanates from every corner of this room. Maybe it's good for business, I surmise, knowing Julian is a master of disguise. I sit down and look up, seeing that he is staring patiently at me. He acts so innocent, as if he can't imagine what I have come to talk with him about. One would think I needed a handbag or something. "I'm pleased to see that things are going well," I say, trying to make polite conversation.

"Yes, of course. Spring is our busiest season. We have a sale in our store where everything is half off. Women go mad. Many of them come in dressed so glamorously and they end up fighting like chickens in a henyard. It's really quite ridiculous. Can you picture this tug of war over a silly handbag?"

"I suppose when you make *the* handbag, many people find that important."

"But you don't?"

"Not really. Not to say I don't like beautiful things, but look at the way I dress. I have more important things to consider."

"I'd say you're still quite a lovely girl, Lauren." He winks. "Even without one of my handbags. Don't worry, I won't hold it against you."

He sits across from me, acting like we're old friends. The tension has dissolved and I admire the ease with which he has led me to where he wants me. I'd better get to the point. "You must be wondering why Jean arranged this meeting. You remember India, of course."

"Who could forget her?" He smiles, but his eyes seem far away. "Sometimes I'll be at a restaurant or in a crowd, and I'll think I see her. My heart still pounds, Lauren, and for a moment, I wonder if her death really happened. It's strange, I know."

"But Julian," I cry, unable to help myself. "A part of India lives on in your daughter, Nélie. She's very much like her mother. The way she laughs, the way she moves, her sense of humor."

"That doesn't surprise me at all. Nevertheless, I have three children by my wife."

His coldness on the issue surprises me, but I refuse to be daunted. Taking another tack, I mention that Nélie is seventeen now. "She's curious and wants to know more about her parents."

Julian nods in understanding. "I'll let you in on a little secret. I never sold India's apartment. Most of her things are still there. I still visit there from time to time, just to remember. Despite what you must think, I loved India. I'll never forget her."

Choosing not to reveal that I'd already discovered his secret, I inquire, "Could I take Nélie there? I know it would mean a lot to her."

"You may visit there if you wish. I'll give you a key before you leave."

"And then what?" I refuse to give up. "What about your daughter? Could you at least talk with her once? Perhaps explain things? I've not told her enough about her mother. That's why she ran away, to find India again. Only I think she'll find you, and I'm afraid she'll be very hurt by it all. She's seventeen now, Julian, and such a lovely young woman."

Julian stands up, walking over to the window. With his back to me, his stance appears unyielding. He turns to face me and says, "No. I'm afraid I won't see her, Lauren. It's too complicated."

Anger surges through me. "She's your daughter, Julian. I raised her, and I've never once asked you for anything. You can't dismiss her so easily. All I ask for now is for you to meet her, just once. Talk to her. Make her understand. That's it."

"You should have told her that her father died in that plane crash with India. It would have been easier that way," he says, pacing a few steps in front of the window as if deep in thought on how to rectify the situation. "That's what I led her to believe. If she stays on in Paris, she's going to start asking questions, and the truth will come out. I don't want it to happen that way. I had hoped you would feel something for her and agree to share the facts in a loving manner. How hard can that be?"

His nostrils flare as he folds his arms in front of him, revealing a gold watch. "India knew when we met that I didn't want any more children. I was very clear on that issue. She defied my wishes and got pregnant, which she confessed to me one night. I loved her enough to forgive her, but I swore then that I wouldn't be accountable to the child. India was a clever one, but she pushed me too far." He then returns to his seat, sighing heavily. "India was young and wild. She always had that impetuous nature that intrigued and irritated me at the same time. I never knew what she was going to do until she did it. In Nélie's case, it wasn't exactly a mistake that could be undone."

"I see," I say quietly. "But the fact remains that you have a daughter, whether you like it or not. Don't you ever wonder about her?"

"No," he replies coldly. "I don't."

"Then how can you have truly loved India? I'm not sure that you did. Maybe you just kept the apartment because you were too lazy to clean it out. Maybe it provides an occasional retreat from your wife. Is that it?"

Julian looks at me and laughs softly, breaking the tension. "You're a tough one, Lauren. I always thought you were India's better half, beautiful, responsible and intelligent. Perhaps you'd like to come to work for me sometime, yes?"

His charm disarms me momentarily, as it was meant to do. "We're not talking about me. Please think about talking with Nélie. I'd hate for her to think that India meant nothing to you." I stand up, and smooth out my dress. "May I have the key, please? It means a great deal to me."

"As you wish." Julian jumps up, probably relieved to have something immediate to focus upon. He walks over to the desk drawer and removes a gold key, handing it to me. "Will you be staying much longer?" he asks politely.

"About a week. Ten days at the most. I'll return the key before I go."

"There's no rush. Goodbye Lauren. It was a pleasure seeing you again."

"Goodbye, Julian," I say, feeling the weight of his rejection on my shoulders as if I were his daughter. As I reach for the door, Julian calls to me, but I refuse to look back at him.

Fatigue consumes me. I have the sudden urge to crawl into bed, throw the covers over my head and hide myself from my present predicament. Once I am outside, the warm air enlivens my spirits, and I plunge forward with no real direction in mind. Glancing at Julian's flagship store across the street, I see a line of well-dressed women outside the door, waiting to take advantage of this semi-annual sale. I stroll down the street until I see a small park in the distance.

The sun feels hot on my face. My high-heeled shoes start to bother me. Glancing at the children, I notice that one little girl in a pink dress has fallen off the swing. Her mother rushes over to pick her up, dry her tears and give her words of encouragement. My eyes fill with tears as I watch them. The urge to mother never really goes away. Nélie has grown up but it hurts to let go. I still see her as my little girl. I want to dust her knees off, then hug away her problems.

My youngest child is almost nine years old. Where did the time go? They grow up so fast. Those precious moments of early childhood have to last a lifetime. All of my girls have brought me such joy that I wonder why I don't include Matt in my thinking.

What would I be doing if I weren't standing in the middle of a park in Paris? At the grocery store? Picking up Matt's dry cleaning? Shopping? He'd want to know what's for dinner or whether I'd gotten the repairman in to fix the leak in the bathroom. He'd ask if I had remembered to call someone to take the lawnmower in for repair. A surge of distaste runs through me, making me wonder if I'm the one who should have run away, not Nélie.

Chapter 11

The apartment carries so many memories I want to share with Nélie. It's time that we talk. Invigorated by my private treasure key, I head to the restaurant to find her. My heart pounds in anticipation as I walk through the door, looking for her familiar brown head.

"May I help you?" asks a young man in dark pants and white shirt, indicating that he works there. Our communication is a bit awkward.

"I'm looking for my daughter. She's new here. Her name is Nélie," I sputter in my makeshift French, taking out a photograph.

His eyes light up. "Yes. But she's not here. She worked this morning, then she and Richard were going to visit a friend in the country for the weekend."

"Richard?"

"Richard Bristol. He's managed this place off and on for years."

I nearly lose my composure. "Do you remember who they were going to visit? I must get in touch with her. It's a family problem, you understand?"

"Of course," replies the young man. "Louis Vernon. He's a well-known vintner in the area."

"Oh, my God!" I say. My heart starts pounding.

"Are you all right?" asks the waiter. "Can I get you a glass of water?"

"I'm fine," I say hastily. "I have to go now. Thank you for your help." Louis Vernon? Does Nélie have any idea she's going to stay with her grandfather this weekend? My mind ticks off everything India once told me about her father. She had hated him, but why? The words come back to me from that afternoon when we spoke of him in a café. *I suppose we'll always be at odds. I like to think of myself as his conscience.*

I race down the street, trying to get back to Paige's apartment. I must sort through this new twist to an already convoluted situation. Would Louis recognize Nélie? I picture mother and daughter in my mind. The similarities seem clearly visible, yet I know them both so well. Could India's father make the connection?

Once inside the confines of Paige's apartment, surrounded by silk, damask and gilded furniture, I bustle around, calling for Paige.

"I'm here. What's the matter?" she asks, responding to the urgency in my voice. "Don't tell me they had a fifty percent off sale at Gucci and I missed it!"

"Nélie's gone away for the weekend with her boyfriend!" I say anxiously.

Paige leads me to the sofa, sitting down beside me. "What's the problem? She's an adult."

"They're staying with Louis Vernon, India's father!"

"Not good," she says, her expression serious for once. "How did that happen?"

"It seems he's a family friend of her new boyfriend. His name is Richard Bristol. I'm not sure whether Louis ever knew he had a grandchild. At least I never met him. I always had the feeling there was more to the story than India let on. She was afraid of him, I think. Do you think he could possibly recognize Nélie?"

Paige shrugs. "I don't know. Let's hope not, or he might be pretty upset that you never contacted him after India's death."

I lean back on the sofa, rubbing my aching temples. "I hadn't thought of that. Why do I have the feeling that this situation is going to get worse before it gets better? Louis must be a prominent figure. Even the waiter in the restaurant knew who he was. He said that Louis is a well-known vintner in this area."

"So how do we get ourselves invited?" Paige stands up, pacing the floor. "I've got it! It's a brilliant idea if I do say so myself!" She claps her hands, her eyes sparkling with excitement. "I'm going to ask Bert to call Louis Vernon first. I'm sure Louis will have heard of him. Bert can talk money and tell Louis that he's thinking about investing in his company. You know once Bert starts throwing out numbers he's hard to resist. He can also mention that you and I just happen to be in Paris and we're old friends of India's. Maybe then, he can pave the way for my phone call this afternoon."

"Great idea! I think it sounds believable. How do we get his phone number?"

"I'll bet Jean would know. Give him a call and see if you can get it," Paige orders, now fully in command of the situation.

Breathing a sigh of relief, I look over at Paige. "I don't know how I ever could have done this without you."

"Save your praise for later," advises Paige. "Bert has a tendency to become the invisible man when he's in the middle of a big deal. The question is whether I can get him on the phone." She grins. "I know, I'll tell his secretary that I just bought a building. Just you wait and see, that'll make him take my call!"

Moments later, I manage to get Jean on the phone, sharing the details of my latest find. I have no choice but to ask for his help again, which he offers without hesitation. Jean volunteers to find the number and call me back immediately.

My next phone call seems like a parody of the first. I ask Matt's secretary to interrupt him in a meeting so that I may speak to him.

His coldness unnerves me. "What's happened?" he demands.

I instinctively recoil from the harshness of his voice. Nervously, I explain the situation, telling him of our plans to visit Louis for the weekend.

"Lauren, this is absolutely ridiculous," he argues into the phone. "We're getting nowhere. You can't just invite yourself to someone's home. What if the girl isn't Nélie?"

His line of questioning shatters my already frayed nerves. "I have to try," I say. "There's no harm in it. If I'm wrong, we'll be back tomorrow night. If I'm right, then I'll finally have a chance to talk to Nélie, maybe work out something. I don't know. I have to try," I repeat, wanting desperately to get through to him.

As soon as I hang up, the phone rings again and it's Jean.

"I've got it," he says, giving me the number. "What do you plan to do?"

"Paige's husband, Bert, is going to call Louis Vernon and say he's interested in investing in his company. He'll mention that we're in Paris and that we're old friends of India's. Paige then plans to make a follow-up call to see if he'll invite us for the weekend. We're hoping it works."

"What can I do to help?"

"You've already done enough," I reply.

"Tell me what happens and promise you'll call if you need me."

"Thank you."

Turning to Paige, I shout, "I've got the number."

Paige takes the slip of paper from my hand and grabs the phone. She calls Bert's office, telling his secretary how she just put a deposit down on this wonderful building. Moments later, she winks at me as she assures her husband that she really needed to speak to him. With her usual flair for the dramatic, Paige explains our dilemma to Bert, asking him to tell Louis that she plans to phone him later on this afternoon. She then wrangles a promise from him to make the call as soon as he hangs up from her.

"Well, so far, so good," she tells me when she hangs up. "We've completed phase one of our plan."

"I don't mean to be rude, Paige, but if Bert is that busy, how do you know he won't forget to call?"

Paige nods. "I promised I'd take that fly-fishing trip with him out to Jackson Hole. God, how I hate the outdoors! All that fresh air and sunshine will just ruin my hair and nails. There'd better be some good spa services out there. I still don't get why anyone would think throwing a fishing line in a cold lake is remotely exciting. Even worse, after all that work, you don't even eat all the fish! Anyway, I'll endure it for the cause!"

"You're the best," I say, grinning.

She checks her watch. "Let's go grab an espresso and wait a few hours before we call Louis. We wouldn't want our plan to look too contrived, now would we?"

"Of course not. I'm sure Louis will be delighted with Bert's call," I say sardonically, reaching for a sweater. "It's not every day a financial guru calls him offering to invest millions in his company when he has no intention of doing so!"

"Ah, details, details," replies Paige. "You never know, Bert may decide to do it. We drink enough red wine in our house— it may save us some money!"

Several hours pass. Paige and I spend our time chatting and drinking coffee at a local café. Finally, we agree that we need to proceed with Paige's call to Louis. Heading back to the apartment, Paige remarks, "I've got enough caffeine in me to really add some melodrama to this call."

"Just don't talk too fast," I remind her. "We need this invitation."

"Don't worry, I think this is even more fun than shopping, if that's possible."

She dials Louis's number, explains who she is to the person who answers, then asks for Louis. Several minutes later, I hear Paige delight in what sounds like a warm reception. "Why, we would love to come!" she replies demurely. Thirty minutes later, she hangs up, shouting, "He invited *us*! Now I really feel like a genius."

"You've got to be kidding!" I say loudly, impressed. "I can't believe you just pulled that off."

Paige takes a bow. "That was good, if I do say so myself! Louis says he'll have several other house guests at his château. I really hope one of them's Nélie." We talk for several more minutes about the trip, the necessary details surrounding our departure and when we'll meet.

I shake my head, scanning my memory. "Now, what do you remember India telling us about her father?"

She says, "I remember India complaining once that her father had too much money for his own good. I still find that hard to believe—you can never be too rich, too thin or too beautiful in this world."

"I do remember India hated her father, but I don't know exactly why. I always sensed that she was afraid of him. Her descriptions of him were filled with such anger."

"You act like we're going to visit Count Dracula or something," says Paige. "This may be a very interesting weekend."

"So, how much do you really know about wine?" I ask, genuinely curious.

"Enough to get by. About ten years ago, Bert and I bought an old farmhouse in Charlottesville, Virginia, thinking we needed a retreat. Bert always has to have a project. He decided to have several acres of our land tilled to plant vines.

Our wine isn't exactly good, but it's gotten better over the years since we hired this nice Italian vintner to help us."

"You never told me that," I exclaim. "How interesting!"

"Lauren," states Paige, "I've seen you less than three times in the last fifteen years. We have a lot of catching up to do."

I stop to stare at her. "Only three visits! That can't be right. What happened?"

"I don't know, you tell me. We grew apart." Paige looks away. "I always thought our friendship meant more to me than it did to you."

"That's not fair, Paige." I sit down on the sofa, trying to determine why we didn't stay in touch. "Maybe it's my fault. I associated you with India and our time in Paris together. It was easier to just close the door than rehash what we had lost."

Paige looks at me in the eye and says, "I've always had the feeling that Matt didn't approve of me. I think he influenced you into feeling the same way."

The denial that should burst forth stays lodged in my throat. "God, I hope not!" I protest desperately. "It seems like I've been such a fool about so many things. Please don't add this to my list right now. I don't think I could kick myself any harder than I'm doing already. I have so much to sort out right now, and not just in my relationship with Nélie. I have so many questions about myself, my marriage and the choices I've made."

"I'm sorry for bringing it up now. I know you've got a lot on your mind. I've just missed you, Lauren. You're a real friend. I don't feel that way about many people in my life. I have too many 'social friends' that I've grown weary of in- dulging over the years. It's nice to be with someone who I know will be honest with me. Now, let's get packing. Let me see, what do you wear to dinner in a château in the south of France?"

"Wait a minute," I say, looking askance at her. "How are we going to find this place?"

Paige waves her hand at me. "Details, details. My driver adores a challenge and his family's from a neighboring town. I'm not worried."

"Fortunately, I have one set of clothes that are just going to have to work."

"Oh, no, you don't," says Paige. "I went shopping this morning while you were out with Julian. I picked up a few things for both of us. Yours are in your room."

"You're lucky I don't have time to argue with you, or enough clean clothes."

As I walk out of the room, Paige adds, with a wink, "By the way, I took the price tags off of everything so you'll have no idea how much to pay me back."

I don't know whether to be upset with Paige or grateful for her generosity. When I see the elegant dress and pants suit she selected, I'm tempted to march back into her room to tell her to return them. At least that's what Matt would have had me do, since it would be an affront to his pride that my rich friend bought me clothes. But since Paige has decided to play Pygmalion, I decide that I don't mind being her subject. Besides, I have too many more important things to consider.

Twenty-four hours later, we leave the city behind. Paige's driver mentions that the drive is a little over five hours so we must get going to make it in time for dinner. The château is in a little town located in a stretch of the Pyrennes.

Seated in the cozy leather interior of Paige's town car, I almost feel guilty at how comfortable I am. "Tell me more about your small vineyard," I ask, suspecting that it probably produces the best wine in Virginia.

Adjusting her pink designer silk dress, Paige explains, "Bert and I bought a farm in Charlottesville called Oaklands on about fifty acres. We thought it would be fun to make our own wine for family and friends. It seemed like a good idea at the start but we had no idea how hard it is to make good wine. And I emphasize the word, *good*. Some years our wine was truly awful but, fortunately, no one spit, choked or gasped for air in our presence."

I laugh. "How often do you visit?"

"Three or four times a year. And I know, we can't expect to make decent wine on the weekends. At first, we had a guy named Larry working for us helping with the vines. We were growing these seyval blanc grapes which take five years before the harvest has the right flavor. Every year, it seemed like we had some unexpected problem. I remember what happened the first year after poor Larry and his crew had worked so hard planting and harvesting the grapes. I'll never forget his phone call telling us the grapes were gone. We were shocked."

"What happened?" I ask.

"Deer," replies Paige. "Some deer hopped the fence and spent a week partying in our vineyard. They munched every single grape in sight. It never occurred to either of us that something like this could happen. But the real challenge was stopping it from happening again. Our hunting friends volunteered to sit up at night and shoot the deer that jumped the fence which, of course, we didn't think was very funny. Then someone suggested we put tiger dung in the fields."

"Forgive my ignorance, Paige," I say with a chuckle. "I don't follow you. Why tiger dung?"

Paige laughs at the memory. "The tiger is a natural predator of the deer and if the deer pick up their scent, supposedly, they would stay away."

"Where ever would you get tiger dung?"

"That's the whole problem with the idea! Larry could have gone to the National Zoo at Woodley Park for some. But can you imagine transporting it back in his truck. Phew! What a smell!"

We laugh. "So how did you solve it?" I ask.

"The truth is just so boring!" says Paige with a sigh. "We

ended up by having Larry build an electrical fence for us with more barbed wire."

"How many bottles do you produce each year?"

"About one thousand," replies Paige. "We give it to friends and family during the holidays. Sometimes we'll sell it in some local wine shops."

"I thought you said it was awful."

Paige responds, "I didn't say we liked our friends and family!" We laugh as she continues. "One year, we even stomped some of the grapes in our bare feet. I once had a 'Bacchus' party and our friends came down to help Larry and his crew. It's was a riot."

"I doubt Louis stomps his grapes by foot anymore. I'm sure his equipment is state-of-the-art. I'm trying to decide whether I'd want to drink wine that some of my friends' feet have been in."

"It's just as ridiculous as it sounds. We have large plastic vats and grown men step into them. More than likely, they've had a few Bloody Marys. Then we put the grapes in an old-fashioned press to take out even more juice."

Paige becomes serious. "Now, for the hard part. How do we convince Louis that I really want to talk about wine? He'll think we used him to find Nélie, which we did, of course."

I shake my head nervously. "I'll have to tell him the truth."

"What!" exclaims Paige. "We can't do that! He'll think I'm a complete charlatan." She laughs heartily. "I can tell him his young friend Richard is the real reason I came, that I have a thing for younger men or even better, that they lust after me." She playfully pats her hair. "While you're at it, you may want to mention that Nélie is his long-lost granddaughter that he never knew existed in the first place."

"What a mess!" I say, leaning my head back against the leather seat. "What are we going to do?"

"Lie," says Paige confidently. "We'll just have to think of something really good."

The driver announces our impending arrival at the château. I roll my eyes heavenward, knowing that we're walking into a potentially disastrous situation. Paige, however, seems to be reveling in the drama.

As we pass the vineyard, I exclaim, "Look at those grapes."

"Now, that's a vineyard!" says Paige, her excitement showing. "Let's just hope I know enough to carry on more than a five-minute conversation with Louis."

The silence of anticipation hangs over us as we approach Louis Vernon's house. Oddly enough, I respect India's feelings about her father and can't help the distaste that crawls to the surface. What kind of man is he? Certainly, he's extremely wealthy, and by the look of these rows and rows of perfectly groomed vines, he's also a successful vintner.

"There it is," says the driver, pointing to the château.

A stone fortress with a beauty that awes me comes into view. I'm certain that over the centuries other guests have felt the same way. The château is immense, sprawled across a landscape as imposing as the trees bordering it. It is both welcoming and forbidding, pulling me closer, yet daring me to come inside. But my daughter is somewhere in there, and I must get to her. Little does Nélie realize that she has stumbled headfirst into her heritage.

"How many rooms do you think there are?" I ask, trying to calm my nervous stomach.

"A hundred is a good guess." She laughs. "And we were worried Louis didn't have enough room for us!"

Chapter 12

When the front door swings open, I watch a tall, broad-shouldered man emerge. Louis appears to stand well over six feet, with a lean frame. The fine cheekbones, graceful movements and mannerisms—not to mention his confident stride—remind me of India. He has a shock of gray hair, but the red shows through. He waves a hand in greeting to us. "Hello, there!"

"Louis, it's so nice to meet you," says Paige. "You're so kind to invite us to your home, and on such short notice. I'm really looking forward to learning about your vineyard this weekend."

"The pleasure is all mine," says Louis with a wave of his hand. "It's not very often I get to connect with India's old friends." He hesitates. "It'll bring back some good memories. That'll help me, you know?"

He introduces us to Claude, a serious-looking man whose thinning hair places him anywhere between thirty and fifty. A member of Louis's household staff, Claude automatically opens the trunk to retrieve our bags. Louis then rattles off a list of instructions about what he should show us, then tells him where to take each of the bags.

"Louis, this is Lauren. She and India shared an apartment in Paris fifteen years ago."

"Thank you again for having us, Louis," I say.

"No, thank you for coming. I'm delighted to spend time with two of my daughter's good friends," he says, walking over to shake our hands. "Now, down to business. You'll be staying in the blue and purple rooms which adjoin each other. Claude manages the household staff and he'll return shortly to show you to your rooms. Please report any problems or questions to him."

"Thank you," I reply, thinking he sounds like a hotel owner.

"Come this way, my friends," he says, ushering us inside the immense building.

As Paige and I enter the front hallway, I am struck by a series of contrasts: the dark beams on the ceiling against the white walls, the play of light against the wall-sized paintings, the rich reds of the oriental rug against a cream-colored marble table with claw feet. Everywhere I look it seems that the warmth of the place is tempered by a cold, hollow elegance.

"I'm afraid I have some work to do. I'll look forward to our getting better acquainted at dinner. We serve cocktails at seven o'clock in the library. Other than that, Claude will take care of anything that you need." He smiles politely, then heads down the hallway with a vigorous stride.

The size of the front rooms commands my attention. Their high ceilings are decorated in decoupage plasterwork with a series of long vines bordered by flowers. The family crest is carved in stone in the center of the front fireplace. As we walk into the living room, a Japanese scroll painting catches my eye. It looks hundreds of years old and must be very valuable. In the painting, a white orchid's last petal floats to the ground.

"What are you looking at?" Paige asks, standing next to me.

"This painting is beautiful. I've always loved the Japanese tradition of honoring things that are old."

Paige quips, "Does that tradition include people? Maybe I should move to Japan in the next ten years so I'll be appreciated." She grins. "I'll tell Bert that it'll be cheaper than all the plastic surgery bills that he's going to get."

"Better yet," I say with a laugh, "you could move to Greensboro and you'd be an instant celebrity without the face-lift."

Paige mulls over this proposition, then shrugs. "I wasn't cut out to be a southern belle." She adopts a pseudosouthern drawl. "Y'all are much too sweet for my tastes. I'll take the bandages."

Fortunately, Claude nudges us forward. Paige looks at me, then nods.

"Claude," I ask politely, "Louis mentioned that Richard Bristol is staying here this weekend with a companion."

"Oui, madame," Claude replies as he marches forward with our luggage. "Monsieur Bristol's family owns the neighboring property. He was here today with a young lady, then they went out there for the evening. They'll be back tomorrow around lunchtime."

"Oh, good," I say. "I'll look forward to seeing him again then."

I pray that Nélie really is Richard's date. But I won't know until tomorrow. Holding in my frustration, I walk along, looking at another crystal chandelier, wondering why I never told Nélie about her true heritage. Once Claude departs, Paige pats my shoulder. "Well done. You see, it's not so hard to tell a blue lie. You did that one pretty well. Just keep up the good work."

"What's a blue lie?"

"Lies come in all colors. You use a green lie when you buy something outrageously expensive that you know you shouldn't have, then tell your husband it cost a third of the price. Red lies are when you lie to your personal trainer by telling him you've been following his eating plan to the letter. A black lie is when you spread a dirty rumor about someone you hate. And, well, a blue lie is done with good intentions."

"I thought it was supposed to be white."

"I hate white. It's too perfect. Blue's better." She slows down to admire a gilded portrait. She whispers, "I could get lost in here."

I laugh. "This hallway's the size of my entire house!"

We walk through room after room filled with gilded paintings, crystal chandeliers and velvet-upholstered furniture.

Paige whispers, "Should we ask him for a map so we can find our way back to the living room?"

I nod, gazing at a wall of family portraits. A large painting of India is located to the far left. I would guess it was completed when she was twelve years old. She looks like a little angel dressed in a white satin gown, but her mischievous grin is unmistakable.

We drop off Paige, then Claude escorts me to my room. I walk inside and admire the large, open space. The window overlooks the back gardens. A bathroom the size of my entire bedroom at home awaits me. Inside, a series of painted angels dance around the walls. I splash my face with cool water, marveling at the turn of events that brought me to India's childhood home. Where's Nélie tonight? Is she spending the night with Richard?

I quickly remove my things from the overnight case Paige has loaned me. Too agitated to rest, I take a long, hot bath, then change into a black evening pants suit, brush my hair and apply some cosmetics to liven up my pale features. I place India's pin on my shoulder, hoping it will give me a bit of courage. I go to find Paige in her room next door. She greets me with a smile, her eyes shining with excitement. Dressed to perfection, she wears a gold-patterned, floor-length satin coat with her dress. "You look marvelous!" she says, staring at me.

"I was just thinking the same thing about you," I reply, thinking that I feel like I'm playing dress-ups. Since I know I am not going to see Nélie tonight, I try to relax.

The drawing room has oak-paneled walls, shelves of leather-bound classics and a fire to warm us on this cool spring night. Louis introduces us to a parade of guests, including a Lord and Lady Mountbridge, a German banker whose name I can't pronounce, an American couple named Mr. and Mrs. Hewitt and their daughters, Candice and Melissa, who look about Nélie's age. As it happens, Paige knows the Hewitts from New York, and they begin a discussion of how each came to be here. A lively old gentleman named Mr. Fox mentions that he breeds horses and loves wine. Finally, Claudia Bristol, with a bright smile and unruly, brown curls, extends her hand in greeting. She mentions that she's Louis's next-door neighbor, but, more importantly, she's delighted that her nephew, Richard, and his guest are visiting for the weekend.

Eager to learn more, I open my mouth to ask about Richard when Louis joins us. He places a champagne flute in my hand. He asks, "Tell me, Lauren, how long did you know my daughter?"

Taking a sip of my drink, "Ten years," I say, nodding to Claudia as she tactfully departs.

Louis shakes his head. "India and I were too much alike—headstrong, opinionated and passionate. She was my nemesis. But, God, how I miss her." His hand trembles, making the ice in his cocktail clink against the crystal glass.

I nod. "I miss her too," I say softly. "She was a rare and special person. I've never met anyone quite like her."

Except her daughter, I muse nervously. How am I ever going to tell this man that I've spent the last fifteen years raising his only grandchild? A premonition of disaster overcomes me and I suddenly feel light-headed. I can't just blurt out everything now; how can I possibly tell him the truth?

Louis glances at me. "You and Paige were kind to come

and keep a lonely old man company for the weekend. I'm delighted that you called. I love visitors. They keep me sane."
I smile politely, my hands feeling clammy. "We're delighted to be here," I respond evenly, wondering how on earth I'm going to get through this weekend.

Much to my relief, dinner is announced.

Lit by candlelight, the table is artfully arranged with a red linen cloth, vases of red and yellow roses and silver place settings. The painting covering the right wall appears to leap off the canvas. I am startled by its subject matter. The larger-than-life figures are illuminated by an overhead light. I make out the image of a woman holding a dagger. A man's head lays on the floor by the bed; he was probably her lover, who she has just killed.

Paige sees me staring at the painting. She says, "Louis has a flair for the dramatic, wouldn't you say?"

"It's rather a gruesome painting to put in the dining room," I observe, looking at the blood dripping from the dagger.

In the next few moments, Louis insists that Paige and I come and sit next to him at the head of the table. As we settle into our places, Louis leans over, whispering in my ear, "I've played a small trick on my guests. I'm serving a nineteen eighty-one Torres Gran Reserva 'Black Label,' which is a Spanish wine. I want to see who notices first."

"I'm afraid I don't know much about fine wines," I admit, a blush staining my cheeks.

Louis smiles warmly. "My dear, I shall teach you. I couldn't have asked for two more lovely dinner companions."

He has instantly disarmed me. Louis is certainly not the monster I imagined. In fact, he seems so congenial that I wonder whether much of India's battles with him were mainly due to her own rebellious nature. Nothing about Louis Vernon seems offensive. What really happened to make India despise her father?

He says, "This wine smells distinctly like a cabernet. Go

on, smell it." He adds, "If your nose were trained, you'd recognize a hint of blackberry flavoring. Now, taste it."

Paige and I follow his orders.

"It's lovely," she says with a smile.

Louis leans over to Paige. "I'll show you around the vineyard tomorrow after breakfast. Does that suit you?"

"That would be wonderful!" cries Paige. "On the drive here, I read your article on creating the perfect Pinot Noir; it was very informative. I'm absolutely thrilled that you're willing to indulge me with a few hours of your time!"

I try not to roll my eyes heavenward at Paige's blatant pandering, but I must admit she's a master at charming anyone. They continue on the topic of wine for a few more minutes until Louis brings me into the conversation.

"Lauren, I hope you'll enjoy the food. My chef's absolutely marvelous. I believe we're starting with a braised breast of squab with wild mushroom ravioli and black truffles."

I nod and smile politely, trying not to let my real feelings show. As the waiter serves our meal, I wonder if the young girls at the table will enjoy such a dish. Laura and Kathryn would rather eat macaroni and cheese than pigeon. Have I raised them to be completely unsophisticated?

"Oh my," I say, remembering that India was the one who first introduced me to squab. It was a bird bred for the royalty, she had said. I remember her laughing and telling me she considered it a royal pigeon.

Moments later, Lord Mountbridge motions to our host. "Louis, you devil. You thought you could slip one over on us, didn't you?"

Louis chuckles. "I knew I couldn't fool you, Charles! The only other wine that's not from this vineyard is our dessert wine, a nineteen ninety-seven Torcolato which is absolutely marvelous. It's harvested from the Vespaiola grape, from the northeast region of Italy. Zeus himself would have enjoyed it!" He salutes him.

"How do you create different flavors in wine like this dessert wine you mentioned?" I ask.

"Good question. We use partially dried grapes that are aged in a 'barrique.' That's what gives it such a sweet taste. But it's really the age of the wine which gives it that extra flavor."

"Ah, I see. That's so interesting," I reply, relieved that I was seated next to Louis, who has been guiding me through the meal.

Dinner, however delicious, has little taste for me. I go through the motions of being a polite guest, hoping that the meal will end before midnight. Meanwhile, I am praying that the girl staying upstairs is really Nélie. It occurs to me that I could leave Nélie a note telling her I'm staying here, but I fear that she'll see it and disappear again before giving me a chance to explain things. Now that she's had this taste of freedom and luxury, our world in Greensboro must seem like a prison to her. My reverie is interrupted when Louis says that after-dinner drinks will be served in the living room.

"What do we do now?" Paige asks, coming over to stand beside me.

"I thought I saw a terrace off the living room. I'd love to get some fresh air before heading up to bed." I stifle a yawn.

"Me, too," says Paige. "I feel like I'm about to pop." She pats her belly. "If I ate any more of that rich food, they'd have to roll me out of this place." She takes the lead. "Let's go walk around for a bit. I need to digest."

I nod in agreement, thinking that I had just played with the food. It really wasn't to my taste. I would have been happier with a simple salad and bread. To the right of the living room, we see a set of glass doors leading out to a brightly lit terrace. The view is spectacular and the rows of carefully tended boxwoods are visible in the evening light.

"It's beautiful here," I comment, smelling the sweet scent

of roses. "It shouldn't surprise me that India grew up in this château, but I guess it does."

"At least now we know she didn't need Julian's money. God, I'd never have left this place. It's paradise!"

I shrug. "This is Nélie's rightful heritage. It pains me to think about it. Once she finds out, she's going to think she grew up in the slums!"

"Lauren!" Paige cries. "Don't be so hard on yourself! I'm sure you gave Nélie a great life with the right values."

I turn to face my old friend. Her face is shadowed in the light. "Could I have been wrong, Paige? Raising her the way I did? Money was always an issue, even though I tried so damned hard for it not to be."

Paige leans closer, her voice low. "I'd be willing to bet you never used any of India's money to raise Nélie, did you?"

Tears spring to my eyes. "No," I reply. "It's hers. She'll have every cent of it when she turns twenty-one. I've secured it in a trust so she'll receive an annual income, but she can't touch the principal until she's thirty."

"I knew it," Paige says softly.

I've just spoken the words that have been locked inside me for fifteen years. My lie is out in the open, but I feel an enormous sense of relief. How many times over the years did Matt ask whether India had left any money for Nélie's care? How many times did I say it had all gone to her relatives? I've always thought he resented, on some deep level, having had to support India's child. Surely, he still suspects I've kept this secret from him, but I refuse to budge on the issue. The more he has questioned, the more I've grown to distrust him. I would never have used India's money.

India left everything to me—her jewels, her paintings, and so many of her personal belongings that I put them in storage under the care of an attorney. India gave me an expensive ruby bracelet and a Matisse. Gustave also gave me two paintings, which I placed in storage. When Matt and I were short on money in the early days, I thought about telling him that I owned these things but I always stopped myself; I was afraid I would wind up telling him about Nélie's trust fund. Nevertheless, I felt ambivalent about keeping these secrets from him. Instead, to assuage my guilt, I would paint someone's bathroom or front hallway or help decorate their house for Christmas to help supplement our income.

My attorney has specific instructions never to contact me directly or write. I've always contacted him over the years. I planned to tell Nélie when she was old enough to understand and showed the maturity I wanted to see in her. As for telling Matt, I would push it from my thoughts.

"I've never told anyone, Paige," I say softly. "Nélie has no idea that she's extremely wealthy in her own right."

Paige laughs, trying to lighten the mood. "Poor Nélie! She's about to find out she doesn't have to work a day in her life."

"She doesn't need to know how much money there is," I reply quickly.

Paige laughs, rolling her eyes upward. "She can take one look at this palace and get a pretty good idea. But, I'm afraid Louis is going to be your biggest problem." She lowers her voice. "Louis may not be easy to handle when he finds out he has a granddaughter and she's under his roof."

Paige folds her arms across her chest, her diamond rings catching the light. "He's a man who gets what he wants in life. His methods aren't necessarily based on any sense of morality. You're without guile, so you couldn't possibly understand someone like him."

"I just want to see my daughter and know she's all right."

"I know you do. That's why I'm here."

"You've been wonderful, Paige. I don't know what I would have done without you."

"Remember that, next time I have a party!"

I laugh, breaking the tension. "Just don't ask me to come to a seventies disco party, I don't think I can take it."

We turn to head inside. "How about a costume party where you have to come dressed as your favorite historical figure?"

"God, I'd have to come as Thomas Jefferson," I say, raising my hands in mock despair. "Who would you be?"

"Jesus," she quips with a straight face. "I bet Bert would love that!"

I nod in admiration of her nerve. "I bet you'd win the cocktail party Olympics!"

"Not a chance," she shoots back. "It's New York. Somebody's bound to come as God."

Suddenly, we hear raised voices in the doorway next to ours. Paige and I look at each other wondering what all the commotion is about. We walk inside to see Louis speaking in rapid French with Claude. Claude looks worried; he's gesturing and pointing upstairs. Louis breaks away, then motions Claudia Bristol over to him. Several suspended seconds pass. Guests exchange uncertain glances, whispering their fears. Suddenly, Louis clears his throat, then looks each of us in the eye.

"I'm afraid we've had an unexpected problem arise this evening." He shakes his head in frustration. "Last week, I fired my top manager. I suspected that he'd been stealing my wine, then trying to sell it under a different label in the States. While I couldn't prove it, the vineyard has suffered enormous shortages in wine exports since he took over. Well, he's made several death threats against me. I didn't take them seriously, until now.

"Claude told me this manager phoned this evening sounding drunk. He threatened to destroy the vineyard and everything that belonged to me. After the call, Claude and his staff searched the house. Someone found several gas cans hidden in an upstairs closet. The police are coming to investigate."

He continues on. "Fortunately, Claudia, who lives fifteen minutes from here, has graciously agreed to allow all of you to stay at her home for the next night or two. I really do apologize for any inconvenience this may cause you. I just don't want to take any chances until this man is caught."

"My God, Louis," says Lord Mountbridge. "I'm furious that some nutcase has threatened your life! There are too many of these types around, if you ask me!"

"Indeed," cries Hugh Fox. "Please don't worry about us. I'll stay here with you until the police come, old friend. This is a travesty!"

Paige chimes in. "My driver was planning on spending the night. We can take two or three more people in my car."

Louis nods his appreciation. "Claude has instructed the household staff to help you with your things immediately. I want you all to come back as soon as we have determined that it's completely safe."

I follow the group upstairs to get our things. My hands tremble as I pack my luggage, wondering about this sudden threat to Louis. All of India's warnings about her father come back to my mind.

Paige bursts into the room, startling me. "So, we're one step closer to finding her!"

I pause to think about the ramifications of arriving at the Bristol house and the scene that may follow. "If it's really Nélie. I've got to find a way not to surprise her in front of the other guests. The last thing we need is a public meeting."

"Well, the good news is that Louis plans to stay here to meet with the police. We'll figure it out. Don't worry. You can stay in the car until the last minute, while I go in and find out what's going on."

"Good idea. Let's go." My heart pounds in anticipation.

Chapter 13

Once I swing open the door of the third floor bedroom, I instantly recognize Nélie's blue duffel bag in the corner. I notice a magazine and her purple cardigan sweater lying on top. Relief flows through me as I grasp the chair for support. She's here, I tell myself, as I breathe freely for the first time in a week. Fatigue suddenly threatens as I rub the tension knots in my neck and shoulders. Pacing the room, I look at my watch several times, wondering where she is. The minutes tick by slowly, escalating my anger and frustration. Where is she? I muse again for the hundredth time. Who is this young man she's with—how much of a factor was he in Nélie's decision to run away?

When the doorknob clicks, I race to open the door.

"It's only me," says Paige as she pokes her head in the room. "I take it she's not back yet." Paige looks over the room, running her hands over the flowered duvet cover bordered in pink roses.

I place my hands on my hips. "Where is she?" I demand. "What does she think she's doing out all night with some boyfriend she just met!"

Paige nods sympathetically. "I know you're upset. But she's seventeen, Lauren, with a mind of her own. There's nothing you can do to stop her. If you question her too much about it, it'll only make her want him more."

"What should I do?"

"Let's get some sleep. You'll feel much better if you talk with her in the morning. Besides, I doubt she's going to be nestled in this sweet little double bed by herself."

I rub my tired eyes and sigh. "You're right. This isn't doing me any good." I get off the bed and stretch. Suddenly, I laugh, "I guess I can't control what's going on, can I?"

"No, you can't. She's an adult with a mind of her own."

"It's hard to let go, Paige," I reply softly. "This wasn't on one of my lists."

"You're a good mother, Lauren," says Paige, putting her arm around my shoulders as we head down the hall to our bedroom. "I know you'll say just the right thing when you talk to Nélie." She adds, "Let's go, I'm beat. This mother business is a tough job. I'd never have made it through."

Sleep proves difficult as I fight my urge to see my daughter. Finally, after tossing and turning for an hour, I hear a soft giggle and the sound of two voices coming up the back staircase. It's her, I realize, controlling my urge to burst in on her and Richard. Paige's snoring provides a steady backdrop to the muted sounds of their passionate hallway encounter. I hear a man's voice say, "I've been wanting to do this all night," Nélie's soft giggle, and the sound of their lips coming together. It's a rather strange moment, knowing my daughter is outside my door embracing some man I've never met. She's also a young woman, not a little girl I can order to bed. In what seems like an eternity later, I hear their door slam and then silence. Somehow, fatigue overtakes me and I doze off.

The sounds of a shower and a rush of footsteps going down the hall awaken me. Listening in the quiet shadows of the morning, I hear the pipes groan as another person turns

on the water. The sound of Nélie humming softly in the bathroom is both a relief and a challenge. Clearly, she's completely enamored with her new love interest. The door clicks
as she pads back down the hall to her bedroom. Giving her a
few minutes to get dressed, I feel so nervous, realizing that
the inevitable confrontation is close at hand. What shall I
say? Will she resent seeing me? I feel all at once the same terror I felt when I realized Nélie would have to grow up without her real mother.

How do you tell a twenty-month-old that her mother is
dead? I remember the moment that I walked into her bedroom in Paris after I heard about the accident. The ring of the
phone had awakened me. I reached for it, sensing something
was wrong. It was Julian who told me that India's plane had
crashed. "Oh my God!" I cried, tears springing up in my eyes.
"Are you sure? There must be some mistake."

I ran into the bathroom and threw up. My heart pounded
so hard that I couldn't catch my breath. "Why?" I cried into
the night. Splashing cold water on my face, I had called
Paige, then Matt. Both of them had arrived shortly thereafter
and we had turned on the news to hear the reports.

Fortunately, Nélie didn't hear us that night. She slept soundly
in her bed, which was one of the last times she had sweet
dreams for years afterwards. At one point, I went into her
bedroom, checked on her and gave her a kiss. She seemed so
innocent that night; I hated knowing I would have to be the
one to tell her the awful news.

The next morning, she knew something was wrong the
moment she woke up and saw my face.

"Nélie," I explained haltingly, "your mommy has gone to
heaven where she's going to be very happy. She's watching us
right now. And do you know what she told me?"

Her eyes welled up with tears. "Where's my mama?"

Pain coursed through me at the sound of her cracking voice. Tears rolled down my cheeks. "Your mommy wants me to take care of you just like I did yesterday. Didn't we have fun? We went to the park, ate ice cream and didn't we see that funny clown on the street?"

Nélie clung to me and said, "Auntie Lauren, I want my mommy. Where is she?"

My fears back then were justified. How could I have ever hoped to replace her real mother? No matter how hard I tried, there was nothing that could replace such a loss. The memory is too painful to recall for long.

Darting out of bed, I throw on a pair of jeans and a T-shirt, then make my way to her room. I tap lightly. When there's no answer, I crack the door to see her long brown hair spread out over the pillow. The imprint of another head reminds me that Nélie has other attachments now. Gingerly walking to the bed, I tap her dozing form.

"Nélie," I say gently. "It's me."

"What?" she says, rolling over. "Oh, my God!" she cries, sitting up, startled by my voice. "Mom? Is that you?" She catches her breath. "What are you doing here? How did you find me?"

"I've been searching for you," I say nervously. My voice sounds so high-pitched, even to my own ears. "Since I got your note." I can't help myself. I start to cry. "Why, Nélie?"

"Oh Mom," she cries, reaching over to hug me. "I never meant to hurt you. It's just that I had to get away. I couldn't stand it anymore." Tears stream down her cheeks.

"*Neither could I,*" I want to reply, wondering at my own defection. An image of our home in Greensboro flashes through my mind.

When we finally separate, Nélie looks away, unable to meet my gaze. Her voice shakes as she says, "Really, Mom. I'm sorry for just leaving like that." Her face is soaked with tears.

As I've done so many times before, I brush away her tears with my hands. "Oh Nélie, I'm sorry. I never knew you were so unhappy."

Her shoulders shake. She smoothes her hands over her tear-stained face. "I didn't belong there. I mean, I never fit in with anyone. I tried," she cries. "I swear I did."

"I know," I reply, smoothing the top of her head. My tears flow freely as I hold my daughter safe in my arms.

"What's wrong with me?" she asks. "I don't know who I am. I wanted something or someplace different, but I don't know what. Does that make sense?"

"Oh, Nélie," I say. "So much of your unhappiness is my fault. You didn't belong in Greensboro. Your mother wouldn't have lasted more than a week there." I pause, with a nervous laugh. "When India and I first met, I told her I was from Greensboro—she looked at me like I was from another planet. Although she did promise to look it up on a map—which I doubt she ever did."

Nélie laughs, breaking some of the tension.

"I wish I had told you more about her." I sigh, feeling the weight of my failure. "My only excuse is that some of my own memories were too painful."

Her gaze meets mine. "I need to know more about her. I feel so lost inside sometimes, like there are all these pieces missing." Nélie rests her hand on my arm; her pupils are dilated into two black moons. "I want to know about both my parents. You never talked about my father at all. But tell me, how did you get here?"

Pausing for a moment, I say, "Can we open a window in here? It's hot." The next few moments are centered around punching open a tiny square window by turning a lever clockwise. The outside air smells like hyacinths.

"It's a long story," I reply. My explanation sounds stilted to my own ears as I tell of my search through Paris, Jean Whitfield and our discovery that she and Richard were staying with Louis Vernon. I mention that Paige just happened to have a connection with Mr. Vernon, who graciously invited us for the weekend. The fact that he's India's father and her grandfather requires more background information so I carefully omit that from the story, knowing I must face the inevitable before long. Then, I go on to tell her about the drama that occurred last night at the château—the disgruntled employee who threatened our host's life. Wiping my brow, I decide to start my story at the beginning.

I return to an armchair while Nélie throws on a pair of jeans and T-shirt. She returns to the bed to face me. "I'll tell you what I know," I promise gently, seeing the look of relief cross her features. "When India first came to Paris, she was twenty-one. She fell in love with a man named Julian DuBusé, a contemporary of her father's who hired her to photograph his three children. She really didn't want to get involved with him, but his persistence and charm eventually won out. Julian had everything: he was sophisticated, wealthy, and charming, and he adored your mother." Looking down at my hands, I search for the right words. "Their love wasn't perfect. No one plans these things. Certainly, India always knew she had fallen in love with the wrong man, but she couldn't help herself. Julian, I believe, wanted to leave his wife for India."

Nélie immediately stands up, her distress evident as she struggles to accept the fact of her illegitimacy. She clenches her fists, but I keep talking, knowing that the time is right.

"Your mother's love affair with Julian was real, Nélie, despite the incredible odds against them. I think love was not something India planned on and when it happened, it consumed her, in a way. India was a passionate person, passionate about life and love."

Nélie stands up placing her back to me. "People used to talk about me at home, like it was some dirty little secret that my parents weren't married. I hated it!"

"When?" I ask, standing up. "Who said things about you?" "I always felt like Grandmother's bridge group didn't approve of me. People like Mrs. Woodlands who always gave me this funny look. No one criticized me directly, but I heard them talking one night when I was about eight years old." Nélie folds her arms across her chest. "They said that my mother was loose and wondered how you ever got involved with someone like *her*. They called you a saint and claimed that I was a burden on you and Matt." Tears well up in her eyes. "I've never forgotten their words. That's why I need to make my own way."

"Oh Nélie! I never knew." I sit beside her on the bed, throwing my arms around her, wishing I could erase her pain. I pull away, cupping Nelie's face in my hands. "Listen to me carefully. India was my best friend for ten years. I wanted you more than anything. It was *my* decision to raise you, it was something India and I had talked about at length. You're my child, Nélie, just as if I'd given birth to you myself. I've always loved you as much as Laura and Kathryn, if not more sometimes because I was trying to make up for your loss."

Tears run down Nélie's cheeks. "I always thought so, but sometimes I wondered."

"How could you ever doubt me like that?" I demand.

She pauses for moment, then says, "I don't know. It's just that you've always acted so strange when I tried to talk about my mother. Matt used to say things like my mother was unique and roll his eyes heavenward. What did that mean? What kind of person was she?"

I squeeze Nélie's hand, observing that it looks so womanly. A memory of her child's hand holding mine surfaces. I can feel the energy in her hand, the slight clamminess of her fingers as they connect to mine.

I pause, considering my words. "India was a unique individual. She had traveled all over the world by the time she was eighteen. She had lived in so many places that it gave her a maturity beyond her years and yet, India desperately wanted to be 'normal' like me, I suppose." I exhale. "India had the financial means to do whatever she wanted, practically whenever she wanted."

"I just don't get it. Is that why Matt didn't like her?"

"What are you talking about?" I ask nervously. "Matt cared about India. He just didn't know her as well as I did."

Nélie shakes her head. "He always talked about my mother's money and then how expensive I was to raise. I've heard him complaining downstairs about money, the high cost of private schools, my dance lessons, my music lessons and so on . . ." Nélie looks away, unable to meet my eyes.

She confirms my worst suspicions. I curse Matt in my mind; he should have known better. "God, I wish I hadn't made so many mistakes. Nélie, your mother was extremely wealthy in her own right. She had enough money to support you for the rest of your life. I didn't want to use any of it. Back then, my motivations seemed right. The money would be yours to keep when you were old enough to manage it properly. But I considered you my child and I didn't want to touch India's things." I search her face. "Your mother left me everything. Nélie, all of it and her valuables are stored in a safety deposit box. Several of her artworks are also in storage. I can show them to you when we return to Paris."

"You mean, you could have had my mother's money at any time?"

"Yes."

"Why didn't you tell Matt that he didn't have to pay for me?"

"I don't know," I reply. The words, *I didn't trust him*, pop into my mind, sending a shiver down my spine. Unwilling to reveal my fears to Nélie, I add, "The first part of the money will be yours when you turn twenty-one. But when I set up the trust, I included a stipulation that you would have to have some sort of education to receive it. Your mother was extremely intelligent and so are you. She would have wanted you to pursue some form of higher education. There's no question in my mind about that."

"My mother left you everything. I still don't get it. Why didn't you use anything? I mean, to buy yourself something special."

"India left you to me. That was all I cared about. You're my daughter, Nélie, and I love you. India was my best friend; we understood each other in a way that defied all of our differences. She taught me how to live life freely without fear for a time. My nature was always more cautious than hers. India had such a passion for things like children, people, art, music, literature, different cultures, photography, and the list goes on. I'll bet I still have some of her photographs in the safe deposit box."

"Oh please, I need to see them."

Hearing the yearning in Nélie's voice, I contemplate why I kept India from her for so long. The pain and hurt are obvious, as I know now Matt never truly loved her unconditionally, the way I wanted. Certainly, he did his best, perhaps more than many men, but the results prove his job inadequate.

"One of my favorite things India and I did together was look for art while we lived here. India loved to spend weekends searching for new talent. Your mother loved so many different kinds of art: Indian, Japanese, African, and Dutch. She was drawn to objects that defied the current definition of beauty, like her set of African tribal masks that lined the hallway to our apartment. That's how India learned about people. She studied their reactions to the masks."

Nélie smiles through her tears. Her face looks red and puffy. "My mother was so incredibly interesting!"

"Yes, she was," I say. "I remember the time India flew to

Japan to find an original Samurai sword to give Julian for his birthday. That was so like her. She didn't say where she was going or why, she just told me to watch you and that she'd be back in a couple of days. She probably would have taken you, but Paige and I talked her out of it."

"Do you have a picture of Julian anywhere?" she asks, standing up to stretch her legs.

"Sit down, Nélie," I ask, reaching for her. "I never told you about Julian because there's something I didn't want you to know."

"What? Please tell me. I must know!"

"He's alive," I say quietly. "He didn't die in the plane crash like I led you to believe."

Nélie gasps and her eyebrows arch in realization. Hope fills her face. "Oh my God, where is he? Did he know I lived in the States? What if he's been looking for me all this time?"

"Nélie," I say firmly. "Julian loved your mother and he loved you, but you must understand he's married with three children. His wife is extremely powerful and wealthy in her own right and didn't take kindly to his relationship with India. I was there the night she confronted your mother."

"What did my mother do?"

I laugh, breaking the tension. "Actually, I think she called India a stupid American. India laughed and answered her in four different languages, claiming she was no more American than Madame DuBusé. Anyway, the Madame despised India, as you can imagine, and claimed she would never give Julian a divorce. She made it clear that she would make trouble for everyone if India continued to antagonize her with her need for marriage. What made India back off was when Madame threatened to harm you. She wanted no one making demands on her family."

"I have a real father," Nélie says quietly. "What's he like?"

"Handsome and charming. Even at seventy, Julian presents a very commanding figure. He inhabits a different world from the one I raised you in, Nélie. In many ways, you're right. You don't belong in Greensboro. You have the power to make a different set of decisions."

"Will my father see me?"

"No, and you must never contact him on your own," I respond. "Madame DuBusé's threats are very real. I believe even Julian fears her wrath. I would guess he may find it too hard. I found out that India's apartment is still intact. I've been there this week."

Nélie stands up, her body trembling. "You mean, I can go see where my mother lived and actually look at her things. Touch them." Nélie's eyes fill with tears of gratitude. "Is there any more?"

Suddenly, a knock sounds at the door and Richard pokes his head in.

"Hi," Nélie says, a blush staining her cheeks.

"I was wondering where you were. Everyone's packing up to head back over to the château. I guess they caught the guy and everything's okay."

"That's great news," I say, standing up to survey my daughter's love interest. He's tall and lean, with a high, intelligent forehead. Soft brown eyes and a wide smile light up his face.

Taking his hand, Nélie leads him over to me. "You're not going to believe this, but this is my mom. Her best friend, Paige Riverton, owns a vineyard in Charlottesville and she's meeting with Louis to get some advice. They were staying with Louis, but came here last night with the rest of the guests."

He gives my hand a good firm handshake. "I guess Ms. Riverton's going to be touring the vineyard with us today. I'll look forward to meeting her. But, more importantly, I'm glad to meet you. Nélie's told me a lot about you."

"Hello, Richard," I say automatically, realizing that he's got no idea that Nélie ran away from home to be with him. Or, if he suspects it's rather odd that I've suddenly appeared, he's polite enough not to bring it up.

With ease, he says, "You two finish up, I'm going to go help the other guests get back to the château."

When he leaves, Nélie smiles warmly and her face lights up. She says, "We met by accident several months ago. We were introduced at a party I attended in Washington when I visited Georgetown University that fall weekend with Diane's parents. We've been writing letters and sending e-mail ever since. He went to school at Georgetown, and now he plans to develop his family's business in the United States like Louis Vernon has done. Mr. Vernon's agreed to teach him about wine-making."

"Are you living in Paris with him?"

Dodging the question, she says, "I met his parents last night. Did you meet them? We got along so well. They even forgave my Americanized French." Her eyes look hopeful as she stares out the window somewhat dreamily.

Dreading the answer, I feel compelled to ask, "Nélie, how much of your decision to run away had to do with Richard? We were all terribly worried about you. Matt has already talked to the police."

"The police?" Nélie replies, genuinely shocked. "I wrote you a note and said I was fine. That I would contact you as soon as I was settled. It's not like I left with no word at all," she adds.

"You could have been anywhere, Nélie, for God's sake! How were we supposed to know? We're in the south of France," I exclaim. "You should have given us more consideration than that. Your sisters are worried sick about you."

Nélie shakes her head. "I'll be eighteen in a month, Mother, or have you forgotten? I trusted my own instincts about Richard."

I rein in my frustration. "I don't know. Do you consider this a serious relationship? I mean, you're already living with him after only knowing each other for a short time. You're seventeen years old. You don't even have a college degree. Think about it! Doesn't all that I've taught you over the last fifteen years about life and choices and becoming an empowered young woman mean anything anymore?"

"How can I become an 'empowered young woman' when I don't know who I am?"

"It's a process. I agree that things are a bit tangled right now, but you'll figure it out. You're capable of being more than a waitress in some French restaurant."

"At least, now I know I'll be able to support myself," she retorts, her gaze a direct challenge.

"Just remember that your mother hated being the 'other woman,' always on some level unacceptable to society. As unconventional as India was, she despised the fact that Julian couldn't marry her. We talked about it numerous times and it gave her great pain. India wanted a garden wedding, you see, with flowers everywhere. She had even picked out her dress, which she placed in the back of her closet for the occasion. Only she never had a chance to wear it. Maybe marriage isn't for everyone, but I do firmly believe that as a woman, it is important to have a passion for something and have choices."

"You didn't."

What I want to say is, *You're wrong, Nélie. I made the terrible mistake of giving mine up.* "I had always dreamed of being an artist." I pause. "I've always believed in finding one's passion and that's what I want for you. I want you to make choices that allow you to develop to your fullest potential. You have so much talent; I'd hate to see you waste it."

"Who says I'm wasting it?"

"I'm not saying you are. I suppose this incident just seems very out of character for you. You skipped your graduation ceremony, left your friends and family with no word. You never even filled out the acceptance to college. I worry that you're not thinking clearly."

"Like you don't want me to get pregnant like my mother did."

"Yes, I do worry about that. I'd hate to see you ruin your life by having a baby when you're so young."

"You don't think I ruined my mother's life and her chances of marrying Julian, do you?"

"Of course not! India wanted Julian's baby. She knew exactly what she was doing. Besides, your mother was six years older than you are now when she delivered you. That's a big difference."

"What are you going to tell Matt? Is he completely horrified at my behavior? You're not going to tell him about Richard, are you?"

"Not all the details are necessary. Despite what you think, Matt does love you and he's been worried sick. I'd hate to think that you ran away because you were afraid he didn't care enough about you."

Once I've shared my fear, I dread her answer. In my heart, I know Matt was never the kind of father to Nélie that I had wanted him to be. Sure, he had made some effort, but I've never been quite convinced of his sincerity. Why? I wonder.

"That was part of it," she confesses. "I got tired of listening to him complain about money." She stands up. "Would it be all right with you, Mom, if we used my mother's money and wrote him a check for it all? I mean, we could include the cost of private schools, food, clothing and all the rest. Then I'd be free and clear, wouldn't we? It's what I want."

I feel my stomach lurch, and I am sickened that Nélie wants to pay Matt back for his financial support. Would he take the money? What an ugly thought. But I'm not convinced he wouldn't. "But it's not what I want, Nélie. His concern over your welfare was very real. Perhaps you've drawn too dramatic a conclusion. I know Matt worries about money; it's part of his job, being in commercial real estate, but I don't know that his complaints were made out of a sense of personal resentment toward raising you."

"You always defend him. Mom, I heard him say it a hundred times. It's not your fault, but I can't change how I feel. I want to reimburse him; please won't you give me access to my mother's money so I can do so. Then, I'll make choices for my future."

"I'll think about it."

Nélie bounces back on the bed, lying with both arms outstretched. "God, I'm exhausted."

"Let's take a break. We'll talk more later."

Paige bursts into the room. "What a sight! Did you kill her?"

"Who are you?" demands Nélie, sitting up with a grin.

"I was your mother's jealous best friend," quips Paige, extending her hand in greeting. "Your mother was too rich and beautiful for her own good or more accurately, my own good!"

"Hi!" says Nélie. "I'm glad to meet you."

"You shouldn't be," Paige says. "Listen kid, you're damned lucky to have a mother like Lauren who chased you across the Atlantic when we both know that all you've cared about is that brown-haired young Adonis out there. If you were my kid, I'd lock you in your room for a month. Just be glad India didn't ask me to raise you."

"So," Nélie says, "I guess I'm not glad to meet you."

"Sure you are. I'll tell you the real scoop on your mother. I'm sure Lauren left out many of India's really good antics in college. She wouldn't want you to get any ideas."

I raise one eyebrow. "Nélie, did you know Paige won the Sarah Bernhardt award in college? She's got a flair for the dramatic."

Paige flops down on the bed beside Nélie. "It was about

the only thing I won, too. The perfect training for my social life now, which was getting a tad boring—until my oldest, dearest friend phones me out of the blue, hysterically crying because her precious daughter ran away."

Nélie shakes her head. "But Mom, I left you a note. You knew I'd be okay. I turn eighteen next month. It's not like I was some runaway!"

"Yeah, sure," says Paige. "Are you pregnant?"

"What?" asks Nélie. "No!" she cries in self-defense.

"Paige," I say firmly, sensing Nélie's indignation. "We've discussed a lot of things."

"But you don't ask the good questions," Paige says, stamping her foot on the floor. "All right, I'm starved. According to Louis's driver, Louis has a luncheon prepared for us that is absolutely divine. Let's just hope the château doesn't burn down before we eat."

I can't help myself. I laugh. So does Nélie.

Once Paige and I arrive back at the château, I head to my bedroom to freshen up. Unaccustomed as I am to a seated lunch in the middle of the day, the ritual seems a bit extravagant. Once inside my room, I head into the bathroom to splash some water on my face.

"I trust everything is all right here," says a male voice.

I scream.

"Oh, my God, Louis," I cry, seeing his figure in the doorway. "I didn't hear you come in," I say nervously, wondering how he got into my room, since I'd locked my door.

He stares at me. Our eyes meet and I feel uneasy. "Lunch is in fifteen minutes. Don't be late," he warns, walking away as if I'd invited him into my room.

I go over my movements in my mind. Didn't I lock my door when I came in? With no apparent answer, I hastily select a long flower-printed skirt and blue sleeveless sweater that provide a sharp contrast to the khaki pants and T-shirt I would be wearing if I were home. Laura and Kathryn's faces come to mind, which engenders a sharp pang of regret.

"Good afternoon, Lauren," says Louis when I see him downstairs. I wonder if I had imagined the whole incident in my room. "I hope you're hungry. I've had both chefs working all morning to prepare a big luncheon. I trust last night's dislocation didn't inconvenience you too much."

"Oh no," I reply. "I'm just glad that they caught the man and you're safe."

"Indeed," he answers stoically. "I've not had anyone threaten my life before this event and it's rather unsettling, to say the least. Now, on to more pleasant topics. Please, sit next to me," says Louis. "I'm delighted to have a chance to chat with you more. So, tell me, how well did you know India?"

I hesitate, realizing that I need to be polite. "We were good friends for nearly ten years." I take my seat next to Louis. "We shared an apartment together in Paris while we were working for Gustave."

"Ah yes, Gustave. He was a genius. I still miss him. I remember how he used to come around when India was a child. He had a soft spot for her. They used to spend hours together in the studio; Gustave was the one who taught India how to draw. One time, she drew a portrait of him in a jester's hat. He was always amused by her. Even as a child, she was full of mischief."

Louis brings the group into the conversation. "India always had a great sense of fun. I remember the time she hid from us for two days out in the gardens. Set up a sleeping bag and supplies and decided that she would learn firsthand what camping was really like. I thought her poor mother was going to go gray trying to keep up with her antics."

"She always did enjoy the unexpected," I add, wondering why it took her parents two days to find her.

Louis leans back in his seat supposedly contemplating his subject matter, a rather unruly daughter. His chiseled features bear the stamp of a man who is accustomed to getting what he wants in life. A high forehead and an intense gaze make him a rather imposing figure. His lips curl on the left side, making him look as if he has a permanent snicker on his face. If one believes clothes make the man, then Louis surely could have been an advertisement for a country aristocrat. A navy blazer, polka-dotted ascot and a gold crest ring give testament to his good taste.

He smiles, his lips askew. "There was another time that Eugenie and I were traveling somewhere. Probably Jordan or Egypt, I can't remember where. A day or so after we returned home, I noticed my priceless Chinese statues were missing from the mantel. Let me remind you, these pieces of my art collection were several thousand years old and extremely delicate. That little redheaded terror had climbed up to the mantel and taken them down to her room to play dolls. You'll not believe what I found when I saw them!"

A smile forms on my lips. It sounds just like something India would do. "I haven't any idea," I respond, tasting a sip of wine.

"She had taken the heads off of each one and switched them around!"

"Oh no!" I cry. "Why ever would she have done that?"

"She was angry that the male statue had the more lavish robes than the female! She didn't show one bit of remorse. I think this was India's first encounter with the women's rights movement! I shall never forget it."

Louis seems very charming and I find him hard to resist. Why did India hate him so much? Over the course of the meal, he launches into a detailed discussion of wine making, from the planting to the pressing of the grapes to the actual process. We discuss sugar levels, the rate of yeast absorption and this past year's drought. "I think we'll have the best harvest ever," he adds.

"Why is that?"

"Because oftentimes, drought works in favor of the grapes. It makes them sweeter."

When Louis isn't looking, I check my watch, wondering why Nélie isn't back yet. The weight of my final confession seems overwhelming.

"Louis, might I have a word with you privately after lunch?" I ask.

He shakes his head. "I'm sorry, it's not possible. I'm afraid I've promised Richard and Paige a tour of the winery. Can it wait?"

"Sure," I reply, thinking it's been fifteen years, what's another few hours? I excuse myself to check Nélie's room but, growing frustrated, I tell Paige I need a walk in the garden to clear my head. She promises to find me as soon as Nélie returns.

Rarely have I seen anything as lovely as this setting. The garden is filled with a wide range of contrasting greens from yew and box to the ivy covering the walls. As I walk through it, everything looks symmetrical, inviting me to the rows of boxwoods in clean rectangular shapes. I walk on, eager to discover the hidden groves.

A walled garden of roses greets me, beckoning me forward. When I get to a small clearing, I sit down to try to collect my scattered thoughts. Nélie's disappearance makes me consider the myriad emotions that have coursed through me. A gentle breeze whispers by, blowing the grass and trees. The faint scent of roses clings to the air. For someone who hasn't contemplated the past much in fifteen years, I feel as if I've made up for it in the past week.

Rage runs through me, mixed with a sense of betrayal that I can't quite fathom right now. Matt has caused Nélie so much pain. Yet, in his own defense, I can say that he's been a far better father than Julian, who did nothing for her. I'm certain Nélie will soon come to idolize Julian and blame his wife for depriving her of her real father. True or not, it's far better to blame her than Julian's perennially weak character. He's refused to be any kind of father to her. I search the sky for answers, rubbing my arms to stay warm. The sun has gone down, creating a steady breeze. My thoughts are so intrusive that I feel as if others can hear my internal conflicts. I keep expecting some answer from the wind but none is forthcoming. It is quiet, almost too quiet, a poignant reminder that I have no peace.

Annoyed at the direction of my thoughts, I get up to walk and clear my head. Negative feelings about Matt have taken root and I am unable to dislodge them. We've been married almost fifteen years. We have three children. I can't discard that fact so easily. Why do I want to? Why do I want to be free again? Tears sting my eyes. I'm not angry at Nélie for running away, because I too want my freedom. I want my life back the way it was before India's death.

My pace quickens, as if movement could obstruct the heresy I am committing in my own mind. I trip over a rock and land flat on my face, tasting the damp grass. Sitting up, I look around me. Through a set of hedges, there is a small wooden house tucked in a corner.

As I get closer, it becomes clear that it's just big enough for me to enter. I push open the little door. There are several child-sized chairs and a table. This must have been India's, I think, running my hand over the rough edges of the wood. She probably played with her dolls here. India always loved to read. I can picture her now, her red hair tied up in a ponytail, absorbed in her favorite books for hours. It seems a rather desolate place, though, tucked in the back of a garden. I speculate whether Louis even remembers it's here. Maybe this was where India escaped her father. I'm beginning to get some sense of why she craved the life I had. I'll never know, but I want to come back here tomorrow.

Chapter 14

Elated from my visit with Nélie, I phone Matt to share the good news with him. His anger seeps through the phone. "When are you coming home?" he demands. "I want a time and a date."

"You're being irrational," I reply. "I'm trying to help my daughter."

"What about your other two daughters, who are asking me every day where you are?"

"Tell them that their mother is just fine, that I've found Nélie. We're patching things up, and I'll be home as soon as I can."

"Is that all you have to say to me?"

"Oh Matt," I reply coldly, "I'll have a lot more to say when I get home."

"Don't blame me for any of this, if that's what you're thinking."

"What would you ever have to be worried about? Haven't you been an ideal father to Nélie? Perhaps you should make an accounting of all you've spent on Nélie and me over the years. I want a number and we'll settle it up."

"What's gotten into you, Lauren? This is crazy. Have you gone as nutty as Nélie?"

"Actually," I reply, "I think I'm finally coming to my senses, if you must know. I'll call you with my travel plans."

Paige greets me outside and tells me about a tennis match. "Louis has some of the best players come here to play exhibition matches. Come, let's go watch. We'll sit with Nélie and her young man."

Grateful for a chance to take my mind off the immediate present, I head to the tennis courts to watch two young men volleying, slicing and serving tennis balls at a breakneck pace. A long, wiry fellow seems to be dominating the play while the other, a Ukrainian who, according to Paige, is going to be a serious contender in a few years time, battles to stay in the match. Long a tennis lover, I keep a file on some of the tennis stars.

"I love tennis," I admit wistfully as I watch one of the players slice a ball over the net. "I haven't even watched a match in years."

Paige shrugs. "You know, I get tickets to Wimbledon every year. If you ask me nicely, I'd take you there."

"You're kidding! Really?" I gasp. "I'd love to go!" Reality intervenes. "I mean," I sigh, "maybe someday."

"Lauren, the opportunities to do what you want exist. You just have to create them," Paige says. The Ukrainian makes a great shot, and she cheers.

We move through the group and seat ourselves on a stone bench beside Nélie, who smiles when she sees us. All eyes are focused on the players while a waiter comes around, offering us some lemonade and iced tea.

"Louis says you can use the studio if you want," Paige suggests as she points to a small building on the property.

"What?" I ask, turning to face her.

"Over there." She points to a pretty shingled shed in the distance. "You may want to go and take a look at the studio that's here on the property."

I nod.

Paige puts her arm around me. "Your mother and Lauren studied under Henri Gustave. She's quite a talented artist."

"That's so cool, Mom, I'd forgotten that. Why don't you paint anymore?" Nélie says innocently.

I shrug. "I don't know. Maybe I'll take a look."

"Terrific!" Paige says, delighted with my response. She catches sight of Louis waving to us. "Looks as if our host wants us to gather on the terrace once this match is over."

We walk over to where Lord and Lady Mountbridge are standing. Within minutes, Paige begins regaling them with her own brand of humor. Clouds are rolling in and I find them almost soothing to my sensibilities at the moment.

"Ah, Richard," Louis says. "I've been meaning to ask if you and this lovely young lady would let me engage you in a tour of my wine cellars later. You might find my collection quite interesting."

"Thank you, sir. I would enjoy the tour immensely. I realize I have a lot to learn about wine and manufacturing overseas, but I hope to get things started as early as next year."

"That's very ambitious of you. Now, you never did share with me how you met Nélie."

"One of my good friends works in admissions for Georgetown University," Richard replies. "He asked me to visit the campus last fall to give a talk on my college experience and how it affected my career choice. As it turned out, Nélie was in the audience and asked several interesting questions. After we met, we ended up by spending the weekend together and have kept in touch."

Louis rubs his chin. "Georgetown University. My God, I can remember when India told me she was looking at that school. She was the quintessential political activist. When there a situation she didn't like, she protested much to the chagrin of her mother and me. That daughter of mine had a fiery temper. I'll never forget the time India organized a candle-light vigil on the green at school to protest apartheid. I was ready to throttle her but good for such a public display!"

"Excuse me," says Nélie. "What did you say your daughter's name was?"

"India," answers Louis. "She's dead now. She died in a plane crash fifteen years ago. Actually, your mother knew her well. I understand they were great friends."

The shock on Nélie's face paralyzes me with fear. How could I have been so stupid to allow Nélie to find out about her grandfather in such a public forum?

"Are you all right?" Louis asks Nélie. Nélie bolts from the table and runs toward the gardens.

"Excuse me," I say to the others, turning to run after her. "I'll go see what's the matter."

Frantic with worry, I run after Nélie, calling her name once I lose sight of the terrace. The garden feels like a maze as I run through each section by the statue, the reflecting pond, the rows of boxwoods, and the rose garden. "Nélie, wait!" I scream.

I catch sight of her ahead of me. I quicken my pace, fear fueling my footsteps. Grabbing her arm, I take hold of her while she gasps for breath amidst tears of anguish unlike any I've ever seen.

"Listen to me," I cry desperately, trying to reach her before she builds a wall of hate against me.

"Louis Vernon is my grandfather, and you never told me about him either. You've cheated me out of the only family I had! How could you? You brought me down to some hole-in-the-wall holier-than-thou southern prison and tried to impose all of these rules on me when you're just a liar!"

"Stop it!" I scream, my chest heaving with emotion. "I understand you're upset but that's unfair."

Nélie shrieks, "I've spent fifteen years not knowing anything and in twenty-four hours I find out my father is alive and living in Paris and so is my grandfather. You led me to believe there was no one but you. I wanted my family—my *real* family, for better or worse—not the pseudomodel you created for me." She clenches her fists.

"All those nights I lay awake dreaming that there might be a blood relative somewhere out there to rescue me, and they exist! How could you look at yourself in the mirror each day?" Beads of sweat form on Nélie's brow. She looks at me with disgust.

"Tell me something, Lauren," she shouts, "were you really my mother's best friend? Why did you lie to me?"

"Listen to me, Nélie. Your mother had stopped speaking to your grandfather. She absolutely hated him. I never knew why. I think she feared him in some way. I was trying to protect you!"

"Protect me?" Nélie exclaims angrily. "Tell me another one. To think that I could have grown up with all this. You kept me locked up in that shabby little house with homemade curtains you sewed yourself. Isn't that special?" she mocks, placing her hands on her hips. "You stole my rightful heritage from me! Do you understand me? You stole it and took away all of the things that made me, me. You were wrong, Lauren. My mother would have wanted me to be with *my* family, not yours."

I inch closer. "I'm sorry, Nélie. I gave you everything I had to give. And I'm sorry you find no value in that shabby little house that you grew up in. I did everything I could to be a good mother to you, and contrary to what you think, Matt and your sisters love you. Have you learned nothing at all about values?"

Nélie's nostrils flare. "Values? How can you look at me and preach values? Lies, all of them. You told me a bunch of lies. I thought my father and my grandfather were dead all this time! Do you have any idea what it was like to feel like an orphan with no money growing up in a home that never felt like my own? I felt like an outsider looking in on this happy family."

Tears stream down my face. "I'm sorry, Nélie. I did what I thought was right. I gave you everything I had to give, but I couldn't afford all this. You're right, I was a poor substitute for your mother. I was twenty-seven when India died, unmarried with no job and no hope of supporting you on my own. I may have even married the wrong man while trying to create a home for you. But I had made a promise to your mother that I would take care of you and I did my best!"

"I have nothing to say to you!" shouts Nélie. "Nothing. I think you're a liar. I hate you!"

The world suddenly seems to tilt awkwardly, but I muster my dignity. On wobbly legs, I turn and walk away from Nélie, filled with regret. Exhaustion seeps through every pore of my being, and I feel as if I could sleep for a week. Making my way back to the terrace, I'm relieved to see it's empty except for Paige, who seems to be waiting for me. She comes up beside me, offering soothing words, telling me she'll take me to my room. As she leads me there, I feel completely detached from reality. Paige shakes me, trying to wake me from my self-imposed trance.

"Lauren," Paige says. "Snap out of it, honey! Everything's going to be all right. So she found out the wrong way. She'll get over it. What's not to like? She's an heiress." Paige laughs heartily. "I can think of worse problems!"

"She hates me and called me a liar and a poor excuse for a mother," I say, looking at her. "I don't know that anyone has ever said anything so awful to me. I never meant to hurt her, Paige. India told me to keep her away from Louis. I don't know why she hated him."

There is a knock at the door, and I look up to find a household servant bringing me a tray with teacups, cream and sugar. "I had them put a shot of brandy in it. It'll make you feel better." Paige hands me the cup and I drink from it, the scalding liquid burning my throat. "That ungrateful little brat! She sounds like she needs a spanking. She's just as spoiled and selfish as her mother! Damn it, Lauren! I hate to see you so hurt. Let her go. You've already proven that you qualify as a saint. Let her screw up her own life, that's her problem, not yours anymore. You've done enough."

Perhaps it's exhaustion that makes me feel like I could cry for a month. "She called my house shabby." I say. "Do you think I live in a shabby house, Paige? Tell me the truth."

"Lauren, although I've never been to your house, knowing you, I'm sure it's lovely. Go home. Make peace with your other children. Let the little princess stay here in the château with Louis. He doesn't strike me as a particularly fatherly type." Paige walks into the bathroom and turns on the faucet. She returns with a cold washcloth, which she puts on my forehead. "Lie down," she commands.

Paige gently places the cold cloth on my head. "That kid has caused you enough trouble for now," she says. "Let her get to know him and make her own decisions on his character. You've warned her."

I sigh, feeling several drips of water from the compress run down the side of my face. "I hope she doesn't do anything foolish."

"She will," says Paige. "It's in her blood. India always pushed the envelope. She never listened to anyone else. Why would Nélie be any different? I'm sure my travel agent can get us a flight out of Paris in the next forty-eight hours. I'm starting to miss Bert, I must be getting sentimental in my old age."

Paige mentions that she had asked a housekeeper to try to determine Nélie's whereabouts. An hour later, there's a knock at the door. Paige opens it and whispers with someone, then returns to talk with me. "Nélie's gone for a picnic with Richard. Louis also appears to have made himself inaccessible. I suppose he'll not be seeing us off." She looks completely forlorn, staring wistfully out at the garden. "Since we're responsible for keeping our host's last blood relative from him, I'm not sure we're going to make the guest list again next year. What do you think?" Paige asks with a grin.

"I'd say you're right," I respond tiredly.

"I was hoping to make this an annual event," Paige says, smoothing out her skirt. "I could get used to this lifestyle"

"Oh, Paige," I joke, touching her arm. "I was just thinking about that damp one-room tenement where you live in New York. And that one dress you wear everyday, scrubbing it by hand at night. Your hands look raw and I fear for your health. "

"Lauren, after this week, I've decided I need to teach you more about mankind's evils—cigarettes, alcohol, chocolate, shopping, spa treatments, naps, paté, mayonnaise, cream sauce . . . Wait a minute, you know about chocolate. But you've no idea what you're missing with the other stuff."

"I'll take your word for it," I reply casually.

"Look at the bright side. Now that Nélie thinks you're a liar, she won't hold you up on a pedestal anymore. Why don't you just send your other girls tickets to Paris and forget about going home?"

"I'm not a liar!" I snap back.

"See!" cries Paige, cackling with delight. "You can't even acknowledge the fact that dear, sweet perfect Lauren did something *wrong*! Okay, you withheld information. Is that the politically correct phrase? Same thing. I think I like the word liar better; it's much more interesting. Face it, Lauren, you may need to lose your candidacy for sainthood." Paige folds her arms in front of her. A set of gold rings flashes in the sunlight.

"I didn't lie to Nélie, I was protecting her," I repeat, eager to get my point across.

"From whom? The evil Louis Vernon? So far, the only bad thing he's done this weekend is not invite us for longer. Do you know that we could have had a masseuse come to our rooms each day and give us a massage? Lady Mountbridge has been here a week and she's cornered the market on personal services."

"You're kidding," I say, gasping at such luxury.

"I wish I were. We could have been drinking champagne with our breakfast, but we didn't know about that either. Now, you need to go find Louis and be as nice as you can. Try to explain why you hauled his only grandchild off to the United States for fifteen years without him knowing it. Do you think you can do it?"

I'm unable to muster a sufficient answer to that one right now.

Paige continues on. "India was difficult, Lauren. She wasn't the paragon of virtue that you've made her out to be. She had the attention span of a gnat and constantly wanted her way. Maybe she drove poor Louis nuts trying to deal with her mercurial moods. Perhaps they would have made amends some day. I don't know."

"I can't be wrong, Paige! Why didn't India even tell her father she had Nélie? Why did she never bring me to meet him?"

"I can tell you why right now. If I had come home from Paris pregnant with the kid of a fifty-year-old married man, my father would have fed me to the wolves. Maybe that's just my parents. But, it might explain India's reluctance to contact her father. What was she going to do, call and say, 'Hi Dad! I just had this kid, do you want to meet her?' Besides, I don't think India put much thought into the whole situation. She was too worried about India for her to consider anyone else's feelings, with the exception of Julian and maybe the two of us and Nélie." Paige eyes me warily.

Paige walks around the room, idly looking at herself in the mirror. She leans in closer, checking her teeth to see if she has any food caught in them. Taking a hairbrush, she brushes her hair into place.

I can't be wrong. The thought simply horrifies me. Louis Vernon has had absolutely no idea of Nélie's existence. I've perpetuated his ignorance, possibly living out India's immature fantasies. Certainly, I knew first-hand that Julian's wife had threatened to harm Nélie, and I did leave word with the lawyer as to how I could be reached. Julian could have found Nélie if he had wanted to have some contact with his daughter or ease his conscience. But Louis, who never knew of Nélie's existence, has never had the chance of knowing her, much less seeing her take her first steps, witnessing the very stages that I thrilled in—her toothless grin in kindergarten, the year she played Sandy in the seventh grade production of *Grease*, reading stories together late at night, the joy of watching her grow up. If I was wrong, it is not a mistake that can ever be rectified.

I sit up, letting the washcloth fall on the bed. My thoughts are too disturbing for me to simply lie down. I walk to the bathroom to grab a towel to wipe all the moisture from my forehead. I'm reminded of Louis's unexpected visit, telling myself it was strange but not necessarily an indication that he's awful. Looking in the mirror, I notice my pale features, matted hair and disheveled appearance. Adjusting my skirt, I try to pull myself into some sort of order, hoping the physical act will transform into a mental calm.

How do you make up for fifteen years of lost time? It seems an impossible prospect and one that does not merit forgiveness. Louis would have to be furious, and I expect retaliation. Will I never see Nélie again? He could easily make me into the villain and, unfortunately, he might be right. To my knowledge, he's never been arrested, holds no criminal record and there's no hint of scandal surrounding the family name. If there were something sinister about him, wouldn't someone have reported him? Why would celebrities, world-class athletes, politicians and aristocrats seek his favor so readily if there were secret arms deals going on behind closed doors? If he's as powerful as India claimed, someone would have found out and exposed him by now.

"Let's go downstairs. I hate sitting in here waiting for something to happen. It's better that we face this situation head on." She pauses, surveying my appearance. "You look like you could use a day at the spa."

"I'll see what I can do," I say, reaching for the hair dryer. In a few minutes, I dry my hair, put on blush to add color to my pale cheeks and add lipstick. I decide I certainly look better, despite how I feel inside.

Paige nods her approval. "Much better," she says. "You've always got to look the part, honey. Even if you don't feel like it. 'Fake it 'til you make it.' That's my motto."

Unfortunately, I come face-to-face with Louis in the library. His expression is cold. He says, "Nélie will stay with me for a while so that we can get to know each other." His tone offers no room for objection.

He looks away, then faces me again, his expression contorted with anguish. "Why didn't you tell me?" he asks. "I've been so lonely. I lost my wife and my daughter."

Fear curls up my spine. "I . . ." My voice cracks. "I'm sorry," I respond in a breathless whisper. "I tried to take you aside several times this weekend."

"Rubbish." His hand slices through the air. "Fifteen years is a long time. You could have written me a letter."

"India didn't want you to know," I confess. "I thought I was doing the right thing."

"So, what was the real reason you were visiting this weekend? I find it hard to believe that Ms. Riverton had a sudden all-consuming passion for grapes."

Paige looks ready to speak up, but I motion her to be quiet for once. "Nélie ran away from home last week. She left us a note saying that she wanted to learn more about India. After tracking her down in Paris, we discovered she was here with Richard. That's the truth. Honestly, I tried to take you aside last night but the situation that arose made it impossible. I had planned to tell you myself today, but Nélie figured it out before I had a chance to tell her."

"DuBusé's her father, isn't he?"

I feel paralyzed with indecision on how much to tell him.

"For God's sake, I'll find out soon enough. Although I had to hear about India's death a month later from a family friend who had heard the news from an art dealer in Paris. Anyway, you might as well tell me, I can hire a private investigator and find it out on my own."

"Yes," I reply quietly. "He wants to remain in the background."

Louis rubs his hands over his eyes. "That bastard," Louis mutters. "I've always hated Julian. He's my contemporary, for God's sake. What was India thinking?" He looks at his hands. "I hope that Nélie didn't inherit her mother's stubborn streak. It'll do her no good."

He stands up. "Lauren, I think it's time I got to know my granddaughter. She's my rightful heir, the last link in this family."

"But," I protest, "I want Nélie to come home to her family."

"I'm her family, Lauren. We're blood relatives. She needs me as much as I need her. This is where she belongs. Not in your world. Not in some Godforsaken southern town. To think I almost died not knowing she existed!" He shakes his head. "You had better leave before I decide to get my attorneys involved and sue you for everything you're worth."

Unable to accept the finality of his words, I exclaim, "But that's not fair. I raised her as my own. I love her!"

"If you love her, then let her come back to where she belongs. She's an heiress, to my business as well as my personal fortune. If you protest too much and use her attachment to you against me, Lauren, I promise you, you'll regret it! I have an entire legal team at my disposal. Now, leave, before I tell you what I really think of you."

Paige grabs my arm. We walk out of his office. My mind is so numb, it refuses to accept the viciousness of his threats. All I can think in my own defense is that India hated her father. I try to remember each snippet of information India shared about him. That same conversation at the café comes to mind. *"Father has an unfailing sense of family loyalty. He sees me as the one who cast him aside."*

Could India's feelings about him have been just those of a headstrong young girl against a father with a strength of will that matched her own? I'd always had the feeling there was something more to the story. But circumstance has offered me no choice. Nélie wants to stay with her grandfather. I can understand his feelings of betrayal, joy at finding out about Nélie, and sadness that he never had any idea that she existed. Who could blame him?

I head upstairs to pack and leave a note for Nélie. The message will be brief. I'll leave her Paige's apartment number and address so she can find me if she changes her mind. Ironically, I feel worse now then when she first ran away. This time, I feel I've lost her completely. There's nothing tangible she needs from me right now. Those things are soon to be taken care of by her grandfather in a far grander style than anything I could afford.

With great regret, I realize I'll be unable to show Nélie India's apartment while I'm here. Since Julian expects me to return the key, I'll take a chance and make a copy, assuming he won't have the locks changed. I hope to return soon so I can show it to her, but this hope seems unrealistic given our present situation. Perhaps Nélie will relent and realize that I never meant to hurt her, that I thought I was following her mother's wishes.

Seated at a writing desk in the blue room, I pause to take

in my surroundings. There is a small sculpture of Apollo, an Impressionist painting of a family descending the stairs to the ocean, a blue velvet armchair. A queen-size four poster bed with a blue toile canopy and a blue bedspread is surrounded by soft, white carpeting. The view of the garden captures my attention for a moment as I look out the windows. The lingering scent of Paige's Chanel perfume fills the air. But mostly, the quiet assails my senses, creating an eerie feeling, as if today's drama never occurred. I half expect to hear Louis Vernon stomping down the hallway shouting my name, followed by the police. He would scream, "She's in there! Take her away! The charlatan! Pretending to be Nélie's mother all these years when she's no blood relation. She poisoned an innocent girl's mind against her own grandfather! She's a liar! Liar! Liar! My poor granddaughter had to endure a hellish existence because of her."

A knock sounds at the door, freezing my thoughts. "Don't get excited," says Paige as she appears in the doorway. "It's only me."

"I thought you were Louis coming to take me away," I say wryly, folding my arms in front of me.

"I don't think you're his priority right now. Nélie is going to be the focus of his undivided attention in the weeks to come," Paige says, catching her reflection in the mirror and turning for a side view. She sucks in her stomach and pats it gently.

"That's what I'm afraid of," I say, finishing my letter and sealing it.

Our goodbye to the château turns out uneventful. We find our way to the door and get into the car. Paige's driver takes us away like outcasts without a farewell, thank you or promise to return again. I feel a huge lump rising in my throat when I recall what happened here. I don't think I'll ever forget Nélie's words as they echo in my ears, reminding me that my hope of rebuilding our relationship is gone.

*All those nights I lay awake dreaming that there might be
a blood relative somewhere out there to rescue me—and they
exist! How could you look at yourself in the mirror each
day?*

Seated in the privacy of my room at Paige's apartment, I call
Greensboro and tell them I'll be home late the following
evening. Matt offers to pick me up and, too tired and frustrated to dissuade him, I agree. Looking around, I see my
suitcase thrown on the floor. My cosmetics, change and hairbrush are scattered on top of the dresser. Several items are
piled on top of an armchair. The task of packing seems
daunting. Fortunately, Paige appears in the doorway, a welcome intrusion.

"I've made arrangements for Lord and Lady Mountbridge
to visit next fall when they take their annual trip to New
York. I hope you'll come to New York too, Lauren."

"Of course, "I say, "I'll make a point of it."

"What happens now?" Paige asks abruptly.

"I go home and try to sort things through. After that, I
don't know." Anxious to change the subject, I say, "Are there
some children's shops around here? I'd like to bring Laura
and Kathryn some presents."

"There's a store down the street. Come on, I'll go with
you. I never turn down an opportunity to shop."

Blocks away in a small jewelry shop, I find several beaded
necklaces that Paige tells me are the rage right now. My home
in Greensboro still seems light years away as we walk the
streets. The rain drizzles on the city, the silver droplets bouncing off a series of beige raincoats. Suddenly, I'm wet and cold,
and my surroundings take on a melancholy tone. We stop at
a café to have an early supper, and then Paige heads back to
the apartment.

Alone, I wander the streets of Paris one last time. The walk
clears my mind as I stare at the pretty window displays on

the Rue St. Honoré. An orange jacket catches my eye. Looking at the price tag, I gasp at the number of francs. When I calculate the sum into American money, I realize that it's five thousand dollars. I shouldn't even allow myself the pleasure of looking in this neighborhood.

Suddenly, I quicken my stride. Crossing several streets, I head for the subway. Surrounded by concrete, billboards, and the odor of gasoline, I look at the map to determine the best way to get to Jean's studio. If he's not there, I decide, then I'll leave him a note. Walking with a purpose now, I wind my way back several blocks to the gallery. Once I spot the wrought iron bench in front, my breathing slows. I see a light on in the back. Knocking on the glass door, I peer inside, hoping that Jean might be working in his studio. Several minutes pass as people glance my way, probably wondering why I can't understand that the shop is closed.

A male form appears in the lit doorway, looking completely irritated. He peers through the glass. Our eyes meet and his expression changes to a smile.

"Lauren," he says, opening the door. "I'm glad it's you."

"I'm sorry, I should have called first. Paige and I are leaving tomorrow morning. I just wanted to thank you for your help before I go."

He leads me back to his office and gestures for me to sit. "What happened at the château? Did you find her?" Jean leans against the edge of the desk, facing me. Flecks of paint mark his right hand.

"Yes," I reply. "She's staying with her grandfather for a time. Nélie's really upset with me. I should have told her the whole story years ago."

He nods sympathetically. "Are you all right? You look a little pale."

"I'm fine," I say instinctively, not wanting to involve him any further. "I just hate leaving Paris when things are so strained between us. It's hard." My voice cracks.

"If it's any help, I've just received two pieces I'm taking in on commission. They're Daumier sculptures. I know Louis's collection and I'm certain he would like to see them. I'm planning on contacting him this week to set up an appointment. When I visit him, I could check on Nélie and let you know how she's doing, or I could give her a message from you."

"Oh," I exclaim, "that would be wonderful. You don't know how much that would help me rest easier, knowing she's okay. She's still just a kid." Our eyes meet. "I can't thank you enough for your help." Abruptly, I stand up, reaching out to take his hand. "I've got to go."

Our hands touch, the warmth of his fingers soothing my troubled spirit.

"I understand," he says, letting go of my hand.

As I turn away, Jean's voice stops me. "Lauren," he says, folding his arms in front of him. "I hope you'll give our earlier discussions due consideration. You really ought to think about painting again. If you ever want an opinion from someone in the business, I'd be willing to give you an honest evaluation of your work."

I nod, then chuckle. "Jean, I can't imagine that you'd find it remotely interesting, given your background. I'd hate to waste your time."

"Let me decide that. In the meantime, I'll contact you after I've seen Nélie. Will you leave me your number in the States?"

"Certainly," I respond, hastily scribbling the information down on a scrap of paper. "I've also included my e-mail address."

"Perfect," he says. "Can I give you a ride home? It's late."

"No, thank you. I don't mind walking."

He shakes his head. "I'll walk you to where you're going."

As promised, Jean accompanies me to the front door of Paige's apartment building. With a friendly handshake, he promises to contact me as soon as he sees Nélie.

* * *

Seated in first class, Paige sips on her sparkling water. "Do you want to talk about it? You know, there's not much of a view up here." She leans over to look outside. "Come on, you're supposed to laugh."

I shrug, offering a small movement of my lips.

"A smile often involves teeth. At least that's what I've heard anyway. Lauren, you know I'm here if you need me in the next few weeks. I can fly down to see you and help. Don't hesitate to call." I can't bring myself to talk, but she continues on. "You're so kindhearted. You didn't deserve to have a brat like Nélie for a daughter. Just thinking about her makes me want to find her and give her a good spanking. That's what's wrong with her, you know. You weren't hard enough on her. You treated her like a princess, and now she thinks she *is* one."

"Paige, she's just a troubled seventeen-year-old trying to find out who she is. I'm not denying that her words hurt, because they did. But I'm trying to put myself in her shoes and understand. It was a big shock for her to find out that both her father and her grandfather exist and that I withheld this information from her."

Paige sighs and motions for the flight attendant to bring her another pillow. "How do we think Nélie is faring right now in the château? I would imagine Louis will throw a big party for her to introduce her to his friends in the next few weeks. I guess I won't hold my breath for an invitation."

"I hope she's all right," I say aloud, thinking about India's warnings.

"What could happen to her?" says Paige, adjusting her seat. "She might break a nail playing tennis or gain five pounds from all of the fabulous food. She might soak in wine at night or pull a muscle playing croquet. She's young and in love, and she's just found out her family is fabulously wealthy. You have nothing to worry about."

"Money isn't everything," I remind Paige dryly.

She sits up, looking shocked. "Since when?"

Chapter 15

Everything looks the same, my street, the neighborhood, our redbrick house with the black shutters. The past week has changed my paradigm for happiness. Matt guides the car into the driveway. Our stilted conversations have been punctuated by long periods of silence. The thought of seeing my girls brings a note of joy to this homecoming. I can hear Laura's voice shouting, "She's here! Mom's home." Laura and Kathryn burst out of the back door saying, "Mom! You're back."

"Hi, girls!" I cry, holding out my arms. "I missed you guys! Tell me what happened at school this week. Anything interesting?"

Matt takes my bags inside while I listen to the excited chatter of our daughters. When I walk inside, my eyes have trouble adjusting to the light. The house seems dark and a bit stale-smelling, as if someone hadn't taken out the trash in a few days. Everything seems different. Looking around the kitchen, I notice the Greek keys that I painted along the wall and the curtains I made in matching fabric. I always thought I had done a professional-looking job. Suddenly, I long for the smell of freshly baked bread emanating from the cafés of Paris. A vision of crystal chandeliers, velvet chairs and gilded pictures comes to mind.

"Was Paris so beautiful?" asks Kathryn. "When can we go and visit there?"

"Someday soon," I reply. "Maybe we'll go visit Nélie before long."

The next hour is filled with questions, descriptions, homework, unpacking and straightening up the house. A large pizza box inhabits the refrigerator, and I consider how well my kids have been eating since I've been gone. They look healthy enough. Matt has left a list of people who have called since I left, and I flip the page to see that the number totals close to thirty. Is this an outpouring of support or, perhaps, curiosity about the real story behind Nélie's disappearance? While I'm shuffling through papers, the phone rings.

"Oh Lauren! You're home!" cries my mother. She sounds relieved. "Oh dear, Matt's filled me in on the details. You must be exhausted. That child was nothing but trouble. I knew it the moment you moved her back here. How could she do such a thing to you?"

"Mom, thanks for your concern. I'm exhausted. Can I call you tomorrow?"

"Of course, dear. I've gone to the grocery store. I'll bring some milk and things around in the morning."

"Thanks," I reply dutifully.

I've avoided Matt since I arrived and now it's getting late. The thought of sharing a bed with him seems strange, as if I've never slept beside him before. For now, I decide that I'd rather read through my mail than confront him. Quiet descends upon the house. I bask in the silence, imagining that I can avoid the inevitable confrontation. His footsteps echo in the front hallway and my body tenses, waiting and ready for what's to come.

"Are you coming to bed, Lauren? You can take care of those things in the morning."

"I'll be along soon," I say mechanically, hoping he'll leave. Rather than take my cue, he walks closer to me, standing in the door frame by the desk. He looks tired, his once-blond hair matted to his head and his eyeglasses perched on the edge of his nose. "What's wrong?"

"Nothing."

"Why do I feel like you blame me for Nélie's disappearance? Like somehow I engineered the whole thing?" he asks, folding his arms in front of him.

"Don't worry, Matt. It was as much my fault as yours. I won't be pointing any fingers at you tonight."

"Why are you acting like this? It's like you're not happy to be home. If this has nothing to do with Nélie, then what is it?"

I seize the opening I've been waiting for, eager to express the emotions locked up inside of me. "I learned a lot on this trip about India, and Nélie, and mostly about myself. I never realized how shaken I was after her death and why I made some of the decisions I did, mainly moving back here. This wasn't the life I wanted when I moved to Paris. But here we are, fifteen years later, living it. I can't even believe that I'm not back an hour before my mother thinks she can call and tell me how she knew Nélie was trouble from the start."

He coughs, probably stifling a snicker. "What is it you don't like about this life? The phone hasn't stopped ringing since you left, family and friends calling to offer their support, bring us dinner, drive the girls to soccer practice and tennis lessons." Matt runs his hand through his hair and stares at me, looking truly baffled by my thoughts.

"Maybe I realized when I got to Paris again how much I had missed it. I lived there for over five years. I was happy."

"You were at a different stage of life, Lauren. I could say I was happy drinking beers at Carolina. That time in my life is over now, and we have two kids to worry about."

"Three."

"Well, the first one doesn't seem to want our help. Haven't we done enough already?"

"What the hell is that supposed to mean?" I snap, standing up and walking over to the center cooking island. "It's about time you admitted what a burden she was, because that's what she told me she felt like for fifteen years living in this house. I wonder why, Matt?"

"Don't you dare start that crap. We did everything for her, both of us, and she never appreciated any of it. She's just like her mother, spoiled and flighty. Happy one minute, angry and resentful the next because she didn't get her way."

"India wasn't flighty."

"The hell she wasn't!"

"Can you watch your language?"

"Oh well, aren't we Miss Etiquette now that you've spent the week with that gold digger Paige, who married Bert Riverton for his money. And you've had a week in a château, while I've been up at six o'clock every morning making sure you have a nice home and our girls can attend private schools."

"Oh please, spare me the *I work so hard lecture*. Don't you ever get tired of listening to yourself?"

"What's gotten into you? You've never acted like this before."

"Maybe you don't know me very well," I say, my eyes narrowing. Years of frustration at not being heard bubble to the surface. Matt's defiant stance infuriates me. "I've decided I'm going to paint seriously again. I'd like to see if I can sell my work through a gallery."

"You don't need to work, Lauren, since I support you. How would it look if all of a sudden my wife started hawking her paintings around town?"

"You can't have it both ways, Matt. One minute you play the martyr because you've had to work so hard to pay for things. The next minute, you turn into the male chauvinist who thinks his wife should be barefoot and pregnant in the kitchen. I wish you could hear yourself."

"I don't want to hear any more, Lauren. We'll talk when

you come to your senses." He storms off, presumably to surf the television channels before bed.

How can I make this work when I'm so unhappy? I wonder, staring at my kitchen with its stainless appliances, white cabinets and countertops. The suburban setting does nothing to soothe my troubled thoughts. I need to sort things through, to figure out what I want. Fatigue overtakes me soon enough. An hour later, I head upstairs to bed. Seeing that Matt has turned his back to me, I am relieved.

The following morning, I hit the ground running, involving myself in a multitude of activities from attending soccer games to doing errands, cleaning cabinets, returning telephone calls, answering questions about Nélie, and assuring our friends and family that she's fine on her extended holiday in Paris. All the while I manage to avoid Matt—anything to keep myself from thinking or feeling too much. On Friday, I venture out to a small shop someone has mentioned to buy a wedding gift for a friend's daughter. The task seems mundane enough. As I wander around the aisles of the shop among piles of rugs, lamps and mirrors, the odor of incense emanating from a brass pot invades my senses.

Selecting a mirror, I head to the cash register to pay. The aroma seems stronger now and there's no mistaking it. As I write the note I've written a hundred times or so before, I'm compelled to ask, "What is that smell?"

"Heat and Passion." The girl grabs the bag and turns it upside down. "This label says it's from India."

"I see," I remark, my hand trembling as I write the message on the gift card. "Is it for sale?"

"Sure," says the girl. She adds the amount to the total and hands me the charge slip to sign.

"What about a holder?"

"Right," says the girl as she gathers the rest of the items and asks me for an additional twenty dollars to cover the cost.

Heat and Passion. As if a magical spell has been lifted from me, I clutch the bag while heading to my black Suburban. Where's Nélie right now? Is she all right? I can suddenly picture myself painting again, envisioning my hands delineating a stormy landscape. The picture comes into focus as I work out how to use color to manipulate the scene.

"Lauren," a familiar female voice calls. I must stop and be polite, but the effort irritates me.

"Hi, Betsy. How are you?" I ask.

"Not me, dear, you. When did you get back?" she asks, observing my appearance to see if I bear any telltale signs of my *ordeal*, as it's being called behind my back.

"A couple of days ago. Yes, I'm fine."

"And Nélie? My Sarah was so sad that Nélie didn't attend the graduation ceremony. It's such a special time in their lives, you know." Her eyes shine with curiousity.

"Yes, I know. Nélie is visiting her grandfather in the south of France for a time. Matt and I agreed that it was the right decision for her at this point in her life."

"Will she be going to Princeton next fall?"

"We don't know yet. I need to keep moving," I say, trying to maintain my composure. "I'll see you soon."

She practically follows me into my car. "Any exciting summer plans for the rest of your family?" Betsy inquires.

"We'll probably all head back over to France to visit Nélie," I say, wiping my brow.

After dinner that night, I sit alone at my desk, trying to compose another letter to Nélie. Matt approaches me and says, "Lauren, we can't go on like this. What do you want from me? We're leading separate lives . . . I miss you. I miss us, the way we were before this whole ordeal started."

There's the ordeal word again, I want to say. Instead, I reply, "I don't know what I want, but I certainly have no interest in returning to the way things were." To diffuse the tension, I idly fold my arms in front of me. Looking him straight in the eye, I say, "I want more out of life, as I told you the other night."

"You think painting again is going to make you happy?" He looks incredulous. "Who's going to buy your work, may I ask?"

"I'm going to pay a call on Priscilla Dabney and see if she would represent me at her gallery."

"You're kidding. She represents nationally known artists. How do you expect to just show up at her shop with a canvas in the trunk, hoping she'll take a look? You haven't painted in years. Besides, you never did your own work!"

"Thanks for your vote of confidence," I reply, turning my attention back to my letter.

"What, you're just going to ignore me again?" he snaps, tapping his loafer on the floor.

"I don't need to listen to any more of your insulting remarks about my qualifications. Why can't you just once say, 'Hey Lauren, that's great! I think it's terrific that you want to paint something new. Go ahead and try. I'll help you in whatever way I can.' Would that be so hard, instead of constantly refusing to accept the fact that I need other interests outside of the girls, our home and you?"

"Well, if you ran this house perfectly, then maybe I might be more engaging. How many times have I asked you to get someone over here to fix the fence out back?"

Disgust crawls through me. "You know, Matt, you can do some of these things to help out around here. There's the trash over there. Do you even know where the trash can is? You live in this house too, so you can help out as well." I stand up to leave the room. He reaches for me.

"Lauren, wait. Things don't need to be like this. I hate fighting with you." I gaze into his blue eyes, suddenly realizing that they can't see me.

I shake my head, then walk away, my eyes filling with tears.

* * *

The next morning, I log on to the Internet, eager to send Jean an e-mail, asking if he's heard anything about Nélie. My message is simple and friendly and I long to say more, but feel silly doing so. At the same time, I'm worried. Why hasn't Nélie answered my letters?

I decide to pay a visit to Priscilla's gallery downtown to introduce myself. After frequenting so many youth hostels in Paris and asking for help from strangers like Sophie, this task doesn't seem so daunting. What's the worst she can do?

With great care, I dress in the black pants suit and printed scarf Paige selected for me in Paris. I put my hair back in a chignon. When I check my appearance in the mirror, a smile comes to my lips. I am indeed excited about the prospect ahead, no matter what the outcome. It's been a long time since I've not let Matt's disapproval stop me from doing things. The feeling is quite liberating and I realize how much I have empowered him to control my life.

Priscilla's gallery has a white brick exterior with two large oil paintings set in the front windows. Willing myself to go forward, I walk inside to look around, admiring the modern and contemporary art. A woman greets me, then asks if she can be of assistance. I ask her if I may speak to the owner.

As I expected, Priscilla appears, neatly dressed in a green dress and black high heels, with big gold earrings framing her face. She's blond, trim and somewhere in her mid-fifties. I introduce myself and ask if she has a few minutes. Quelling a rush of nerves, I say, "I'm an artist. I studied under Henri Gustave in Paris and I'd like to know if you'd be willing to see a sampling of my work."

Her voice brightens. "Henri Gustave? Really? Why don't you come into my office?" She leads the way, moving a pile of papers from a leather chair. I sit down, noticing her mahogany desk stacked with files. Covered with little yellow sticky notes, files line the bookcases. Large art books decorate the floor.

"Tell me about yourself," she inquires with a warm smile. "Well, I've been at home with my children for the last fifteen years. They're grown now. I've decided I'm ready to paint seriously again. When I was in Paris, I worked with Gustave for four years on various projects, but mostly I work on canvas."

"Do you have some things that I could see?" she asks.

"I'm not going to lie to you. Establishing yourself as a professional artist today is extremely difficult. However, if your work is good enough, it can happen. The fact that Gustave is so well-known and you were one of his students would help you get started." She pauses. "What are your paintings like?"

"Landscapes mostly. Some portraits. I'm very interested in using color in unexpected ways."

"I'm intrigued, Lauren." She motions to one of the stacks of files. "I'm so embarrassed by the way things look here. My assistant just went on maternity leave so I'm looking to replace her. Why don't we plan on meeting in, say, two weeks? You could bring several of your canvases here and I'd be willing to take a look at them. How does that sound?"

Wondering how I'm going to put together several canvases in that short a time span, I reply easily, "Of course. I'll look forward to it."

"I'm going to impress upon you that I take on only what I think I can sell. Nearly all of my artists are known nationally," she cautions.

"Priscilla, I'm looking for an honest evaluation of my work. It would answer a lot of questions for me personally."

We continue to talk for another twenty minutes. Afterwards, energized and delighted, I feel so elated that I've made progress that I call Paige and leave a message on her machine.

That night, having decided that a public forum seems the best approach, I break the news to everyone at the table.

"Why do you want to paint for some gallery?" cries Laura. "What's wrong with the things you make for my school?" Matt gives me a knowing look.

"It's something I need to do for myself." I reply firmly, gazing directly at Laura so she doesn't challenge my authority.

"Does this mean you won't be there in the afternoons for my soccer games?" Kathryn whines.

"Sure sweetheart, I'll be there. I'm just going to need to paint as much as I can in the next two weeks. We'll make it work, I promise. Why don't you girls head upstairs. I'll be up in a few minutes to help you."

"Well, Lauren," Matt offers politely, "if painting landscapes will make you happy, then I won't stand in your way. But I just don't want you to be disappointed." That's the closest thing to an approval I'm going to get.

Feeling conciliatory, I smile and say, "I just want a chance to find out if I have the potential to make a go of it as a professional. That's what Priscilla Dabney's giving me."

"You mean you want to sell your paintings!" says my mother, her face scowling with disbelief. "You don't need to work now, Lauren. Matt makes enough money to support the two of you."

"That's not the point," I say, taking the bag of groceries from her. "I want to do something for myself."

She scratches her head, seemingly perplexed by the whole conversation. "What's gotten into you?" she asks, looking at my pants suit with distaste. "It seems like Nélie's disappearance has turned this whole family upside down. What going on here?"

"That's not it," I reply. "This has everything to do with me, with my life and what makes me happy. It's important."

"What does Matt think about all of this? You know, he really did a terrific job with the girls while you were gone. It was a lot for him to take on, especially after getting that promotion." She places her hand on her ample hip.

"What promotion?" I ask, noticing her plain dress and sensible shoes.

"He didn't tell you?" she replies, looking at me strangely. "He's just been made a company vice president, with a huge salary increase and benefits. He'll soon have twenty-five salesmen working for him."

"Oh. Well, he's worked hard. I'm pleased that he received such recognition," I say, giving a worthy boilerplate response to the news.

"Are you?" asks Mother, surprised. "You don't act like it. You sound like you could care less. Did you meet someone in Paris?" she asks pointedly, staring at my features.

I look her in the eye. "Of course not. I just realized how much I missed being in Paris and how happy I was when I lived there with India and Paige. Those years seem like a lifetime ago."

"Of course they do! You kids had no real responsibility except to yourselves. Now you have a family to take care of that demands your constant attention. You can't look back, Lauren. You must go forward and make the best of things." She busily opens up cabinets as she attempts to organize several of the items sitting on the counter. "Where do you keep your flour?"

"In the jar by the stove," I reply instantly, thinking that nothing ever changes.

"Why not keep it up in this cabinet. It'll be easier to reach that way." She places it in just the right spot. "There," she says with a sigh of satisfaction.

"Because I don't want it there, Mother," I snap, wondering why I've let her come into my kitchen and tell me how to run it for the past fifteen years. "Would you like me to come to your house to show you how to arrange your pantry?"

"Tsk!Tsk!" she says, backing away. "Lauren, I don't know what's going on with you, but it sure isn't pleasant. Poor Matt! You'd better watch out or you'll lose him, honey. He's a good man—and successful, too. Now, I loved your father, but Matt's done a lot more for you than your father ever did for the two of us."

Oh Lord! I think, wondering at the life cycle. No wonder I'm here now, living in this small town, worrying about how to keep my man and where to put the flour in the kitchen. "Mother, maybe you should head home and start figuring out what's for dinner," I offer, trying to keep my sarcasm at bay.

"You know," she says, "I'm planning on making the most marvelous new recipe for meatloaf. I'll drop it by tomorrow if it's good."

Meatloaf. My mother's main concern is meatloaf. She wants me to feel the same way. She's been a good wife and mother and her greatest pleasure was serving her husband meatloaf. There's nothing wrong with that. *It's not what I want. I'm a different person.*

I want to tell her to go to the bookstore to check out a book on Elizabeth Cady Stanton, one of the founders of the women's liberation movement. Perhaps I'll buy my mother a copy for Christmas. She'll look at me blankly and say, "That's nice, dear." Instead I say, "Don't forget about the onions, Mom. You know the kids won't eat it if you put in too many."

"You're right," she replies, pleased with this bit of input. "Don't think too much, Lauren."

I refuse to respond to her unique brand of male chauvinism. It really is no accident that I married Matt. I just perpetuated another cycle that has been maintained in my family for generations. The man is clearly the king of the castle, with no room for reinterpretation. Such a costly dynamic to my self-esteem. I have been unwilling to question the only family system I know.

An image of Paige's apartment comes to mind. I hold my breath, trying to figure out what to do next. I walk around the center island in my kitchen three times, hoping the answer will come. What do I do now? Indecision gnaws at me and I am immobilized by years of training in responsibility. For some crazy reason, I feel I owe it to Matt and my children to at least try to make this marriage work. Perhaps if I incorporate more of my needs into our lives and assert myself professionally, Matt and I can be happy.

"Damn it!" I cry into the empty room, wishing I could change my life. The risk seems too high at the expense of my children.

India knew how to follow her bliss, I think. She was a master of doing what she wanted without once worrying about the consequences. Out of a desperate need to preserve my sanity, I race upstairs in search of that bag of incense. Rushing into my room and to the bottom of my closet, I find the bag tucked in there, as if it contained some secret mystical spell that would exorcise years of restricted living from my being. I remove the brass holder and incense from the bag, then go in search of matches. Grabbing a pack off the windowsill in the kitchen, I race back upstairs to my bedroom and, after much fumbling around, I manage to light the oil and incense. Smelling a waft of Heat and Passion, I am tantalized by the aroma and I lay back on my bed, clasping my hands behind my head, and stare at the ceiling.

My mother's face comes to mind and anger unlike any I've known surfaces, bringing with it a barrage of scenes like the one we just had in the kitchen. Each incident seems minor enough, yet her messages remain clear—that I'm so lucky to have married Matt and that I should hold on to my man at all costs. Happiness isn't necessarily one's objective in a marriage, peace must be maintained, she always says, and I should set aside my needs for those of my husband and children. India's face appears and I immediately think of Nélie. She has forced me to question the choices I've made and my servitude to a set of outdated ideas.

With a deep breath, I get up to go in search of my paints in the garage. For the next few hours, only the furious pace of my brush strokes eases the pounding in my head. It's as if these feelings inside me must come out. I paint the outline of India's playhouse, using bold strokes of green in various forms. Color replaces form in the image as I recall the gardens at the château. An image of a young girl comes to mind and I draw her brown hair and slim figure as she glides through this imaginary forest. *Is it Nélie?* I wonder, pausing at the image. The young girl looks lost in the woods as I dab in hints of red roses sweeping over a brick wall.

"Mom!" shouts Kathryn. "Where are you?" She enters the garage, licking something from her finger.

"I'm right here!" I say, getting up from my stool. "I'm painting," I tell her, giving her a hug. "Did you finish your homework?"

"What are you painting?"

"Just a scene I had in my mind. I took several photographs of one of the gardens where we stayed in France. Painting helps to keep me from worrying too much about your sister."

Kathryn nods in understanding, displaying a maturity far beyond her years. She walks over to survey my work.

"Wow!" she exclaims. "That sure is pretty. Is the girl in the picture Nélie?"

I nod.

"I wish she'd come home. I miss her!" Her eyes well up with tears. Leaning over to give Kathryn a hug, it's hard not to feel sad about Nélie's absence. "I miss her, too. But she's getting to know her grandfather right now, honey. It's important that they have that time together."

I check my watch, remembering that I have several errands to run, including picking up Laura from a friend's house later on and chauffeuring her and a friend to a school function.

Matt's out of town on business for the next three nights, and I am grateful for the brief respite from him.

Three days later, seated in Priscilla Dabney's office, I look askance at the two canvases that I have completed in record time. Thanks to Matt's business trip, I've worked nearly all night the last two nights. Actually, the experience was rather cathartic. At least I was productive, rather than tossing and turning all night worrying about Nélie. The muscles in my fingers, unaccustomed to holding brushes for long periods of time, ache, but I feel good. It's time I started to make a realistic assessment of my own artistic abilities. Not that I think one person's opinion should make or break my renewed enthusiasm. But Priscilla Dabney is a highly respected art dealer in the south, and she could be helpful.

A shiver of anticipation hangs over me. This is the part of painting that I dread. It's hard to detach emotionally from work that I've poured my heart into producing. I remind myself that not everyone is going to like my work.

Priscilla enters the room dressed in a crisp black dress and high heels. A double strand of gray pearls is her only jewelery. How incredibly tasteful she looks, I think.

"Good morning, Lauren," she says, coming forward to shake my hand. Her face wears a comfortable mask of professionalism.

My stomach lurches as I anticipate her reaction. Seized by anxiety, I say nervously, "Good morning," while feeling the hard grasp of her hand in mine.

With a polite smile, she announces, "Well, I'm certainly curious to see what you've brought me."

I nod, suddenly wondering whether I should grab my paintings and run out of the room. Taking a deep breath, I reply, "I completed two sixteen-by-twenty canvases for you to see. The first one is called, *Little Girl Lost*." With trembling limbs, I reach for the canvas and turn it around to show Priscilla.

"Can you bring it closer," she requests, leaning forward. She looks me in the eye and announces, "It's absolutely beautiful! Look at the detail of the roses. You captured those perfectly." She pauses. "May I see the other one?"

"This is more abstract," I explain, removing my canvas of reds and blues for her to see. "I've called it *Passion*; I did some experimenting with color here."

She nods. "I can tell you studied with Gustave. Your work is very alive and your use of color is excellent. How long do you think it would take you to put together a show?"

"Are you saying that you're willing to sell some of my work?"

"Yes," she nods. "You'll have to work mostly on commission sales. But I would be willing to hang these in my gallery if you'll let me."

"Really?" I smile broadly. "That would be great."

"Since you're an unknown, we have to price them accordingly, but I think you have real potential. My gut reaction is that we'd try to sell them for say, a thousand dollars each."

"That's two thousand dollars," I say, trying to control my surprise.

"Lauren," she says, "in all my years as a dealer, I've never had someone walk in off the street, who just happened to study with Gustave, and be this talented. There are so many false leads. You're obviously a gifted artist."

Suddenly, Matt's predictions of disaster come to mind. "Priscilla, I can't commit to a show right now. I'll be honest, I'm flattered. How about if you try to sell these two works first?"

She nods in agreement. "I'm willing to wait. In the meantime, I'll have these framed and displayed appropriately. I'll need more information from you in terms of the years you studied with Gustave, and your training and background, so we can design some marketing materials."

"Fair enough. I'll send you that information this week," I reply, my confidence soaring.

Around six o'clock, Matt walks in the door, carrying a bouquet of flowers.

"Hi!" he says, smiling and holding out the flowers for me.

"What are these for?"

"A peace offering. I've phoned your mother. She said she would come over and take care of the girls so we could go out to dinner together."

"How thoughtful," I reply, wondering why I feel so indifferent to the offer.

Dutifully, I head upstairs to change into the appropriate clothes. I select one of the things Paige purchased for me in Paris, a pretty blue dress with beaded flowers on the hem. My enthusiasm grows as I spray on some perfume, brush my hair and contemplate an evening with my husband. I remind myself that Matt has committed to me for life.

"It's been too long since we've done this," Matt says, taking a sip of red wine.

I lean back in my seat, enjoying the candlelight, the red wine, the flowers, and the tentative truce that has formed between us. "This is lovely," I reply. "Thank you."

Matt looks at me and says, "Lauren, I really want our marriage to work. I know sometimes I don't tell you how much I appreciate everything you do for the girls and me, but I really do."

"Thank you," I say, pleased to be acknowledged. "Mother told me about your promotion. You haven't said a word."

Matt's face lights up. "I'll run the company's southern division. It means a bit more travel, but the pay and benefits are well worth the sacrifice."

"Congratulations!" I say. "That's great news. And while

we're on the topic, I spoke with Priscilla Dabney today. She's offered to sell two of my paintings in her gallery." A feeling of personal satisfaction delights me.

"You don't have to work, Lauren," he assures me, then changes the subject. "As I said, my promotion practically doubled my salary. I've also been given more stock options in the company. I was thinking we might want to look to buy a summer house at the lake. Do you remember the one we looked at several years ago but couldn't afford? Things are good now and we could manage something like that."

Matt launches into a discussion of all the things we could do together as a family, from water skiing to a trip to Europe. He looks at me and says, "I was thinking that perhaps you could hire someone to help with the cleaning and chores around the house. That way you'd have time to volunteer for some benefits in town. Those charity functions would be a great way to meet the right kind of people."

"Matt," I say. "I'm trying to paint more and establish myself as a professional artist."

"Lauren, you don't need a job. Your job is helping me with my career and then taking care of our kids who need you. You're great at that. This art thing of yours will just make you unhappy. I know you. You have a perfectly happy life with the girls and me."

He's really trying, I tell myself, to make me happy. Even a month ago, before Nélie's disappearance, I would have been thrilled by all these changes in his work situation. Do I owe it to the children to make this work? Am I kidding myself into thinking I really am talented enough to appeal to serious art collectors?

The questions hang in the air as we finish our meal, heading back to the car. Matt reaches for my hand. I let him take it, the familiar touch bringing me a certain amount of comfort. Tonight, we head to bed and, accustomed to our union, I feel the warmth of his body next to mine. I fall asleep on my side, awakening at three o'clock in the morning with a longing so deep it hurts. I stare at the ceiling and the man next to me and, suddenly, a vision of another pair of eyes pierces my consciousness. There's a part of me Matt does not see and I'm puzzled about that. Why am I having this realization now, not fifteen years ago?

Chapter 16

The month of June passes in an array of outdoor cook-outs, weekends at Nag's Head with friends and doubles tennis matches in the evenings. Laura and Kathryn are both going to camp up in Maine for the month of July. This year, Laura's going to be the counselor for Kathryn's group. I busily help them prepare for their yearly trek north.

"Why hasn't Nélie called or written?" asks Laura. "This is so weird. I can't believe I haven't seen or heard from my own sister in almost two months! What's going on?"

I shrug my shoulders, trying to lighten the mood. "Honey, you've got to understand. Nélie is with her grandfather, getting to know her own family. I don't think she realizes how long it's been. Her grandfather never knew of her existence until a month ago, so he's probably spending lots of time with her and introducing her to other relatives. Nélie's also learning more about her mother."

"I've written her a long letter. Can you mail it for me?" she asks, checking to make sure her name tags are sewn in her socks. She looks up and then says, "I wish she'd come home so things would be back to normal again."

"Oh, sweetie," I reply, "I know you miss her. I do, too. I'm going to call my friend in Paris this week to see if he has any news. Maybe when you get back from camp, we can all go and visit Nélie."

"Really?" she says excitedly. "I hear it's beautiful, with all of the old architecture and the paintings. Could we really do that? Please?"

"I'll talk with your father about it while you're gone."

Why couldn't we take a family trip to Paris? I could bring the girls even if Matt couldn't come. We could visit Nélie and, maybe as a group, tour the city together. This trip might also give me a chance to show my work to Jean.

That night, after everyone else has gone to bed, I sit at my desk, sketching some ideas for pictures, using Nélie's senior portrait as my guide. The movement of the pencil against the drawing paper commands my full attention. I look again at my photograph to go over the line of her nose. There is an empty space in my heart and I long to talk with her to ask her forgiveness. The shock of learning about her past may have worn off by now, so why hasn't she answered my letters? Leaning back in my chair, I sigh before closing my eyes.

"Why don't you come to bed?" asks Matt, standing over me.

"Just a few more minutes," I reply, surveying his T-shirt and sweatpants.

"What are you doing?" he asks, eyeing my sketch of Nélie. "Why do you insist on torturing yourself over her, Lauren? She let you down, not the other way around. Poor little Nélie just found out she's an heiress. We'll probably never hear from her again!" he chides me, leaning back to fold his arms in front of his chest. His look seems smug.

Annoyed at his intrusion, I reply, "Let's not go over this again. I'm working on a sketch for my opening, if you don't mind."

"Come on, Lauren," Matt sighs. "Get real! You have no

formal art background, why in the world are you wasting your time? We don't need the money and you're just setting yourself up to be disappointed. You're not some undiscovered talent just because you studied under Gustave. No one cares. Now, come on, let's go to bed."

The thought, *I hate him*, rolls through my mind. Its eerie presence stuns me. This man, who is supposed to be my soul mate, has not the slightest notion of who I am. I ponder my relationship with Matt. If I play the role of dutiful wife and mother maintaining a clean and nice home, presenting a positive image to the community and involving myself in the proper charities, then our marriage works. When I express views contrary to his idealized version of the perfect wife, he turns ugly, critical, and condescending. Sure, on the surface our marriage seems fine, but I have serious doubts. I miss the way I felt in Paris, and I worry about Nélie. I promise myself to call Jean tomorrow to find out what's going on.

The next morning, Matt and I take Laura and Kathryn to the airport to meet their group, five other girls from this area. As much as I miss them each year, this month will give me a certain amount of time to travel to Paris without worrying about their well-being. Being alone with Matt does not bring me much solace. Uneasiness creeps in as I contemplate the discussion we are soon to have. At least the weekend will pass quickly, since Matt plans on playing golf with his friends.

Matt's attitude serves only to fuel my desire to work harder on my painting. With the kids gone, I have all day to paint. The hours seem to pass too quickly, and often, only the rumbling of my stomach halts my process. My mind feels clear, with images floating inside, longing to be put on paper. The blending of color and light consumes me as I nurture each of my canvases, tending them as if they were small children in need of constant care. My approach has been almost chaotic as I've scattered ideas across several different canvases, trying to find my direction.

Feeling frustrated one morning, I am reluctant to head to the garage. Suddenly, the phone rings.

"Lauren," says Priscilla breathlessly. "Do you have a minute?"

"Yes," I reply. "What is it?"

"I just sold both of your paintings! A woman just came into the shop and adored your work. She bought both of them!"

"Oh, my God!" I cry. "You're kidding! I can't believe it! You really sold both of them?" Unable to help myself, I keep thinking that's at least a thousand dollars for me. I calculate how many wineglasses I'd have to paint to earn that kind of money.

"She even said she'd like to buy more of your work. She's refurbishing her home down in Florida and would like to meet you. You should be very pleased with yourself. Now, I really think you ought to consider putting together a show."

"We'll see," I respond, elated. "Priscilla, thank you so much for everything!"

When I hang up the phone, I can't contain my glee. I jump up and down and shout in my empty kitchen. *I did it!* I cry breathlessly. My exuberance is suddenly dampened, though, when I realize that it's been several days since I contacted Jean. I wonder why he hasn't responded yet.

"Lauren," Priscilla says, "your work seems to be blossoming. I love seeing these projects in motion. I do hope you'll let me help you get started."

I sigh. "I can't tell you how many times I've thought about committing to an opening. But part of me is afraid I'm too old to start now."

"Heavens, no! You're still young, dear. Look how easily I sold your first two paintings!" cries Priscilla. "You have so much talent; it's a shame not to let people enjoy these beautiful paintings."

"My husband thinks I've gone mad now that I spend my

days locked in the garage, painting. I'm not sure where all of this will lead, but I do feel compelled to finish some of these projects."

While there's a ten-year age difference between Priscilla and me, we seem to understand each other. I am pleased that she seems willing to overlook my fifteen-year hiatus from painting and focus on my progress. Summoning up my courage, I decide to phone Jean to check on Nélie.

"Lauren," he says. "I'm glad you called. I'm sorry I haven't gotten back to you, but I've been staying at the château with Louis and I just returned this afternoon. I've spent some time with Nélie."

"Really?" I reply. "Is there something wrong? You sound worried."

"Frankly, Lauren, I am," Jean says somberly. "She doesn't seem like herself. I don't know whether she's having boyfriend trouble or she's upset with what happened between the two of you. She's lost a great deal of weight and she seems subdued. Certainly, I asked her many times if she wanted to talk, but she always refused. Then again, she doesn't know me particularly well. Nevertheless, Louis seems extremely possessive of her, which I can understand to a certain extent, but he won't let her meet with her boyfriend. He claims they need to become 'reacquainted.' I don't know. Maybe I'm worrying over nothing."

"No, no," I cry. "I've spent the last month in limbo trying to figure out what to do. I just didn't feel right leaving things the way they were, but I felt I had no choice. I've written her several letters, but she hasn't written back."

"Perhaps she hasn't received them. As I mentioned, Louis seems wildly possessive of her and won't let her out of his sight most of the time."

"I need to see her. I'm worried about her. How much weight has she lost?"

"Enough for me to notice that she looks thin and pale," says Jean.

"I've got to see her. I'm going to check on available flights. Is there somewhere we can stay nearby? An inn or something?"

"Let me check into it and call you back. Where can I reach you?"

I hesitate before giving him the number at the gallery. "You can call me at this number and let me know. Thanks again for checking on her."

After hanging up the phone, I become aware that Priscilla is standing in the doorway, staring at me. "Is everything all right, Lauren? You look as if you've just received some bad news."

My instincts tell me I can trust her and I explain that I'm worried about my daughter, who is in France with her grandfather. "We had an angry confrontation, you see, when I was over there. It's not been resolved yet, and I feel I need to do something."

"By all means," says Priscilla. "Why don't you fly over there and check on her? That's what I'd do. Nélie's an interesting name. Is it French?"

"Yes," I reply, sharing the whole story with her. Just talking about Nélie with someone who understands my feelings eases my troubled spirit, especially after listening to Matt these past few weeks.

"You're right, Lauren. I'd try one last time. If you can sort things through, I think you'd feel better about leaving her there."

I have almost a thousand dollars of my own money in the bank; I can afford to pay for a plane ticket on my own. Matt shouldn't complain about the cost. But *shouldn't* is the operative word. I had been meaning to tell him I planned to go to Paris in August, but I was delaying the inevitable confrontation as long as possible. It looks as if I'll have to address it with him in the next day.

I'm worried about Nélie. India's warnings come to mind, and hearing that Louis is very controlling doesn't surprise me. As I think back to the night at the château, it seemed rather odd that a disgruntled employee went so far as to threaten his life. How often does that happen? I'll wait until I hear back from Jean before I broach the subject of Nélie and this trip with Matt.

Our détente has lasted for several weeks, simply because we have avoided certain subjects. Matt doesn't mention Nélie's name and it pains me. It's as if she has ceased to exist for him. He seems glad to be relieved of her presence. Some days, I find myself alone in her room, touching familiar things. I hate feeling so out of touch with my daughter. I hate that we haven't spoken in weeks. Is she all right? This uncertainty makes me feel so helpless, even though my painting and weekly visits to the gallery have helped me to mask my frustrations.

When Jean calls, he sounds even more worried than before. "I've talked with Louis. He refuses to include you in a visit to the château again despite your relationship with Nélie. I'm sorry Lauren, I tried."

"I have to see her, Jean. Something's not right."

Jean sighs. "I found a little inn in the town where you can stay."

It dawns on me that without Paige, I will be completely alone in this endeavor. Indecision gnaws at me.

"Thank you, Jean. I'm going to call Paige to see if she'll come with me."

"I want to help, Lauren. I'm worried about Nélie."

"All right. My other girls have just left for camp for a month. I'll make arrangements to fly over again on the next plane. I'll phone you once I know what we're doing."

"Very good, then," Jean adds quietly. "I'll wait to hear from you."

While I feel strong, a ball of fear forms in my stomach. *Please let Matt support me on this one,* I pray, knowing the answer.

"You're what?" he repeats, his look incredulous.

"Going to Paris on the next flight out. I'm worried about Nélie. My friend, Jean, says she's lost weight and appears pale and unusually quiet. I need to know that she's okay."

He slams his fist on the counter. "I can't believe this! Nélie made her choice when she moved out of here. She didn't give a damn about us—she just left with no indication of her whereabouts after all we've done for her. You chase her across the Atlantic Ocean to find she's living with some boyfriend she met a few months ago. The kid is just like her mother."

"That's not fair, Matt!" I cry. "Don't you dare criticize either of them!"

"Wake up, Lauren!" he shouts. "India was a spoiled, selfish rich bitch who didn't give a damn about anybody but herself. She certainly didn't care about the family she destroyed when she had her affair with Julian—nor did she ever take responsibility for Nélie! You were the one she used to pick up after her."

"How dare you! India was my best friend. I've always loved Nélie. That's your problem. I always wanted you to love her and treat her like your own daughter. But you never could, could you? You were always too busy calculating how much it cost to raise her."

"Damn it! I work for a living. I paid for everything, Lauren, her clothes, her private schools, the dance lessons you insisted she have. She wasn't my kid, for God's sake! What did you want from me?"

Tears run freely down my cheeks. "I wanted you to love her, just like you do Laura and Kathryn. Why was that so hard? Are you so arrogant that you couldn't get past the fact that she wasn't your own flesh and blood?"

"I did more for that kid than anyone else in her family and

she never appreciated it. She was born a snob just like her mother."

"And you had no idea why she left. She knew how you felt. She *heard* you every night, complaining about the cost of her care. Do you have any idea how much that must have hurt a young girl, especially one who was an orphan? How could you be so cruel?"

"I don't have to listen to this. You're not going to blame me for anything. Where's her real father? I don't see him anywhere. Julian never offered to give us one dime for Nélie's care, did he? Yet, you hold him up on some pedestal like he's some hero. He did nothing, Lauren."

"How much?" My voice sounds like a hiss, unrecognizable even to my own ears.

"What are you talking about?"

"How much did Nélie's care cost over the years? I want a number and I want it now! A hundred thousand dollars, perhaps two hundred thousand. How much?" Matt shakes his head in disbelief. While we are separated by the center island that measures only a couple of feet, our emotional distance is beyond measure. I stare at him, seeing someone who repulses me. "I'll give you a check for the full amount."

He glares at me, his nostrils flaring. For a moment, I'm afraid he's going to leap over the island and strike me. "She left you money, didn't she?"

"Millions," I spit out, wanting to hurt him. "It's locked in a bank in Switzerland and you'll never have any of it unless you do as I say. I still control Nélie's money."

"You bitch!" he cries. "How could you betray me like this? All these years, I've been working my tail off and you had *her* money all along. What's wrong with you? Are you demented or something?"

"I must have been when I married you," I shoot back. "It's over, Matt. And you'll not see a dime of that money unless you agree to give me custody of Laura and Kathryn."

"What?" he cries.

"You heard me," I say, feeling stronger now. "I can afford to give you a handsome settlement. If not, you'll not see a penny. The choice is yours."

He turns and walks out the door, slamming it behind him. I take a deep breath and sigh. It's over, I tell myself, and I refuse to look back. In a way, I'm so shocked by myself that I don't feel a thing, yet. For some reason, the house seems eerie. On trembling limbs, I walk over to lock the kitchen door. Matt's anger frightens me and I don't want to be alone. Checking my watch, I make the inevitable phone call to Paige.

"Paige," I wail. "I need you. Can I come stay?"

"Are you okay, Lauren?"

"Matt and I just had a terrible argument. I'm afraid to be alone. He was furious."

"Where are the girls?"

"They've gone to Maine, to camp there."

"Pack up your things and come on. We're off to a cocktail party now, but we'll be back before you get here."

Feeling a strange sense of déjà vu, I run upstairs to pack, not once thinking about the enormity of what I've just done. As if on automatic pilot, I fill two suitcases full of belongings and race back downstairs. I figure I'll call my mother once I get to New York. I can already hear her voice; she'll probably tell me I've lost my mind, just as Matt did a few minutes ago. For the first time in fifteen years, I feel that I am in control of my destiny.

I reach the kitchen to find Matt standing there. Surprised by his presence, I scream. His eyes narrow and he places his hands on his hips. "Where do you think you're going, Lauren?"

"None of your business, Matt. I think we've said everything for now."

"Have we?" he replies quietly. "I'm sorry for losing my temper. I still love you, Lauren. We have two children together. Remember that?" His humble apology does not deter me from leaving. Nor do I trust his motives.

"Goodbye," I say, firmly. He takes hold of my arm.

"Don't forget what I said," he says again, remorse written all over his face.

I'm ready to snap, *Why don't you take an anger management class while I'm gone?* It sounds like something Paige would say. Instead, I nod, walking out the door.

After a quick flight to New York, I arrive outside of Paige's apartment building feeling as if I were reliving a bad dream. Upstairs, Paige's housekeeper greets me, saying she'll be back in an hour. I make myself at home, contemplating my future with and without Matt. Despite his apology, the scene replays itself over again in my mind. *You bitch! How could you betray me like this?*

What feels like moments later, Paige waltzes in looking festive in a cherry-printed dress and red high heels.

"You made it!" she says, walking over to give me a hug. The smell of expensive perfume, cigarettes and wine emanates from her. She perches on the bed across from me. "I can't sit in this dress," she admits, "or I'll split one of the seams. I just need to lean here like this."

"You look great, but don't you want to change?" I ask.

"Of course not," she scoffs. "Do you have any idea how much this thing cost me? I need to get my money's worth out of it, so I'll wear it for at least another hour."

"Oh," I mouth, sighing. "Here we go again! Jean says that Nélie looks awful. I'm going to fly over there and check on her."

Paige reaches into her handbag for a cigarette. "I take it Matt didn't take too kindly to your leaving again?" She lights up, drawing in a mouthful of smoke, and exhales, keeping her movements to a minimum.

"He's not who I thought he was," I say, leaning forward in my seat.

"I could have told you that fifteen years ago," Paige offers, raising one eyebrow. "I'm having my niece's bridal shower here tomorrow afternoon. I can fly out tomorrow night. I'll give you the key to my apartment so you can stay there."

"Thank you, Paige. You're wonderful."

It really hasn't hit me yet that I'm walking away from a fifteen-year marriage. Should I be consulting a divorce lawyer? A headache is forming in my temples, pounding layers of guilt over my decision.

"I'm sure Nélie is just fine, Lauren. She's probably having boyfriend trouble. Maybe Louis won't let her see Richard as much as she wants to. Ah, the irony of it all." She flicks her ashes into a silver ashtray on the night table. "She's found her long-lost grandfather but she'd prefer to be spending her time with her boyfriend. Louis probably won't let her out of his sight. I've got it! Nélie is suffering from acute boredom."

"Paige," I exclaim, "you have an answer for everything."

She chuckles. "Maybe not the *right* answer, but an answer just the same."

The flight to Paris seems unusually long as I worry about Nélie. It's been nearly eight weeks. Unable to sleep, I grope for the ear phones to listen to some classical music. Right now I would welcome even Paige's litany of complaints for amusement. An eternity later, as the plane lands, I immediately reach for my compact to brush my hair, powder my nose, apply perfume and attempt to remove all traces of travel fatigue from my face. Smoothing my black pants, I grab my bag from the overhead.

Jean's waiting for me. We decide to have a quick drink before he takes me back to Paige's apartment. Jean parks the car, then takes my hand. "It's good to see you again."

The touch of his hand makes me feel safe again.

"Most people don't stay in the city during August. They're in the south of France, sunning themselves on a beach."

Emerging from the car, I say, "You were kind to stay in the city to help me find Nélie."

He nods. "It's no problem. I'm in the middle of finishing up a commission."

Moments later, we're seated in a café, talking like old friends. "What have you been painting?" I ask, relaxing and taking a sip of my wine. It seems the most normal thing in the world to be back in Paris again, having just left my husband at home. Greensboro seems a million miles away. Have I really escaped?

"A sunset. I've wanted to experiment more with color these days, brilliant color, to make my landscapes less traditional, perhaps more realistic." He signals to the waiter, ordering us a light meal of cheese and bread.

Blushing, I blurt out, "I've painted some things, too. God, I never realized how much I missed my work! Anyway, I contacted a dealer in Greensboro who thought my paintings were good. She ended up by selling two of them. She actually wants me to do a show for her."

"Don't act so surprised. Although I've never seen your work, I trust that Gustave knew what he was talking about," he says, nodding in approval. "You've accomplished a great deal in the past few weeks, Lauren. I'm proud of you."

His compliment seems so natural. Flustered, I think of all of the years Matt criticized me at every turn.

"Thank you," I reply easily. "But I have no training. It would be foolish of me to say otherwise." I look down at my feet for a moment, avoiding his gaze.

"What does training have to do with talent? There are many successful artists who lack formal training. Don't let that stop you."

"You're right," I reply, nodding. I contemplate whether I can successfully do a show. The idea of creating so many canvases seems daunting, yet my excitement is helping me feel less afraid. In any case, I'm not here to talk about my work. "Now, back to Nélie. Paige should be here tomorrow morning. We'll figure out a plan then."

Later, Jean drops me off at Paige's, where I settle in. I mention that I want to go to India's apartment just one more time to see if it's intact. It would be wonderful to show it to Nélie.

That night, I fall into bed, sleeping soundly despite my guilt at feeling so relieved to be away from my husband. How am I ever going to tell Laura and Kathryn? Yet, since standing up to Matt, I feel so alive again. I don't know why I gave away all of my power to him. It was as if I had been in some sort of trance that was suddenly broken by Nélie's disappearance. The strength of my love for her has given me courage that I never thought I had.

The next morning, key in hand, I make my way to India's apartment, hoping Julian hasn't decided to remove everything before I could show it to Nélie. As I enter the courtyard, I look up to see Sophie emerging from her apartment. Anxious to say hello, I dart up the stairs, walking briskly to greet her.

"Sophie," I call, waving to her.

She halts, turning to face me, while her little dog barks his disapproval of my intrusion. "Lauren," she answers. "I had wondered when you would return. How have you been, my dear?"

"Very well, thank you. You look well, Sophie. I trust you're having a pleasant summer." I lean my hand on the rail, catching my breath.

She adjusts her straw hat. "Of course. I enjoy each day I'm alive. When you get to be my age, you look at time as a gift. I've wondered if you ever found your daughter?"

"Yes." I smile, not wanting to go into detail. "She's well, staying in the south of France with her grandfather. You know kids these days. She seemed to think leaving me a note was sufficient cause for me not to worry about her!"

"I'm happy for you both. She seemed like such a lovely young girl from the picture." She pauses, rubbing her chin. "You know, there's something I've wanted to show you, but I forgot about it last time you were here. That's what old age does. Do you have a minute, dear?"

"Of course," I reply with a gulp, fearing that she's going to head inside to put on the tea kettle.

She opens her apartment door again, explaining to the dog that he can relieve himself in just a few minutes. I wait in the corridor as she begins opening a series of cabinets and closets. "Now, where is it?" she asks aloud. "It has been almost fifteen years!"

"What are you looking for?" I call, watching her retreating form head into what appears to be her bedroom.

"A box," she replies. "A Gucci shoe box, to be exact."

What in the world is she doing? I ponder, checking my watch. Jean and I are due to head to the château to find Nélie in about an hour.

"Here it is!" she says with a triumphant gleam in her eye. "I'll bet you thought that I'd never find it." She brushes some dust from it, handing it to me. "I thought you might be interested in seeing these things. A young man came to the complex with it a few months after your friend's death. He looked lost, so I offered to help him. As I recall, he was a strange-looking fellow with big ears and a cleft chin, said he worked for the government or something. But no matter, he gave me this box to give to the appropriate person. Apparently, they couldn't find anyone else to give it to. He said I could throw it away if I didn't find the right person. I suppose it contains some of your friend's belongings." She pauses, rubbing her temple. "You know, I do remember that the man mentioned the fact that she was so beautiful, too young to die."

My puzzlement increases as I look at the box, wondering what could possibly be inside. "Could these things have been recovered from the ocean?"

"I don't know," she answers. "I've forgotten what's in there. I don't know why I didn't throw it away. "

"Thank you, Sophie. I am going to head down to India's apartment and take a look. You've already taught me how to get in. I wanted to bring Nélie back in the next few days to show her some of her mother's things. It would mean a lot to her," I say, gripping the box in both hands.

The dog barks several times, reminding Sophie of her promise to take him for a walk. "It looks like I've delayed long enough. Good to see you, my dear." She eyes my tight grip on the box. "I hope seeing India's things again doesn't upset you too much. I'll be back shortly, if you need someone to talk to."

"You're very kind," I say, walking out behind her. "I'll be all right."

Clutching the box, I follow Sophie back downstairs before heading to India's apartment. My key works, allowing me easy entry to the past. All of the windows are closed and the curtains are drawn. The faint scent of ammonia permeates the air, indicating that the housekeeper has recently left. I immediately open the drapes to let some light into the place. The windows come next. I unlock one, opening it up to the courtyard.

The box waits for me on the coffee table, stirring up feelings of fear and sadness. What lies inside? A soaked license, some sort of clothing, one of her rings? I take a deep breath, thinking of Sophie's offer to talk. With trembling hands, I remove the lid, preparing myself to see India's last earthly possessions. Inside, I find her brown Louis Vuitton wallet, a set of gold rings, and a billfold, all perfectly intact. Looking at her license, I notice that it says India St. Clair, not Vernon. I remember when India had her last name legally changed in college, after her fight with her father. It was her ultimate revenge to take her mother's maiden name. Was it just another act of rebellion? Rubbing my fingers over the grainy leather of the wallet, I remember India, wishing that things had turned out differently. Frowning, I open the billfold to reveal an unused plane ticket tucked inside. "What's this?" I say aloud, thumbing through it. The information jumps off the page. Turning it over, I see that it is for Flight 974 to New York City, leaving on March 18—the day her plane went down. *What is her wallet doing here?* I wonder. I flip through her charge cards, license and a card for a local salon indicating that she'd had an appointment a week later. These are her things, I know, but they look perfectly intact. Even if they were in her purse, they would have had some sort of damage if they had been in the ocean. What could this possibly mean? I immediately grab the ticket and India's wallet, stuffing them into my black handbag. Suddenly, I wonder if India is still alive somewhere. Could she have survived the crash and be walking around with amnesia? The idea seems far-fetched. Surely, though, she would have been treated somewhere and the doctors would have tried to find her family. My mind reels at the implications of this find. A piece of this puzzle is missing and I intend to find it.

Anxious to talk with Jean, I race to the gallery, hoping to grab his attention for a moment. Breathless, I arrive there and ask his assistant to locate him for me.

"He'll be with you in just a few minutes," she says, offering me a cup of coffee, which I decline. Trying to distract myself for a moment, I walk around the gallery, looking at some of the new works he's acquired since my last visit.

"Lauren," says Jean, coming up behind me. "Is everything all right?"

"I'm sorry to interrupt," I say, turning to face him. "But could I talk with you alone for a moment?"

"Certainly," he says, motioning me into his office.

"Remember I told you about his wonderful woman named Sophie who let me into India's apartment? Well, it seems she's had a box of India's possessions in her apartment for the last fifteen years. I guess she didn't want to throw them away. Anyway, look what I found."

Removing the items from my purse, I show him India's wallet, rings and the plane ticket. He frowns, looking at me. "Why would these still exist?" he asks, examining each one. "They seem to be in perfect condition. If they had been recovered from the ocean, they would have had some water damage, wouldn't you think?"

"That's not all," I say, holding up the unused plane ticket for his inspection.

"It's odd," he says, looking at the date of the ticket. Scanning the information again, he turns a perplexed stare at me. "What do you think?"

"Is there any way she could still be alive?" I ask, careful not to show the drop of hope that has crept into my consciousness.

"Highly unlikely," he responds, rubbing his chin with his hand. "Maybe India didn't die in the plane crash. Maybe she was murdered."

Shock overwhelms me. "Murdered? By whom? Why?" Suddenly, the memory of the night of "Isu's" opening comes to mind, when Madame DuBusé threatened India.

"The only person who wanted India dead would have been Madame DuBusé. But isn't that obvious?" I ask, sitting down in the leather seat across from Jean. I feel hot and sweaty, with stabbing pains in my stomach.

Jean picks up the plane ticket, looking over it again. "If India had gotten on that plane, the end result would have been the same. She'd still be dead. There's a piece missing here. An error was made when someone delivered these goods to her apartment. Or were they meant to be found?" Jean puts his hand on the phone. "I think we should talk to Julian. Why wasn't he with India in the first place? Do you remember where she was going?"

"She wanted to attend her childhood friend's thirtieth

birthday party in New York. You know how India was; she liked to come and go as she pleased. As I recall, Julian had to go elsewhere on business. India was annoyed that he had canceled at the last minute."

Jean picks up the phone to dial Julian's office. He identifies himself, telling the receptionist that it's extremely important that he get in touch with him. He shakes his head as I listen to him repeating that Julian will return around one o'clock today.

As I look around Jean's office area while he talks, the signs of his success catch my eye. The space is neat, clean and modern. The black leather and steel mix well together. A Toulouse Lautrec painting of the Moulin Rouge hangs in the background. His gallery is like the one where Gustave used to show his work. I dream that someday my work might be good enough to display here.

Jean hangs up. He says, "I have one last meeting before we head out to the château to find Nélie. Are you okay? I don't have any answers right now. We're just going to have to wait to talk with Julian. I have a feeling that his wife might know something more. Let's make photocopies of the ticket, the contents of the wallet and the rings and lock these up later."

"I'll do that if you'll just point me in the direction of the copier."

He walks over, rubbing my arms to comfort me. "It's going to be all right, Lauren. We'll find the truth."

He hugs me close. The smooth scent of sandalwood assails my senses. I think again about the night of his opening, over fifteen years ago. I was young and innocent, never once believing that my life could change so dramatically as it did with India's fatal crash.

Looking at my watch, I decide to check in with Paige to see if she's going to make the seven o'clock flight out of Kennedy Airport. When there's no answer on her home phone, I dial her cellular phone. She answers breathlessly; she wants to delay her trip one more day unless I need her. I assure her that I'm fine and that Jean is going to help me contact Nélie.

Jean secures us a meeting with Julian at his office hours later. In the luxurious waiting room, I see a statue of Ganesha, which I didn't notice on my earlier visit. "Jean, look," I say, smiling for the first time in hours. "Julian has Ganesha, the 'God of Good Fortune' here."

Jean nods, observing the piece. "I found this for Julian years ago on a trip to India. I've always liked it. When Louis saw it, he asked me to find him a similar one. He's rather proprietary about it now. He can be very territorial when it comes to his possessions."

"I hope Nélie doesn't fit into that category," I remark, wondering if my daughter is all right.

When he ushers us inside the white office, Julian has a distinctive frown marring his features. "What's this all about, Jean? I've never known you to be an alarmist."

Jean shakes his head. "I hope it's nothing, Julian. Lauren found some things of India's this morning." He explains about Sophie and the shoe box she had saved. "We have reason to believe that India wasn't on that plane that crashed. Take a look at this." Jean takes out the ticket, offering it to Julian. He then shows him India's wallet and rings.

Julian's hands tremble as he caresses the items. "Yes," he says. "I gave these rings to her. How can this be, if the plane went down in the ocean?"

"Precisely," says Jean. "There's a piece of the story missing here. I was hoping you might make some inquiries in town. It sounds as if a government official delivered the items, but I can't be sure. We want to know why they exist. Where might they have come from?"

Julian's olive skin looks pale as he clutches the objects in his hand. "You can be sure that I'll do some checking around.

I'll let you know the moment I find something. Where can you be reached?"

Jean apprises Julian of our whereabouts over the next few days. He makes no mention of Nélie or whether we've found her and Julian doesn't ask. Even Sophie, a complete stranger, remembered to ask about Nélie—why couldn't her own father take just a little bit of interest?

Once inside the car, Jean turns to face me. "He knows something more than he's telling us. Maybe that's why he's stayed away from Nélie."

Sitting forward, I say, "You can't think Julian had anything to do with this."

"I don't know," Jean shrugs. "I'm certain he'll question Madame DuBusé before the day is out."

"Could she have killed India?" I say, fearing exactly that.

"My hunch is someone else was involved. But who?"

I shake my head, trying to grasp the magnitude of this mystery. Certainly, it pains me to think that India's death was not an accident. I close my eyes against the sun's glare.

Chapter 17

I speculate on what Nélie will think when Jean tells her I'm here. I've missed her terribly, yet still feel wounded by her angry words. Right now, I can't help but feel a sense of dread all over again. Poor Nélie—hasn't she endured enough without me soon having to tell her I don't think her mother's death was an accident? How am I ever going to get her away from Louis, who probably hates me?

The inn's charm is lost on me as I grapple with engineering my next meeting with Nélie. With his usual grace, Jean books us into two rooms down the hall from each other. Despite the mystery surrounding India's death, my concern over Nélie's well-being is paramount.

After a brief lunch downstairs, we devise a plan that seems simple enough. Jean will make a social visit to the château this afternoon, when he'll try to tell Nélie I am nearby so that we may arrange to meet. There is no way I can gain entry to the château or possibly get inside unnoticed. Our meeting would have to be tonight, perhaps adjacent to the vineyard. Nélie will have to want to see me for this to work easily. If not, I'm not sure what I'll do.

How has Louis treated her? A nagging feeling about Louis keeps surfacing, one that is so heinous that it terrifies me. Could he have been involved in India's death? Perhaps not directly, but he could have had some type of explosive planted in the cargo hold. He is a powerful man. There's no denying that he could have carried out such a maneuver. Now I have such fear for Nélie's safety that I find myself pacing the floor nervously. I consider whether I could find my own way over to the château, but I reconsider, reminding myself that Jean knows what he's doing.

Time moves agonizingly slowly. I notice the cracking plaster on the wood frame of the window, the carvings of a sheep and a lion on the dresser, and the white stucco ceiling that slopes to the left. I pace the room, trying to occupy myself by reading a fashion magazine, scratching notes on a piece of paper, staring out the window at the partial mountain view, and praying. Mostly, I pray that Louis has not harmed Nélie in any way or poisoned her mind against me. India was such a free spirit that his possessive nature must have played a part in her decision not to have any contact with him. Again, I worry, uncertain whether her rejection might have fueled a deep-seated hatred of his only child. Was it strong enough for him to plan her death? If I hadn't found the unused ticket, her death would have been the perfect crime.

The sound of the key in the lock snaps me out of my musings. Jean arrives, a scowl darkening his features. His face appears tense and drawn.

"What is it?" I ask, practically jumping out of the chair to run toward him.

He rubs his hands over his eyes as if to blot out the afternoon. "I saw Louis this afternoon, but he wouldn't let me see Nélie. He seemed distracted, rambling on about these philosophical concepts of life and death. I've never seen him behave in such a confused state of mind. He kept referring to Nélie as India, saying his long-lost daughter had returned." He walks into the room, puts his key on the dresser and takes a seat on the edge of the bed. Rubbing his beard, he sighs. "I hope this works, Lauren. I'm starting to get very worried that

Louis is holding Nélie prisoner in her room. He won't let her see anyone. That way, he says, she can't escape."

"Oh, my God," I say, absorbing the seriousness of Jean's findings. "How could this have happened? I should have forced her to come with me two months ago, kicking and screaming, if I had to."

Jean touches my arm. "You must believe, Lauren, that I had no idea Louis would behave this way. No one has seen her in days."

My heart thuds in my chest at this piece of information. "What did you do?"

"I gave a note to a housekeeper named Sara whom I recognized from my earlier stay. Who knows if she'll give it to Nélie? She may take it to Louis, which would really be a disaster." He wipes his brow. "Is it hot in here, or is it me?"

"Both. There's no breeze today," I say. "What are we going to do?"

"My note told Nélie that we would meet her in India's playhouse, as you suggested. I thought Louis wouldn't pay much attention to that area. Let's hope Nélie has had enough time to explore the grounds so that she can figure out where to go." He gets up and walks over the window, trying to cool himself. "We can leave at dusk. I know how to slip into the garden through a back pathway I discovered years ago. We have to hope that Nélie receives the note. More importantly, let's hope she can find a way out without Louis knowing."

"Why hasn't anyone said anything or alerted the authorities?"

Jean turns to face me. "You must remember, Louis is a powerful man. He also provides one of the main sources of employment in this community. No one here is in a position to challenge his authority. It's as if he has his little kingdom here."

"No one is that powerful," I say, wanting to believe my own words.

After changing into dark clothing, we proceed to the château. The sun wends its way slowly across the sky, unmindful of my desire for complete darkness. Jean takes us down several back roads to the outer reaches of Louis's property. Jean uses the small flashlight on his key chain to help us as we make our way through the overgrown path. If the situation weren't so serious, I would laugh aloud at this novice attempt at abduction.

It is hot. The air feels humid, making my skin clammy. It smells like summer, a combination of dry grass, roses and mountain air. The only sound I hear is that of Jean's movements in front of me as I stay close behind him. "It's about two miles from here," he whispers before turning around. My running shoes enable me to keep pace with him, and I'm grateful for once for my practical taste in clothing.

Our steps are even, steady and rhythmic. I try to stay calm by focusing my mind on the present, not the past or fearful imaginings of the future. An inane ditty comes to mind and I recite the words over and over in my mind. *One, Two, Three—Nélie will soon be free. Four, Five, Six—We'll get out of this fix. Seven, Eight, Nine—She's just fine.* Each minute ticks by so slowly as we move closer to her. Suddenly, Jean stops, waiting for me to catch up to him. "See, down there. There's a break in the fence. It's another half-mile walk from there."

Quickening our pace, we move forward cautiously, wondering what awaits us on this dark, quarter-moon night. My breath quickens as I match Jean's strides. We finally reach the small hole in the barbed wire fence that's covered by brush on both sides. "I can't believe you found this!" I exclaim, marveling at his ingenuity.

"You're not going to believe that I was out wandering the grounds looking at the light for a canvas. I backed into the bush and fell backwards into the hole. I had completely forgotten about it until now. Fortunately, I also forgot to tell

Louis that it exists," he says, wiping his hand on his black T-shirt.

"What if she doesn't get your note?" I cry, panic setting in.

He takes my hands in his. "We'll wait all night and leave at dawn."

Once we reach the playhouse, we crawl inside, hoping that no one will see us. Louis employs several guards, but they have never appeared to be overly efficient. Crouched in the playhouse, my ditty plays in my ears. *One, Two, Three— Nélie will soon be free. Four, Five, Six—We'll get out of this fix. Seven, Eight, Nine—She's just fine.*

We pass the hours in near-silence, each lost in our own musings, waiting and listening for any movement outside of the playhouse. With my knees tucked up to my chin, I tap my foot impatiently, hoping that Nélie will arrive. Suddenly, we hear the sound of footsteps outside. Jean grabs my arm, motioning for me to be quiet. The door is flung open. Nélie arrives, sobbing when she sees us.

"You're here!" she cries, clutching me. Her tears drench my shirt.

Feeling her frail form, I grab her face, looking into her eyes. It's too dark to see her clearly, but I can tell they look haunted. Why did I allow her to stay with him? "Are you all right?" I say.

"He's nuts!" she says, burying her head in my shirt. "A complete lunatic!"

Jean interrupts us. "Nélie?" he asks. "We've got a two-mile walk to the car, are you strong enough to make it?"

She nods. "I just want to get out of here, please! Hurry, before he finds out I'm gone!"

With no time to lose, we race into the darkness. Nélie clutches my hand. She seems weak, not the strong, athletic girl who led her lacrosse team to the state championships last spring. Nonetheless, she keeps moving, her fear propelling her forward. The night remains quiet, although I expect an alarm to sound any minute. Fortunately, thanks to Jean, our bags are in the car so we can return to Paris immediately.

Crawling through the hole, I feel the wire scratch my belly and my arms, but I don't care. I know I must be bleeding some because I feel the sticky wetness on my shirt. I grab hold of Nélie's hand just to be sure she's all right. The sight of the car, untouched in our hiding place, brings tears to my eyes.

"You may need to give me a slight push to get it out," he says. I nod, observing Nélie's thin form, thinking she looks as if she hasn't eaten a proper meal in weeks. Seeing the direction of my gaze, she says, "I'm all right, Mom, really." She starts to cry again. "Thank you for coming to get me. And after all those terrible things I said to you."

Interrupting our conversation, Jean says, "Let's get out of here!" We immediately return to the task at hand, getting behind the car as Jean pushes on the accelerator. After a few good pushes, the car slides into place and we hop into the backseat. I hold Nélie close, trusting that soon enough, we'll talk about what happened. For now, my daughter is safe in my arms where she belongs. She puts her head on my shoulder, promptly dozing off. I rub her hair to soothe her troubled spirit, which I know will take time to heal.

When we return to Paige's apartment, Jean tells me not to answer the door for anyone. He says he'll bring us some food within the hour. "This is the least likely place for Louis to look for Nélie. I'm going to call Julian. I want to know about his findings and see what he knows about Louis Vernon." Unmindful of Nélie's presence, I hug Jean before he waves goodbye. Nélie watches me from the door, a quizzical expression on her face.

"Where are we?" she asks, yawning and stretching.

"Paige's apartment. Remember her? She was also a good friend of your mother's," I say, opening the refrigerator door to find something for us to munch on while we await Jean's return. "Are you tired?" I ask, going over to give my baby a hug.

"Oh, Mom," she weeps into my arms. "How could I have been so stupid? Why didn't I listen to you? I know you'd never do anything to hurt me. Now I know why my mother refused to see him."

I hug her tightly, trying to blot out the memory of these past few weeks. "He's just a lunatic," she says. "At the end, he would lock me in my room, telling me I couldn't ever escape him the way India did. It was like I was one of his possessions," she cries harder. "And Richard, who knows what he told him? I know he threatened to kill him one night."

"You're safe now, Nélie," I say, stroking her hair. "I'm here. You'll always be my little girl, no matter what."

She breaks away. "How can you ever forgive me after what I said? I didn't mean it, I swear I didn't! I was so angry that you didn't tell me the truth." She wipes her nose. "Now I know why."

"I never meant to hurt you, Nélie. I just wanted you to be old enough to understand. Some relationships are complicated."

She laughs as we break apart. "Complicated?" she says, walking over to find a tissue. "That's an understatement. How did my mother deal with it all?"

She hands me a tissue and I wipe my eyes. "India very rarely spoke of her father. When she did, she warned me to keep you away from him. She was very clear that if anything ever happened to her, she wanted me to raise you." We walk into the living room arm-in-arm, sitting next to each other on the couch. "There's so much to say." I pause, realizing that Nélie is going to have to deal with the truth.

"What is it?" she says, looking at me.

I look at her skinny body in shorts and shirt. Her weight loss makes her look years younger than seventeen. "I found some things of your mother's yesterday. Jean and I have been very upset about it."

She frowns, taking my hand. "I can handle it, Mom. What?"

"I went to India's apartment, you know, the one I told you about. There's a lady named Sophie whose been there forever. She's had a box of India's things in her apartment for the last fifteen years, if you can believe it. Someone had delivered that box after the crash. When I opened it, I found India's plane ticket, a wallet and some rings Julian gave her."

Nélie is quiet for a moment. "You mean she wasn't on the plane?" She shakes her head, covering her eyes with her hands.

"No," I say quietly. "Jean and I are trying to figure out what happened. We're not sure if your grandfather was involved or not."

With a maturity I had not seen before, Nélie straightens up, gazing directly into my eyes. "It wouldn't surprise me one bit," she says. "If he's guilty, I want to see him pay. How can we prove it?"

"I don't know. We may never be able to prove anything," I say, sighing heavily. "The most important thing for me is that you're safe."

"I love you, Mom," Nélie says, hugging me fiercely. She starts crying again. "You're the best."

I try to control the lump in my throat. Tears flow down my cheeks. "I love you too, Nélie." *You'll always be my little bunny.*

After a long silence, we break apart. Nélie looks at me. "I need to see my mother's apartment."

"Now?" I say. "Jean will be back with some food shortly. You should eat something before I take you over there. Are you sure you're up to it?"

"Yes," she replies. "I'm ready."

Jean drops off our food on his way to his meeting with

Julian. I tell him we'll be at the apartment if he needs to find me this afternoon. He nods, looking troubled. "I told him about rescuing Nélie," he says. "He was extremely upset. He knows something. He's going to meet me at a café now." Jean squeezes my hand before he departs. "I want you to use Paige's driver to take you over there. Why don't you call her and get his name, and have him wait outside for you both?"

"Yes," I reply. Bringing in the bag filled with croissants, I place them on a plate.

"I still can't believe you found me. Where's Matt?"

"We'll talk more about Matt later."

"I'm surprised you were able to get here." She pauses. "I mean, how did you get away?"

"It's a long story, but we have a lot of talking to do."

"Oh," she says soberly. Then, she blurts out, "Why didn't Julian marry my mother?"

"He loved her, Nélie. I'm certain of it. Perhaps his wife was too powerful to let him divorce her for another woman."

While we finish our meal, Nélie plies me with a host of questions about India, ones I am ready to answer. She wants to know little things, such as India's favorite color and her favorite song. After a few more minutes, I hold my hands up. "I need to take you to the apartment. Your answers are there, Nélie." I pick up our plates, feeling stuffed. "I'll call Paige's driver and see if he can take us over there. I think he actually lives right nearby." Luckily, I reach Paige in New York, who volunteers to send the driver over immediately. She's thrilled to learn that Nélie is safe, but I choose not to tell her about the plane ticket yet. After a few minutes, she says, "Matt called me looking for you. He sounds very upset, far from the conceited man I remember."

"What did you tell him?"

"Nothing," she replies. "I would have liked to tell him that it was too little, too late, but I refrained. You would have been proud of me."

"Good," I say.

"He said he plans to fly over to find you, to apologize," she says. "He's left me four messages already. What should I tell him if he calls again, which he will, knowing him."

"Tell him to book a room somewhere. Where? Do you know any place across town?"

"There's a little inn over by the Musée somewhere—it's relatively inexpensive for Paris. That should make him happy," she adds with a chuckle. "I can't remember the name, but I can look it up. I'll leave the name on your machine so you can contact him. This time, if he wants to talk, he'll have to wait for you for a change. Serves him right," she says, exhaling. "Or I don't have to call him back at all. I can tell my housekeeper to tell him I've left the country for good."

"No," I say, filled with remorse. "He's the father of my children. We're going to need to talk to sort things through."

"Don't let him talk you into anything," she warns.

"I'll be fine, Paige. Thank you so much for the apartment, and for your concern. I can't wait until you get here."

"Me too. I'll call you with that name and my flight plans."

Fifteen minutes later, Paige's driver, whom I recognize from my last visit, arrives. Nélie and I take a seat in the back of the town car. As I observe her profile, it pains me to see her bony elbows and collarbone and her hollowed-out face. Oblivious to her appearance, Nélie stares out the window, tapping her fingertips on the edge of the leather seat. Once we arrive, I tell the driver to wait while we head into the courtyard.

Nélie's eyes light up as I point out the bench where her mother and I used to sit and sip white wine in the summertime. Once I unlock the door, I realize how little she really knows about her mother.

"It's beautiful," she says, walking inside, reverently touching her mother's things. "And so chic." She walks to the picture of India and Julian on the coffee table, picking it up. "Is this my father?" she says.

I realize she has no idea what he looks like. "Yes," I say. "He was quite handsome."

"They look so happy together, so in love." She traces her fingers lovingly over their faces.

A male voice sounds in the doorway. "We were happy," says Julian, staring at Nélie. "I loved your mother, Nélie, very much."

Nélie's eyes fill with tears. "What are you doing here?" she says.

"Ah Nélie, it's a long, ugly story." He walks over to embrace her.

I feel like I'm intruding on their private time, so I motion Nélie over to me.

"Are you all right?" I whisper, putting my arm around her.

"I'm fine, Mom, really. Would you give us some time alone? I've got a lot I want to talk to him about."

Reluctant to agree, I search her face, seeing a look of determination in her eyes. I decide to let her handle this situation by herself. "One hour," I concede. "I'll send Paige's driver back for you, okay?"

"Thank you," she replies, giving me a hug.

Jean is waiting for me out in the corridor. "I'm going to let them have some time alone together," I whisper as Jean ushers me along. "I hope he'll at least try to explain some things to her. He owes her that much. He's got to see what a beautiful young woman she is."

Jean nods. "Julian has a way of charming everyone. I'm sure Nélie will be caught in his spell before the day is out. But he's never going to be any kind of devoted parent."

I nod, then stop myself, wondering if I made the right decision. Should I go back to the apartment to offer Nélie some moral support? I just don't feel right leaving Nélie alone with Julian. "Jean, can you wait a minute. I'll be right back."

"I'm afraid we have a meeting, Lauren. Madame DuBusé would like to speak with you. I'd like to come with you if you'll let me—especially since we don't know exactly what happened to India."

Feeling the need to assert myself, I say, "She can wait a few minutes." I turn back upstairs, pausing outside the front door which is slightly ajar. I wait for a pause in the conversation, then push the front door open. "Nélie, can you come here for a minute?"

She walks over as Julian eyes me curiously.

"I'm sorry to interrupt. I was worried about you. Are you sure you're okay?" I look at her ashen face, shaky limbs and bewildered expression. The shock of seeing her father for the first time seems to have rattled her completely.

"Not really," she says, her eyes filling with tears. "He was never there for me. Now, he acts like I'm interviewing for a job or something."

"I know, honey," I reply, placing my arm around her. "What do you want to do?"

Julian clears his throat, clearly annoyed at my intrusion.

Nélie turns around to face him, then says, "I'm afraid I need to get going. I forgot that I have somewhere else I need to be. It was nice meeting you," she says too politely, clearly mocking Julian's lack of paternal instincts.

"Of course," he replies, surprised.

We head out the door together and I watch her face for some sign of what she's thinking. She seems so bewildered that I'm afraid to say much.

She turns to me when we reach the courtyard. "Mom, I'd like to go and see Richard right now, if that's okay. I have a lot I need to sort through. I don't want to hurt your feelings or anything."

"No, of course not. Do you know where he is?" While I'm

talking with her, I motion to Jean to show him that I really am coming.

"I called him before we left. He's at his apartment," she says.

I nod in approval. "That's fine with me. We'll talk when you're ready. Paige's driver is waiting for us. I'll have him take you there. Okay?"

"Sure," she nods, giving me a hug. "I love you," she says. "I couldn't have asked for a better mother. I'll call you later on."

After I put Nélie in the car, I turn to Jean who has been waiting patiently for me. It's such a welcome change being around a considerate man. The sun is making me feel warm, but I shudder in anticipation of my meeting with Madame DuBusé. "Now, where were we? I have a funny feeling we're about to find out what happened to India. What did Julian tell you?" I ask as Jean unlocks my car door.

"His story was brief. He knows Madame DuBusé was involved, but still doesn't know who helped her. I think we'll have our answers shortly."

Silence pervades our ride through the streets of Paris. My stomach churns in anticipation. If Louis Vernon conspired with Madame DuBusé, then it's a wonder Nélie is still alive. How could I have left her there, all the while knowing India's warnings? Chilled at the possibilities of what could have happened, I grip my fingers together, trying to remain calm.

I remember the gallery opening when she threatened India. She was so intimidating. She seemed to be a person who delighted in overpowering others. Relieved that Jean is with me, I feel some measure of calm. I am, however, ready for the truth. I owe it to India to find out exactly what happened to end her life.

We arrive at the stone building where Madame DuBusé's family crest is carved over the front entranceway. Jean rings the bell, as I feel a bit queasy at coming face-to-face with this formidable woman. A butler answers the door, ushering us into the front hallway which is grand, yet dark. There's a mosaic on the floor, depicting Aphrodite, the Greek Goddess of Love and her son, a winged Eros on her shoulder.

Jean raises one eyebrow. "Rather ironic, don't you think?" he says, looking around him.

"Have you been here before?" I whisper, feeling as if I were on the inside of a stone fortress. It is quiet, almost too quiet. I hear the shuffle of the butler's feet as he steps across the front hallway to alert Madame DuBusé that she has visitors.

"Once, several years ago," Jean replies, taking in the wall paintings from floor to ceiling.

I look around me at the painted Doric columns and the scenes from the ancient world. It seems so civilized. Somehow, I had expected a wall-sized painting of Napoleon and perhaps his fleur de lis everywhere. Maybe even sketches of some bees, symbols of France's former glory. Indeed, I think a painting of a bumblebee would have been more fitting. The sound of footsteps clicking along the tiled floor interrupts me.

"Madame DuBusé will see Ms. Wright now. Mr. Whitfield, you may wait in the salon to the left." Jean looks at me for approval.

I nod to him that I'll be fine on my own. He walks over, squeezing my arm. He whispers, "Are you sure?"

"Yes," I reply firmly, ready for the interview.

The butler takes me into a back drawing room that is dark, with its brocade curtains mostly drawn. A red Persian rug decorates the floor. Madame DuBusé is seated behind a large mahogany desk. "Come in," she says, offering no other salutation. Her red fingernails point to a seat, which I politely decline.

"So you found the plane ticket," she says with a smirk. "You're feeling quite clever, aren't you, my dear?"

I look at her coiffed, jet-black hair, her stiffly tailored black suit and ruby necklace, suddenly thinking that she should be wearing a witch's hat. "Cleverness has nothing to do with how I feel. I want to know what really happened to India."

"Ah yes, India," she says with a sneer. "The redheaded charlatan who thought she could outmaneuver me. It doesn't matter now. Let's discuss Julian's illegitimate daughter. Nélie, isn't it?" she says, her left eye squinting.

"Yes," I say, holding my ground. "She has no interest in your money or your family name."

"But I'm interested in her," she says, leaning forward in her seat, propping her weight on her elbows, and looking like a bee ready to sting.

Panic sets in when I look at her flat brown eyes. "We're not here to talk about Nélie. I'm here to talk about India. I'm not going to rest until I find out what really happened to her."

"How noble of you, Lauren," she says. "You always were a respectable young girl, unlike your friend. It's a shame you didn't choose your friends more carefully. She didn't care about anyone but herself. I believe everyone gets what they deserve in the end. More importantly, you should have been more careful in whom you chose to marry."

"What are you talking about?" I reply, clenching my hands, thinking the woman is completely crazy.

"Your husband, Matt Wright, was the one ultimately responsible for India's death," she says, standing up to face me.

Things feel a bit fuzzy, but I quickly recover. "Matt," I croak, suddenly feeling light-headed. "You're lying to save yourself."

"I don't deny, my dear, that I was involved. You'll never be able to prove it, of course. But your husband has the answer you seek. You may want to ask him what happened fifteen years ago when India left for the airport. He's the one who took her to her death. Not me."

"Prove it," I snap, anger welling up inside. "He had no motive."

She throws her head back, laughing. I can see the gold fillings in her yellow teeth. "Ah, Lauren, you're so naïve," she says, opening up the drawer to the desk. "Matt Wright was the ideal candidate to help me. His greed far exceeded anything else on his mind. But he failed, so he never did get all of the money promised. Isn't it ironic that he was still so in love with you that, to win your hand, he took on Julian's illegitimate daughter in the bargain. The irony of it all." She takes out a gold St. Christopher's medal and places it on the desk. "Recognize this?"

My hands tremble as I reach for it, remembering the day I asked Matt where it was. He told me he had lost it somewhere. I grab the necklace, clutching its smooth surface in the palm of my hand. I look Madame DuBusé in the eye, unwilling to let her see me crumble to pieces before her.

"You could have stolen it from his apartment," I counter.

"That's possible," she says. "But highly unlikely. She must have pulled it off his neck in a struggle. I had it removed from her personal belongings so no one would ask questions. It didn't suit me to have Matt implicated. You see, the night of that gallery opening, I listened outside the door while you and India were talking. I heard her ask you to raise Nélie. At the time, I also knew Matt wanted to marry you. When I met with Matt the first time, he told me he couldn't afford to pay off his college loans and support you. I found it humorous knowing that Matt would have to raise India's daughter in order to have you.

"In any case, every official I paid off did his or her job, except one. No one would ever have known if that government worker hadn't brought back India's things to her apartment. What a fool he was. I do admit it was my only mistake in an otherwise perfect production."

She rubs her hands together, gazing directly into my eyes.

"This is a copy of the medal. I have the real one in a safe to protect my investment. If you choose to incriminate me in any way, I will see the father of your children behind bars for the rest of his life. The choice is yours, Lauren. To see justice done, you're going to have to give up something. Your girls will be sentenced to a life with a criminal for a parent. It would be quite a stigma for them, don't you think? Is that what you really want, to ruin the lives of your innocent children over an accident?"

Dazed, I manage to spit out, "How can you possibly live with yourself?"

She smiles. "My money provides me with all the comfort I need."

"You're despicable," I say, turning away from her.

"And you, my dear," she says with a laugh, "are a complete fool. Good day."

Feeling as if I were in a trance, I leave the room. As I do so, Jean steps forward to take my arm. Seeing my face, he says, "Lauren, are you all right?"

"No, Jean," I respond, my voice cracking. "I'm not. Please get me out of here before I become ill."

Chapter 18

My husband of fifteen years killed my best friend. The thought seems so heinous, so surreal that I want to disregard it. Yet, somewhere in my heart, I know it's true. Lies, deceptions, and greed mark the character of the man who fathered two of my children.

"What happened?" asks Jean, taking my hand. "I'm worried about you, Lauren. You are so still."

"I'm not ready to talk about it," I say. "Can you make sure Nélie's all right? I'm going to need to be alone for a few hours."

"Of course," he replies. "I'll take her out to dinner. Lauren, you can trust me. If you need me, I'm here for you."

"I know that, Jean," I reply, staring straight ahead, too shocked to focus on our conversation. He drops me off at Paige's apartment. "I just want to be alone for a while."

There's a message on the machine from Nélie, telling me she and Richard plan to have dinner together and Richard will bring her home around eleven o'clock. The next message is from Paige, telling me that Matt has called her. He's on his way to Paris to meet with me to talk about our future. He'll be staying at a small hotel called the Madame Bovary, waiting to hear from me. Looking at my watch, I realize he's on his way. I take a deep breath, wanting to scream my frustration to the outside world, but all I can do is fall on the floor to sob out my grief. The rug scratches my face as tears pour down my cheeks at the deception I have lived with for fifteen years.

For several hours, I lie crumpled on the floor unable to move or think about my anger. I want to see Matt punished for what he has done to me and to India. Yet, how can I sacrifice the lives of our children in the process? I know Greensboro. I know that world. Laura and Kathryn's lives would be destroyed, knowing their father was a criminal. Could Madame DuBusé possibly be lying? I'll know the moment I confront Matt.

I finally sit up, wiping my eyes. The phone rings again. It must be Jean calling to check on me. I refuse to answer it. I must be strong right now. This battle is mine alone. Checking my watch, I realize that as his wife, I can gain access to Matt's hotel room before he arrives. The thought brings me some level of comfort. What about my personal safety? If he could kill India, I think, he might lash out at me. I hurriedly find a piece of paper and leave a note for Jean telling him where I'm going. After that minimal precaution, I'm too angry to care.

I walk across town, the exercise clearing my mind and revitalizing my spirits. Anger propels me down streets with a purposeful stride. I am conscious of the sound of my breathing and the click of my sandals. I can hear the Madame's voice in my mind, see her ruby pendant and imagine her catlike eyes. My imagination fills in the rest of the scenes from fifteen years ago. Matt would have been an easy prey. He's always been greedy. I ponder how much money she offered him to make sure India got on that plane.

Arriving at the front desk of the hotel, I am met by an older woman with kind eyes. Introducing myself as Matt's wife, I explain that I would like to surprise my husband when he arrives. Removing my passport from my purse, I lie to her, explaining that I've been in London on business and he's not expecting me. It's our anniversary. She smiles knowingly. Nodding conspiratorially, she eagerly leads me up four flights of stairs to a small room with a blue print bedspread. "I'll just wait here."

Darkness falls over the city as I wait for the sound of the key in the lock. Looking out the window, I see a young couple holding hands, an elderly woman clutching her handbag and a group of kids walking down the street. Before long, I hear footsteps, those that I've known for the last fifteen years. I hear Matt thanking the concierge, who tells him to have a pleasant evening.

My heart thuds in my chest, but I am determined not to give in to fear. Matt walks in, searching for the light. He finally turns on a lamp, his shock turning to excitement when he sees me sitting on the bed. "Lauren!" he says with a wide grin. "What a wonderful surprise after a long trip. I didn't expect you."

I simply stare at the face that has deceived me for so many years. "I've had an interesting day today, Matt," I say, moving away from him as he tries to kiss me. "I met with Madame DuBusé."

He becomes very still and eyes me warily. Putting down his bag, he stares at me, waiting for me to finish. "And?"

"And," I say, "she's convinced that you're responsible for India's death. Is it true?"

"How much did she tell you?" he counters quickly, instantly removing any of my hopes that he was not involved.

"You bastard!" I cry, shaking my head in disbelief. "You killed her, didn't you? No wonder you hated Nélie so much."

"It was an accident, Lauren," he says, coming over to me. "It's not what you think. Listen to me, I still love you. You've got to believe that."

"Don't you dare touch me or I'll scream this place down," I say, pointing to the window I have left open. "I want the truth, all of it. After fifteen years of marriage and two children together, you owe me that much."

He sits down in a chair, rubbing his hands over his face. "All right. When we lived here, Lauren, I was poor. I wasn't like you, living in that fancy apartment. Being broke gets old, you know. One day, Madame DuBusé approached me. She offered me a million dollars if I would take India to the airport and make sure she got on a particular flight. She didn't tell me why." He breathes out heavily, as if to exhale any guilt he has over his part in her death. "I knew that one way or another she was going to succeed in getting rid of India. So, I accepted her offer."

He turns to face me. "It was a million dollars, Lauren. Fifteen years ago that was a great deal of money. More money than I had ever dreamed of at the time. I needed to pay off my college loans, to buy you a ring and start a life. It all seemed so easy."

I feel a prickly sensation on my skin, but I stand there, willing myself to listen to his version of the story. "Then what happened?"

"I offered India a ride to the airport. I said I needed to talk to her about you. She was reluctant, but accepted my offer. While we were driving there, we got into a fight. I suppose I realized the enormity of what I was doing so I told her she should give up Julian and start a new life in another city. I told her that she should skip the party in New York and find a new focus in her life or something. Anyway, I tried to warn her not to get on that flight." He pauses, searching my face for some sign of understanding.

"Go on," I say, refusing to exonerate him for this meager act of conscience. The fact that he was even willing to enter into such an appalling arrangement with Madame DuBusé sickens me.

"India became enraged." He pauses to wet his lips. "You remember what a temper she had. She told me I had no right to offer such 'ridiculous advice' on her relationship. That her life was none of my business, but, more importantly, that I wasn't good enough for you. She screamed at me, calling me every name in the book."

"And what did you say to her?" I retort, knowing Matt's temper.

"I told her the truth. That she was a whore and that Julian would never marry her. She became enraged, then jerked the handle of the car door open and went out into the street. She was struck by an oncoming car and died instantly. But it wasn't my fault, Lauren. I swear to you."

"What wasn't your fault, Matt? That India died on the street and not on the plane? I suppose you managed to get away unnoticed. Or perhaps Madame DuBusé paid off the witnesses to keep the accident a secret—wasn't that convenient."

"I didn't force India out of the car."

"What a shame!" I cry. "I guess that's why you couldn't collect all of your money from Madame DuBusé. No wonder you were in such a hurry to get married. And it was you who comforted me about the plane crash that night."

"Either way, Lauren, it was a lost cause. If India had gotten on that plane, she would have died anyway."

I exhale, trying to control my revulsion. "You seem to think you've done nothing wrong."

He stands up. "I admit I wanted the money, and I got some of it. How do you think we put the down payment on our first house? But I did realize my mistake. For that, I'm sorry. I don't want to lose you, Lauren. I have always loved you and our children." He holds out his hands to me.

"And Nélie. She left because of you, you know. She was smarter than me. She could see through you." I wipe my brow, wishing that I hadn't made such a terrible mistake.

"I did more for that kid than Julian did. Why don't you condemn him for abandoning her instead of pointing a finger at me?" he asks, pulling at his left ear. "When you look at the big picture, you'll realize how much you need me. You couldn't function on your own without me."

"Really?" I say, reining in my anger. "I wouldn't be so sure."

"You're a good mother, Lauren," Matt warns, his voice getting lower. "You know that divorce would kill Laura and Kathryn. No matter what, they're still my children, too."

"Finding out that their father is a criminal would harm them more," I counter. "Don't you think?"

"You can't prove anything," he sneers. "And I know you too well, Lauren. You would never poison the girls' minds against me. You're too honorable a person. I knew that when I married you." He grins smugly.

I've heard enough. I take the medal from my pocket and throw it at him. "Here," I say smoothly. "You lost this fifteen years ago."

He takes the medal, smiling at its return. "Thanks," he says.

There are so many things I want to shout at Matt to make him realize that he has no conscience, but I know it will do no good. I head for the door. He doesn't stop me. It's over for me, I think, as I turn to look at him one last time.

"If you walk out on me, Lauren, I'll sue you for full custody of the girls," he threatens. "If I have to, I'll tie you up in court for years. My reputation at home is impeccable."

For the first time in fifteen years, he does not frighten me. "You wouldn't want to do that, Matt. I'll fight you until you haven't a dime to your name."

He steps forward. "I always hated India, Lauren. I knew she would come between us somehow, even dead! You're just an idiot!"

"You just don't understand, do you, Matt?" I say, backing away. "This has nothing to do with India anymore." I close the door on the last fifteen years, only I have no regrets.

Chapter 19

"If you are a gardener and find me,"
said the little bunny, "I will be a bird
and fly away from you."

"If you become a bird and fly away from me,
said his mother, "I will be a tree that you come
home to."

"Mom, you've been so quiet all morning. I hope you're not upset that I'm seeing Richard again today. If you are, I can cancel." Nélie looks at me, her brown eyes filled with worry.

"I'm sorry, Nélie. There's something I have to talk with you about. Can you come sit down for a moment?" I say, motioning her over to Paige's silk couch. "You're the first person I'm going to tell." I swallow hard, carefully considering my choice of words. "I'm not going to stay married to Matt any longer. I'm not happy and I haven't been for a long time."

She takes my hands. "Oh, Mom! I hope it's not because of me! I mean, I have my problems with Matt but we can get past them, I promise. I just want you to do what's right for you." I look into her trusting face, wondering what good it would serve if I told her that Matt was responsible for India's death, even if it was an accident. It's one secret that Nélie need never know. I pray I'm doing the right thing this time by withholding this piece of information from her.

"You're a sweet girl," I reply. "But this is what I want. It may actually mean that I bring Laura and Kathryn here to Paris with me temporarily. How do you feel about that?"

She practically leaps off the couch. "Oh my gosh!" she cries like a small child. "That would be great. All of us living here!"

"I'm not sure yet where we're going to live. I need to give it more thought," I say, remembering my confrontation with Madame DuBusé. Picturing the expressions on my girls' faces when I tell them about the divorce, I feel my heart tighten. I hope I can make them understand the reasons behind my decision—it will be the best for everyone. Matt will probably remain in North Carolina.

A vision of Matt kidnapping the girls comes to mind but I shake it off, deciding I don't need to escalate my worries. Certainly, the possibility does exist, so I'll have to work out some way to protect them. I say, "I'll need to fly home to talk with them. I'm hoping that you'll come with me. They've missed you. And I spoke with Julian this morning. He's going to allow you to live in India's apartment when you turn eighteen next month."

She grins happily for a moment. Then, her expression turns serious. "What about my grandfather? Or Julian's wife, for that matter?"

"I'm not going to lie to you. We may have problems from both of them. The more I think about it, I'm not sure we should stay here."

Nélie bites her upper lip. She looks at me hesitantly. "Did Madame DuBusé kill my mother?" she asks, staring at me intently.

"I'm not sure," I lie smoothly, deciding that I need to be

careful about how much information I reveal. "India was killed in a car accident on her way to the airport. But I'm not certain what Madame DuBusé's involvement was. We'll never know for sure if the crash was simply a coincidence or not."

She shivers, hugging herself. I notice the goosebumps on her thin legs. "I know in my heart that Julian will keep you safe. He's a very powerful man," I say, hoping that this time Julian is true to his word.

"I know you'll find me wherever I am," she says.

Realizing that I can't avoid seeing Jean before I go, I finally return his phone call. He asks to see me, to which I readily agree, telling him that I have only a few hours before I head home to take care of some unfinished business. As I pack up my things, I think of the challenges ahead. Is it safe for Nélie to come back here? I may need to think of a better option. Maybe London, I think, and, for some reason, I recall that Paige once mentioned she had several friends there.

I don't have any money stashed away and I've already used the commission from the sale of my paintings. I had always believed Matt and I would be together forever. Being a single parent is going to be tough. What about the Matisse that India gave me? I'd hate to sell it but I may have no choice. There's no other way to support us. I'll eventually try to make my living as an artist, but that will take time. Perhaps I could get Jean to take a look at the paintings I own and help me decide which one to sell. I know Matt won't part with a penny more than the court makes him.

Glimpsing my reflection in the mirror, I am astonished at the woman who stares back at me. My face looks the same, a bit thinner perhaps, but my eyes look calm. The promise of a new path awaits me now that I've found Nélie. It's amazing that I've learned so much from such a painful experience.

But, despite the pain, Nélie's disappearance has shown me that somehow I can find the strength to tackle difficult situations. My love for my children will keep me strong. The road ahead may not be easy, but I know I can start a new life. Never again will I go through the motions, pretending in my mind that things are what I want them to be. Never again will I allow anyone to dictate my life or my decisions, or determine my needs. Suddenly, an image of my mother's face stares back at me with the same old disapproving tone, the finger-pointing and the unrelenting advice on how to live. I would love to tell her the truth about Matt. It might make her question everything about her own life, I think.

But then, I envision a scene in which my mother and I are talking in her kitchen. She would be working on dinner, probably meatloaf.

"Where's Matt? Can you two stay for dinner?"

"No," I would say. "I have to tell you something. It's important. Can you come sit down?"

"Of course," she would reply, removing her apron. "What is it? Is everything all right?"

"No, it's not," I would admit quietly. I would tell her what Matt had done, complete with his confession.

"Well," she would say, "he can't be all bad, if he tried to stop her. Besides, he's been an excellent husband for the past fifteen years. Doesn't that count for something? And he is the father of your children."

"Mother!" I would cry. "The man's a criminal. He killed India!"

"You know I don't believe in divorce. That's what's wrong with our society. Too many broken homes!"

"So you think I should stay married to him?" I would ask incredulously.

"I'm just saying that you have your children to consider, that's all. This is going to kill them."

My mother would never approve of my decision to divorce Matt, no matter what the circumstance. Why try to explain? Paige's driver takes me to Jean's gallery before heading to the airport to pick her up. I reflect on what I'm going to say, how I'm going to explain to him what a fool I've been. He's sitting on the front bench, waiting for me. I smile when I see him, a real smile. Funny, I think. I'm not afraid. I know what needs to be done now, and I intend to do it quickly and efficiently.

He motions for me to join him. As I sit, he leans back, placing his arm on the back of the bench behind me. "Nélie's safe now. You must be delighted. Julian has finally taken control of his wife. Now that he knows she was involved in India's death, he despises her."

"I'm glad we found out the truth," I add, considering the impact of a simple shoe box.

"Julian claimed that fifteen years ago, Madame DuBusé prevented him from divorcing her because she controlled the leases to the stores. Over the years, he has changed that arrangement. Now, he's frozen whatever control she had over their joint assets. He's told the police everything he knows about Madame DuBusé's actions fifteen years ago."

"What's to stop her from harming Nélie even if she goes to jail?" I say. "After all, she plotted to have India killed and no one even knew she was involved until now."

Jean shrugs. "Julian has a signed confession from two officials involved in her death. One of the men claimed that Madame had paid him to alter the flight's manifest to make it appear that India had been on it. He also said Madame had had a large box placed in the cargo hold. The other government official signed the paperwork to take India's body from the hospital, then arranged for her to be cremated. What no one had counted on was a routine procedure: before her body was moved, one of the morgue staff had collected her personal belongings. It was he who brought the box to her apartment building. Anyway, Julian pulled some of his own strings with the police. I'm sure he made several large contributions to the necessary officials for their help. The police are now questioning Madame DuBusé."

I reach into my purse to grab my sunglasses. "Madame DuBusé deserves everything that happens to her. I feel no pity for that awful woman. India was too young to die. She deserved to live a full and happy life."

Seeing me cover my eyes, Jean motions for me to stand up. "Come inside, I have something I want to talk with you about," he says.

My eyes don't adjust to the light easily as I walk behind him to the rear gallery. He falters for a moment, turning around to face me. "Don't shut me out now, Lauren. Like it or not, I'm involved in this, too." He pauses. "Why won't you let me help you?"

I look into his eyes. Can I trust my instincts? "Matt was involved," I whisper quietly. "Madame DuBusé offered him a million dollars to make sure India got on the plane."

"I'm sorry," he says quietly.

"The way he tells it, they were en route to the airport. He claims he then regretted his decision and tried to get India to take a different flight.

"How could I have been so incredibly stupid as to let that man ruin my life?" As I continue, my tears are edging their way to the surface. "They had a terrible fight, he said, and India jumped out. She was hit by an oncoming car." Tears of regret soak my face for India, for my marriage, for the lives of my children, for all of our losses. Yet, a calm takes hold of my being along with a sense of rightness in this moment.

"I'd like to give you something," I exclaim, taking a deep breath. Pulling a gift-wrapped box out of my bag, I hand it to Jean.

"What's this for?" he asks, his brows furrowed in confusion.

"I wanted to thank you for everything you did to help me."

He shakes his head. "That wasn't necessary. I'm just glad that you and Nélie are reunited."

"Go on, open it," I say, watching him tear off the paper, then lift the lid of the box.

He removes my painting and stares at it thoughtfully. "This is amazing," he whispers, nodding his head in approval. "Gustave was right about you. When did you do it?"

"Last month," I reply, exhaling. "I was so worried about Nélie that I painted out my frustrations. I wanted to give it to you two days ago, but in all the excitement, I just forgot."

Our eyes meet and he holds my gaze for a moment.

He studies the painting. "I recognize the mountains in the background and a hint of the château. I love how the pathway leading to the garden doesn't disappear as your eye follows its direction."

"I wanted to show that life is full of possibilities, there's no right answer. I realize that we must learn from both good mistakes and bad mistakes. It makes us stronger when we're tested. While I wish Nélie hadn't run away, I can honestly say that it forced me to see things in a different way. I also know she'll never doubt my love for her again."

He nods, then turns back to the painting and points to a cricket on the grass beside a young girl playing.

"My metaphor for India. She had a passion for life which I admired, a free spirit that will never die. I learned so much from her."

He says, "We were all lucky to have known her."

"Jean, I feel my life is about to begin."

Suddenly, the sound of Paige's voice interrupts us. She bursts into the room with her usual flair for the dramatic.

"Lauren, there you are!" she exclaims. "Phew, I've had some trip. We sat on the runway for nearly two hours with a mechanical problem. Then, if that wasn't enough, we hit a headwind, which delayed us for another hour. Fortunately, they served us ice cream every half-hour along with some decent wine. So . . ." She pauses to catch her breath. "I found Nélie and Richard gazing at each other back at my apartment. So it was just as I suspected—boyfriend trouble, wasn't it?

I shrug and look at Jean, who suppresses a smile. He says, "That's one way of looking at it."

Paige thinks for a moment. "Does this mean Louis might have us back to the château?"

"Not exactly," Jean says, peering at me. "What do you think?"

"Paige," I reply, "I wouldn't count on it." Seeing her look of utter despair, I add, "Look at the bright side, we're back in Paris together again."

"There'd better be a big sale going on somewhere," she cracks, sitting down on one of the benches.

"How about a painting?" Jean retorts with a grin. "I'll give you a great price on a Picasso."

"Will you?" asks Paige, raising one eyebrow. "How much?" Then she becomes serious for a moment. "So, really, did I miss anything?"

"No," I reply evenly. "I was just telling Jean that I'm going to make a fresh start now. I feel like my life is full of infinite possibilities again."

"That's the way it ought to be," Paige replies. "Our lives are filled with too many things we think we must be or should do. I think the secret to life is to enjoy the little things, like a bowl of butter pecan ice cream."

"Covered in guilt-free chocolate sauce," I add with a smile.

About the Author

Kathleen Reid is a freelance writer who lives in Virginia. Her first children's book, *Magical Mondays at the Art Museum*, has been enthusiastically endorsed by the former First Lady of Virginia. She is a frequent guest speaker at elementary schools throughout the state. Her articles have appeared in such publications as *Richmond Surroundings* and *Southern Living Magazine*. This is her first novel.